Third Eye's a Charm

DOROTHY CALLAHAN

author of *Loving Out of Time* and *Taming the Stallion*

Crimson Romance
New York   London   Toronto   Sydney   New Delhi

CRIMSON
ROMANCE

Crimson Romance
An Imprint of Simon & Schuster, Inc.
1230 Avenue of the Americas
New York, NY 10020

CRIMSON ROMANCE and colophon are trademarks of Simon & Schuster, Inc.

For information about special discounts for bulk purchases, please contact Simon & Schuster Special Sales at 1-866-506-1949 or business@ simonandschuster.com.

The Simon & Schuster Speakers Bureau can bring authors to your live event. For more information or to book an event contact the Simon & Schuster Speakers Bureau at 1-866-248-3049 or visit our website at www. simonspeakers.com.

ISBN: 978-1-4405-8014-7
ISBN: 978-1-4405-8015-4 (ebook)

To: Craig, Janet, Lisa, Sheria, Mary, Laurie, and Lorraine, with love (and thanks).

Acknowledgments

Many thanks to the wonderful editors at Crimson Romance who have helped further my love of writing. You gave me a chance to share my passion for storytelling with the world. Thanks to my wonderful friends and critique partners for helping out in a pinch when a scene was in jeopardy. And, of course, many heartfelt thanks to my wonderful family for always believing in me, even when you didn't understand how I could be a slave to the voices in my head.

Chapter 1

I'm going to divulge my biggest secret: I'm psychic. Really psychic. Now, I'm not saying I'm going to start my own TV show, or work for the police department, because really, I don't want that kind of attention. Once a psychic's face gets out there, she's a bigger attraction than Channing Tatum.

No, I'm much happier channeling my talents to other outlets. And I'm not afraid to admit, my abilities really don't work that way, anyway. I can *see* with my "third eye." I can sometimes hear voices in my head—usually if a deceased person is really trying to get through—and if I have a strong connection, like physically talking to someone, I can actually see through the other person's eyes, making me a bona fide telepath. It's wicked cool, for sure, but it totally destroys that whole "phenomenal cosmic power" one needs to become gratuitously rich.

And, trust me, I've tried that whole Mega Millions thing. Epic fail.

I reach for the phone at my work station, my hand hovering, waiting and ready. It rings once, then I pick up on the second ring. "Pet Pearls Behavioral Helpline, this is RoseAngel. How can I help your pet today?"

"Hi, Roxanne, this is Bev Stein again. Now my cat keeps getting up on top of my bookshelf and knocking off all my knickknacks. She's driving me crazy!"

Yup. This is what I do. I can visualize her home, because she's got the image foremost in her mind. I *feel* these aren't just knickknacks to her; they are souvenirs of places she went with her husband before he died of cancer last year. This would be the owner most likely to relinquish her pet, but only because with every broken trinket, Bev will feel like she's losing a memory of the last thirty-seven years of her married life.

Last time she called, her cat was "rolling around like a floozy." I explained the importance of spaying her, and the behavior stopped. We have a rapport, now, she and I, and I'm hopeful she'll listen to me again.

I hone in on her cat, a mischievous brown tiger female of eleven months. I spend about fifteen minutes with Bev, telling her to pack away the valuables—just for now—put some empty boxes up there to block access, add some motion-activated spray deterrents, and above all, to play with her. Even without a sixth sense I can tell she's a senior citizen, so I inform her that five to ten minutes of high-quality interaction daily should stop the attention-seeking behavior.

Grateful gushing carries over the line, and I give her my name again—RoseAngel, not Roxanne—and tell her I'll follow up with her in a week.

This might seem like a menial job to some, but right now keeping pets in their homes is my primary goal. It's better for the pet, it teaches the owner to work through snags in their relationships, and most importantly, it keeps our intake numbers down.

Sometimes I wonder what it would be like if I were more outgoing, braver, like my brother, who flaunts his power like a side-ring circus act. He's not afraid to embrace his sixth sense, enjoy each adventure it brings. Me, I had a chance, and I choked, and now I live with that knowledge and regret each day.

Maybe someday I'll want more excitement in my life. Right now, I'm happy living *la vida incognito*.

I log my call in my book with the owner's name and pet's name. I already entered her into our computer system the last time we spoke, so there's less data to input this time. By doing this, we can check and see if our outreach program really works.

I'm proud to report that I'm *really* good at keeping pets in their homes; few of my callers relinquish their pets, and those that do don't shock me.

The phone rings again. I press the enter button and log my info, then grab the phone on the second ring. "Pet Pearls Behavioral Helpline, this is RoseAngel. How can I help your pet today?"

A pause. "RoseAngel. That's the prettiest name I've ever heard."

He has a great voice. Rich. Smooth. I'm talking a ribbon-wrapped gold-foil box of perfectly-shaped Godiva. My mouth waters at the comparison. "Thank you. I had no say in the matter." I laugh and repeat, "How may I help you today?"

"It's my cat," said on a sigh.

A sense of darkness washes over me, like being in a wooded cabin at midnight on a new moon with all the drapes pulled shut.

I kind of get a case of the heebie-jeebies from what my third eye is seeing but plow ahead. "Okay, let me just get some info from you first. Name?"

"Pringles."

I laugh and say, "That's my favorite chip."

"Mine, too. And the day he came home, he wouldn't stop stealing and begging for them, so he totally named himself."

I chuckle and clear my throat and ask, "Your name?"

I see *av … rav … Travis …* but he says, "Trevor."

I frown. "Last name?" I see *att … attison … Mattison*, but he says, "Matthews." My game must be off, big time. Maybe I've got my T and M names confused, but more likely I assume he's ashamed of what his cat's doing and wants the anonymity.

Whatever.

Except … I *really* don't like the blackness that still surrounds this caller, and I'm not surprised when the address he gives me seems faked. I hop online and confirm no such location. He gives me one by Preston, a blip on the map just a few miles east of us, which I've heard has the population of an elevator at maximum capacity.

He's not a client in our system, either.

I rally my forces and ask, "Now, tell me about Pringles. Age?"

"I'm thirty-two."

I sense his tease and come back with, "That's a mighty old cat." I can sense his smile and press, "Your *cat's* age?"

"*Oh*." Playfully, like he was confused. "Four."

"Sex?" I can't wait for this one.

"I prefer women … but never on the first date." His voice drops. "I'm kind of old-fashioned that way."

I choke out a laugh, but I feel my eyes light up and my heart go pitter-pat. He is? I totally have a thing for black-and-white movies, Fred Astaire, and any man who opens doors for me. I stumble, "Um, I meant, your cat?"

"Nah, he's an only pet, so I know he's not getting any. Besides, he's neutered."

Okay, so I like his humor. I can tell he's smiling. Flirting, even. The recorders are running like they do for all calls, but I don't mind. I'll just claim that he's the nervous type who deals with stress by cracking jokes and that I played along.

Really, I'm enjoying playing along. Next I ask, "Declawed?"

"I'd never do that to any pet of mine."

Me, neither, but I don't want to get too buddy-buddy with Mr. Nightfall here, no matter how much I like the cocoa-butter tones of his voice. I've never met anyone who actually darkened my vision before, and frankly, it's a little unnerving. Usually with those ultra-dark, moody, depressed people, I see visions of churning storm clouds, not the La Brea tar pits like this guy. I lick my lips and marshal on with, "Does he live inside only, or does he go out?"

"Inside only. I used to live on the twelfth floor."

City man. Probably lived right here in Norwich, Connecticut, and recently bought a house, though why he lied about Preston, I can't say.

Hmmm …

The apartment I see clearly: some pretty-nice furniture, a large flat screen, a king size bed with a really sharp comforter in chocolate and tan hues—something I would totally buy for myself. I shake off the sight and continue, "Now, tell me exactly what he's doing."

Another long sigh. The image of the bright apartment snaps off like a TV. Now, although I still see darkness, I can see a longhair tuxedo cat, quite beautiful, with yellow eyes. He's hiding under an end table. "He seems so stressed all the time."

Well, since he's not declawed, I know there's an actual stressor in the cat's life versus a perceived one. From the shelter's experience, cats who've been through this surgical procedure stress easily. Hiding, aggression, and random urination are the hallmarks of declawed cats—the single common denominator at relinquishment and ultimately euthanasia and the biggest reason we discourage it being done at adoption time. We don't want a cat to be put down a mere two years after adopting it out.

I close my eyes to *see* what the cat's real problem is. Soon I detect piles of cardboard boxes, so I ask, "What's changed in his life?"

"I moved." Begrudging tones tell me it wasn't his choice.

Ah. A reason. "Not happy about moving, are you?"

"Not at all."

"Well, neither is Pringles. Is he hiding?"

"All the time."

I jot that down, and while I'm writing I see an image of an auburn-haired little boy, with one freckle for every year of his young life brushed across his little nose. His eyes are so light brown they look like caramel. "Children?"

"No, he was neutered young."

I have to laugh. "Human children?"

A pause. "I'd have to call *Ripley's Believe It or Not* if he managed that one, but no," he states, "no kids here."

That one really throws me for loop, and I feel my mouth drop open. Could my visions be totally wrong? This kid is adorable, so cute I want to scoop him up and swing him around. His name is Charlie, and I'm wondering if he's been kidnapped.

Darkness. I get the heebies when I wonder if my caller could be tonight's top feature on *America's Most Wanted*, or an escapee from the local prison, and a full-body shudder works through me. Holy schnitzel, I need to get this man off the phone. I glance at Tina, but she's knee-deep in dog training and can't take this call.

The little boy reappears again, and he says, "I want my mommy and daddy." I mentally ask him where they are, but he disappears, and my first instinct is to try to lure an answer from the boy. I find myself wanting to hasten through the phone call, but remind myself I'm a professional and muster through, even though my hands are still shaking over my keyboard and I'm holding back an urge to panic.

Guilt crashes into me, and I vividly recall Britni O'Reilly's body, the 19-year-old girl who worked at the local convenience store where I sometimes buy my gasoline. She came to me as a vision when I was out walking my dog last summer, beckoning me inside my head to follow her into the woods. The hot sun and cool shade seemed like the perfect excuse to do as my third eye bade, and soon I found her grave in a small clearing. Since the sunken dirt gave me the perfect excuse to report it to the police—*sans* ESP—I did.

The cold case could have been solved that week if I merely told them her bag of clothes—and thus the perp's DNA—were buried not ten yards away, right where Britni pointed.

But I was too chicken.

Icicles stake into my spine, and I force myself back to the topic at hand, trying not to choke on the memories and my promise that I would never let another ghost down again. Perhaps I'm just jumping to conclusions. How many times have I made a bad assumption? After all, I know how wonky my visions can be, so I give myself a mental shake and blink away my empathic tears. I focus hard on my caller and what is around him and his troubled kitty.

Although the couch beside the cat appears to be black, I can tell it's really only tan colored. The table lamp, though brown, shows me glimpses of being light yellow. The more I talk to him, the clearer I see, which makes me want to know more about Charlie and how I can help him. "Does ... *Pringles* have any place safe where he can hide?" Britni didn't. Does Charlie?

"That's all he does. He used to be such a loving lap cat before *this*," he pauses, his voice dropping lower, the playfulness now gone, and a thread of agony trembles the air. "Pringles is my little buddy; really, he's the only thing that's kept me sane these last few years, and the thought of how bad he must feel just breaks my heart."

The image of the boy is gone, and I wonder if he's a ghost and not a vision of a living child, which doesn't really help my predicament any. How can I help him if I don't know if he's alive or dead? Do I have any evidence that I can take to the cops?

Now that my own heart has stopped its frantic pace and I take that moment to assimilate the disparity between what my ears and third eye are telling me, I realize the darkness is now more of a metaphor for how the man feels about his life versus any literal location or electrical shortage, and find myself taking a fortifying breath of relief.

"Have you taken your cat to a vet to rule out any medical issues?"

"No, I haven't. Do you think I should?"

"Well," I reason—which is a fantastic antidote for panic, by the way--, "the stress of moving can make a normally healthy animal develop medical problems. If a cat is sick or injured, it will usually hide."

"No," he tells me again, "I haven't. I'm new to the area. Do you have any place that you'd suggest?"

The ghost child has disappeared, so I run with my daily role. "We have a list of all the vet hospitals in the area. You can find it on our website online, or I can mail you a copy, or email one to you."

"Hmm," he says. "Where do you take your pet?"

We're not allowed to endorse one place over another, and I tell him so.

But Mr. Nightfall whispers, "Come on, I won't tell."

Delicious shivers work up my arms, giving me goose bumps, and I stare at them in disbelief that his voice can elicit such a response from me. Wondering if he's some kind of mystic who lures people to their demise, I shoot back, "Who said I have pets?"

He seems very logical and forthright when he states, "You're too passionate about your job to not have any. I'm guessing ..." I could see him looking up, "one dog, and one, no, two cats."

He had it right the first time, but I pretend to be impressed. "Wow, are you psychic?"

He chuckles, and I can tell he's enjoying himself, while I'm trying to reconcile myself to this strange situation. "Am I right?" his low voice asks, and I would totally be flirting with him had I met him in, say, a bar or at a party.

Something less ghost-y.

"No," I tell him, since he's not. "Now, are you going to make that vet appointment, or am I going to have to follow up with you?"

"*Oh.*"

I realize my—inadvertent?—slip.

"You, RoseAngel, definitely need to follow up with me."

I feel a blush crawling across my face, and I slide a glance to my coworker, Tina, taking another call in her own foam-walled cell.

Her eyebrows shoot up, and she smiles and indicates my phone call. I nod, and she gives me the thumbs up.

"Is Pringles still hiding now, or has the sound of your"—I almost add the word *melodious*—"voice lured him out?"

"Wow."

I like that I impress him with that kernel of insight.

"He did come out. He's rubbing on my slipper."

Ooh, I like a man in slippers. And little else.

Oops. I didn't say that.

I say, "Sometimes hearing their owners speaking in a relaxed tone lures stressed animals out of hiding. If possible, sit on the floor by him, wherever you know he's hiding, and just either talk to him, or pick up the phone and call a friend."

"Can I call you? Say, tomorrow?"

My heart revs at that, but I tease, "Oh, so *you* are going to follow up?"

"Oh, I'll call." Like he was going to make darned sure of it.

"*After* you take him to the vet. Otherwise, I'm just plain not going to be very helpful." In a sing-song voice, since I think that will get through to him better than being stern. Plus, I really want this cat to see a vet, and I think Mr. Flirtypants will do it if he thinks it will make me more likely to take his call. Since Pringles is a male cat, and stress causes urinary blockages, I want to make sure he's not a medical time bomb.

The cat, that is.

Trevor chuckles, really happy, and I see he's in a cabin, just like I first thought, with rustic furniture, a small TV, heavy clunky stairs in the back corner. It's a nice place.

But he hates it.

"Okay, okay, I'll take him to the vet. But if the doctor doesn't find anything wrong, then you owe me."

"Oh, really." I'm so flirting I don't even know myself.

"Dinner."

I really wish I could see his eyes when he said that. I bet they're brown and piercing and really keen, and then I give myself a proverbial kick in the rear because I know I'm merely hoping he's a brunet. I can hear my heartbeat thumping away in my head. But I parry with, "If the doctor prescribes any medicine, then no dinner for you."

"Deal."

What the hell did I just get myself into?

Chapter 2

The rest of the afternoon, I'm glad to report, passes anticlimactically. Tina wants all the juicy gossip, so I replay the tape and watch her while her fingers dance lightly along her bottom lip every time Travis … um, *Trevor* is speaking.

"Ooh, he might need some extracurricular assistance," she fans her face, and I note the slow crawl of excitement highlighting her eyes and cheeks.

I think, *easy, killer*, and counter with, "He could be a cellar-dweller." I'm never possessive about my callers. I'm not. But I reach over and snap down the stop button a little faster than I normally move.

Tina perhaps understands, for her tone lowers and she says, "Not with that voice."

I have to admit I'm mighty curious about Travis/Trevor. I can't see his face like more powerful psychics; I can't hold his comb and pinpoint his location on a map. Basically, I can't spy.

Abilities I aspire to have: Hear thoughts, see ghosts, foretell the future beyond when the phone is going to ring (especially where Mega Millions is concerned), and maybe even pinpoint someone's location on a map. (I'd have to go work for the police department at that point, but the pay better be phenomenal.) Other psychics tell me that the more I use my abilities, the stronger my perceptions will become. It's like a muscle—this unused eighty percent portion of most peoples' brains—and, by golly, I like to flex it.

Well, secretly, at least. I'm not ready to buy the crystal ball and gold shawls and open my own shop in Mystic Village.

What I can do, however, is recall that adorable boy. Is he in danger? Harm's way? Is it a son of that Travis/Trevor guy? A runaway? A hostage? I remind myself that the child might be his deceased brother, or even a spirit guide, and allow myself to silence the warning blares going off in my head. Even though I don't want to go to the cops—ever—about my abilities, I did promise myself I would use my powers to help others, which I can't do unless I know what I'm up against.

We return to our cubbies, and I dart a glance to Tina to make sure she's ignoring me. I pull up Trevor Matthews' account and leave a big memo—*RoseAngel only*. I'm hopeful that by speaking to him (not flirting—*speaking*), I can see if I need to help this little Charlie.

I head out at five and go home, take my tri-color Sheltie mix, Titan, for a walk, then feed both him and Grimm, my salvaged longhair black cat.

When I open my pantry, I see Mother Hubbard has forgotten to go shopping. I hate hitting the store at this hour; it's always so crowded. Alas, I'm out of milk and bread, so it's either I go now, or I buy lunch tomorrow and *still* have to go shopping anyway.

I grab my purse and head out.

I'm equidistant from two stores; I elect the one east of me, as it's a little more rural and I don't have to drive into the setting sun.

RoseAngel equals pragmatism.

The lot is only slightly less busy here. I find a spot, park, and grab a cart.

Two days before payday leaves me little spending money, so I grab the essentials only.

Today, this includes some perfectly-shaped, foil-wrapped Godiva.

No reason.

I see a man at the deli counter, very handsome, with another man in a black suit practically standing guard over him.

Whoever thought pasta salad could be so dangerous?

The suit has one of those curly-cue ear pieces and looks like he has never cracked a smile a single day in his life. I'm serious. His features are granite.

The other guy doodles around the counter like he has all day and intends to spend it on a major decision: shaved chicken or sliced ham?

I only see him in profile, but he has short brown hair and brown eyes, and a really nice nose and chin. Sparse hair covers his jaw, a sexy rogue look like he never tried to grow a beard, but, whoop, there it is. I'd peg him at about six-three, making him the trinity of tall, dark, and yummy. I want to put my hands on him and sculpt him like a piece of clay.

I have a type, and he's it. Only problem is: I don't seem to attract my type. Nope, the men who are drawn to my torch-top and big blue peepers are *always* blonds. I guess they figure a girl with freckled milky-white skin probably wants another paleface, but not me. Nuh-uh. Give me a brunet any day if you want to watch me swoon. I turn into a regular Weeble Wobble.

Here's where it gets weird: I'm passing by, eyeing the mac and cheese for dinner, and I see another image of Charlie, not crying or distressed, just … there. Either these two men are connected to my caller, or one of these men *is* the caller.

I'm kinda hoping it's Hot and Hunky and not Mr. Matrix.

I need to know. I ease up to the counter, my heart kicking me repeatedly in the chest. The closer I get, the shallower my breathing becomes. I know on a rational level that I'm trying to see if Mr. Hunky and Mr. Nightfall are one and the same, and if he's got Charlie chained up in a secret bunker for some nefarious plan, but on a deeper level I'm responding to a serious thrum of *bawr chikka bawr bawr.*

I squelch that thought and pretend to know him. "Oh, aren't you Charlie's dad? How's his arm?" I try to swallow but I can't while holding my breath.

The man looks me down and up, a quick glance that tells me he doesn't recognize me. His eyes lock on mine, and I watch his pupils expand.

Mr. Hunky likes me, then, does he? I dig my fingernails into my palms, wondering if I'll recognize his voice.

He leans one confident elbow on the counter and says, "No, I'm sorry, you have me confused with a very lucky someone else."

It's him. My heart loses its rhythm, and it feels like someone is playing hacky sack inside my chest for a few erratic seconds. I stutter, "N-no Charlie?"

"No," his eyes soften, "but I really like the name." He offers me his hand. His jaw is warm and relaxed, and his smile is rather inviting. "And you are … ?"

"Dobson." I shake his hand, and a wave of darkness hits me. It totally conflicts with the intense light I see in his gorgeous eyes. "Miss Dobson."

"Pleasure to meet you. I'm Trav … Trevor." I watch both interest and hesitation cross his features when he asks, "Do you have a first name, Miss Dobson?"

So, I had it right! *Travis.* I still smile, but I release his hand, because I'm wondering what in the name of Jiminy would make a guy lie about his name? My fingers feel warm from his touch, and I close my hand to contain the warmth. "Yes, I do." I grin even wider. I don't want him to know I'm the same woman he flirted with just hours ago. It frankly seems too weird, even by my standards. I mean, really, what are the chances?

He likes this game; I can tell by the way the corners of his eyes move. "Well, Miss Yes-I-do, I'm new to this town. I only got here two days ago, so I have to say, you're pretty much the first person I've officially met." He looks at his right hand and holds his closed, too, like maybe he enjoyed that brief moment of hand-holding as well, and I think my suspicions are confirmed when his next expression offers me mock sadness. "And I'm not even the one you were looking for."

Oh, I'm not too sure about that, but I merely smile. I have to continue the farce for another line or three, so I take a step back and say, "New neighbor I only met once a few months ago. I saw his kid in a cast." I shrug like it's no big deal. "I'll bump into him at home, I guess."

His expression softens, and he gives me this little heart-stuttering grin and leans forward, like I moved too far away. "I wouldn't mind if you wanted to bump into me again. It's been a long time since I've met someone with a voice as pretty as her eyes." He grins and indicates the main entrance with a nod of his head. "I saw a nice little café right at the front; would you like to join me, say, Friday night?"

I feel my face turning as red as my tresses, but I cross my arms and give him my bravest stare. That whole "pretty name/voice/eyes" thing I see is now just a pick-up line, and not a compliment. "Here I thought I was speaking with a neighborhood dad, not the neighborhood *cad*." I'm thinking he's the type who flirts/hooks-up/schmoozes anything remotely female, and I know for a fact he's hit me up twice now, although he's only aware of in-person me, not phone me.

He grabs his chest. "A near mortal wound." But he grins when he says it, his eyes riveted to mine. I can't tell if he's a rake, or just really, really into me.

I'm completely leaning toward A.

I grab my cart, sparing him another grin, because, hey, he's really *that cute,* and say, "I've got to get going. Nice meeting you, Trav-Trevor."

I know I'm not imagining the sheer terror that flickers in his eyes for the barest of seconds. If I blinked, I would have missed it, and I feel a clamminess settle along the back of my neck. Did I just spill my psychic beans? But he wobbles a smile and tries to act nonchalant when he says, "It's Trevor."

I have had the distinct fortune to have met both a Travis and a Trevor in my life, and he don't look nothing like no Trevor.

Just saying.

Somewhere in the back of my skull I hear "Wooga! Wooga!" and the assorted cacophony of warning bells joins in. I don't know what this hottie is hiding, but I'm getting a serious case of the heebies.

The funny thing is: *He* is the one who takes a step back at this, like I just frightened him or something.

He seems a little pale when he asks, "Do I know you from somewhere?"

Since I've honestly never seen his face before now, that's what I tell him.

He stares at me, clearly unconvinced. "Do you know me?"

Now I'm thinking he's crazy, or at least spouting delusions of grandeur. "No, should I? Are you rich or famous or something?" *Or infamous?* I almost add, but shut my pie hole.

"No, it's nothing, never mind." He seems relieved, and then his warm smile returns, and I'm wondering what he's hiding.

I hear static in my left ear—a psychic signal that someone is trying to get through. I'm wondering if it's Charlie, and the only way to find out will be to hang around.

He steps after me, Mr. Matrix tagging up the rear. "Hey, before you go," he pulls out a piece of paper and places his hand on the front of my cart to forestall me. "Can you show me where I might find some of these?"

With a knowing smirk, I take the sheet of paper. I'm now leaning toward B. I scan the list: milk, bread, cheese, cereal, frozen meals, frozen pizza, hots, hamburger, salt, pepper, ketchup, soup, paper towels, TP, pens, paper, envelopes ...

He's starting over.

I get an electric tingle of a nearby ghost, but I can't see anyone. I search inwardly, but my third eye is blind. Huh.

Trevor offers an innocent shrug. "It's a big store, and I've never been here."

I level him another knowing smirk as I wait for ghostly intervention. None comes, even though I'm staring into the nicest eyes I've ever seen.

He returns my gaze, his brown eyes locked purposefully on mine.

I see myself crushed in his arms as he bends me backward with his kiss, and I'm assuming this image is coming from him, but I can't swear to it. It might just be my superego playing tricks with my head. He *is* my type, after all.

My pulse kicks up a bit.

He's still holding my eyes.

With my chin, I indicate the rest of the store. "Come on. I'll show you around."

Chapter 3

About halfway through his list, my stomach starts to do that acid thing, and when I tell "Trevor" I need to eat, he leads me to the front café and treats me to a nice hot veggie sub (my choice).

We leave our shopping carts just outside the dining area, blocking the oranges, but apparently no one really needs any right this moment because no one complains.

Perhaps I'm a bit too distracted to notice.

Who's to say?

For the record, I can't decide if I'm acting desperate or being spontaneous. Misha would say desperate, but Darlene would tell me *carpe diem*. "Trevor" pulls out my chair for me and I think I stop breathing with his chivalry. He sits down and opens my soda for me and pours it into my cup and offers me a straw.

I'm totally serious.

And I'm totally taken. I clear my throat and say, "Your mother raised you well." I catch a glimpse of her: gray/brown hair, brown eyes, great smile, but then another wave of sadness from Mr. Hunky. Luckily, I don't need ESP to see he's looking at his pizza and feeling down. I suck in air and say, "I'm sorry. I didn't mean to—"

A palm forestalls my apology. "Don't." But then, I watch him gather up his memories like so much old newspaper, crumble them up and toss them aside. His smile now is warm, interested.

Mm … inviting.

The suit has taken a seat with his back to the wall, and he watches us. Watches *me*. This guy doesn't trust my motives, and I'm more than willing to bet he's armed and could shoot a fly out of midair.

I ensure I make no sudden moves. I sip my cola and ask, "Are you a politician?" I indicate his bodyguard with a minute tip of my head.

"Hell, no." He holds my eyes with a dead-serious look, but then smiles, and I get another vision of Charlie as he giggles and runs away. *Who is this boy?!* But "Trevor" says, "I'd rather talk about *you,* Miss Yes-I-do."

His grin weakens most of my resolve. "All right, all right. You may call me ... " I sit tall in my chair and angle my head as I lean back. "Marie." It's my middle name.

He must have really good deductive skills, for he scrutinizes me and says, "You don't really look like a Marie to me." He tips his head to the side as well. "Middle name, perhaps?"

I concede with a wink, "Well played, Trevor."

A smirk. "You know," he shifts in his chair, casting a glance at the suit before continuing, "as a kid, my family called me Opie. Would you mind calling me that?"

I think I swallow my tongue. "Opie? As in, Ron Howard?"

One nod. "I looked just like him at that age. Especially in black and white." His intense grin makes my insides flutter.

Maybe Travis/Trevor is trying to get in touch with his inner child. Maybe "Charlie" is part of his psychosis—his multiple personality disorder.

Except I'm guessing there's a lot more going on here than meets my third eye. My spider senses are all a-tingly. The darkness is lifting the more we talk, but something really bad has happened to him ... or around him. He's smart and funny and doesn't seem to notice the other women parading in, some of them straight from their jobs, sporting high heels and fancy dos.

Nope. I'm the only person in his private snow globe.

I shiver as I feel the inevitable *shake.* I venture, "Are you married?"

He looks up, and I figure I've found the catch, the red herring. I wait for the married-guy evasion: *Why do you ask? Am I wearing a ring? Would I be here with you if I were?*

He looks off, his mouth and lips slack and sad, and says, "Not anymore."

Sometimes my visions use Tarot cards as a way to explain things. This time I see the three of swords (heart-stabbing), Tower (shock or surprise), and Death.

He didn't take her passing very well.

I see the three of swords again and he tells me, "She died suddenly three years ago."

I don't want her coming through to me in spirit because I'll be wheedled mercilessly by her to pass along a message, so I apologize and adjust the sails to change tack.

That's when I hear it, loud, front and foremost in my head: *I never should have shot him.* I sit upright in my chair and look at him, but he's reaching for a napkin and doesn't seem to have said anything. But my heart is clambering up my throat, my lungs are shriveling up, and I think my eyeballs just dried out. Ghosts speak into the left ear, which is nothing at all like what I just experienced. I'm wondering if I actually just *heard him thinking*. I ask, "What was that?"

"Hmm?" He looks up as he shakes open his napkin, his expression one of melancholy. "I said it's been three years since she died."

Okay, so, I know he thought it, which freaks me out because I've never actually heard thoughts before. He seems repentant, but, surprisingly, that doesn't really make me feel better if he's a killer.

It certainly hasn't toned down my heart and lung functions. I swig some of my drink and bore my fingers into my eyeballs to rehydrate them.

Now, I know most of my abilities are not one hundred percent readable or accurate. I *know* this. What other types of "shot" are there? Alcohol, bullets, photos, vaccines … what about a long shot? Take a shot? Shot put?

Right now, I'm really hoping I'm not captaining the *SS Delusion*, sailing straight down the River Denial.

He clears his throat and cocks a brow and says, "You look like you just saw a ghost."

One ability I'm now afraid to ask for. I nervously laugh it off.

He smiles wanly at me and says, "Things haven't been the same since." He looks down, sad, then looks up and smiles again. "I have to say, it's a little scary stepping out into the public realm again. I mean," he spares a little grin as he scratches the back of his neck, "I've actually forgotten which one of us is supposed to talk about their dysfunctional families first."

I laugh, the scary moment dissipating. "It's a rock, paper, scissors thing. Oh, and the girl always wins."

He snaps his fingers, shakes his head. "I knew I'd forgotten."

I eye him and say, "You are, however, as the man, supposed to practice questionable hygiene habits at the table."

He makes a cross-eyed, tongue-biting face and tries sticking his knuckle in his ear.

I laugh. I like that he plays along. I'm really not sensing he's dangerous, and I've truly met my fair share of *creepy* masquerading as *normal*. This totally conflicts with my first impression of him on the phone, and I'm wondering if my psychic abilities took a sudden hiatus. "Are you passing through or staying?"

He smiles, and somehow it warms me straight to my toes. "Oh, I'm pretty sure I'm staying." Like meeting me just solidified his decision. It's a powerful feeling, I have to admit.

"Doing … ?"

"Bank manager." He leans over the table. "Would you like to visit me Monday and discuss CD rates?"

Palm up, I grin and back up in my chair. "No, thanks. I'm good." Good-n-poor.

"Marie … ish … what do you do?" He knows it's not my name, and his wolfish smile reminds me he knows.

I'm an *ish*. I fashion a version of the truth. "Reception. Desk job." I shrug. "Nothing glamorous." I stare at my drink and start spinning it in place.

He nods a bit, like he knew that or something, but then he asks, "Where?"

I work at the Lucky Clover Animal Shelter right here in Norwich, but I really don't want to tell him that. All he'd have to do is describe the girl with flaming shoulder-length red hair and blue eyes, and boom, I've blown my cover.

For the sake of this unknown child, I evoke classic evasion. "I'm sensing you're a stalker, so, for now, I'm not telling you." I give him the cheekiest grin I can share, and he chuckles and shakes his head.

"No," he tells me, "you do something far more valuable, I can tell. I bet you help people. Really help people."

Maybe he really is a stalker. Did he recognize my voice? I evoke classic evasion and say, "Help is relative."

He holds my gaze for a long moment, then tugs a pepperoni from his pizza and breaks off the cheese strand without looking at me. "You make it awfully hard for a man to get to know you."

I want to see if he'll call me, RoseAngel, at work tomorrow the way he said he would, so I say, "Tell you what. I'll meet you here Friday night."

He drops his morsel, hopeful. "Seven?"

"Sure."

"Deal."

He likes that word. I've finished eating, and I offer him my hand. "It's been very nice meeting you, Tr—" I cut myself off and instead say, "Opie," which makes him smile. I need to get to the bottom of his identity issue, so I don't want him to know I'm on to him.

His fingers caress my hand. I feel shivery as he holds my eyes and says, "I'll wait with baited breath."

I leave while I still have mine.

Chapter 4

Around two, the phone rings, and I answer it with my usual, "Pet Pearls Behavioral Helpline, this is RoseAngel. How can I help your pet today?"

"Ah, you answered."

It's him. His voice is so warm that I want to curl up in it, regardless of the fact he just made my breath catch so fast I jerked the glass of water in my hand. But, I elect to play dumb. "Yes. May I ask who's calling, please?" I pull up his account to document our call.

"Trevor Matthews."

He gets his name right this time. "Ah, with Pringles, the cat. Did you go to the vet?"

"I did."

"And?"

A sigh. "He prescribed an anti-anxiety pill, which I have to give him every day."

I type that in and guess, "Amitriptyline?"

"Yeah, how'd you know?"

"Believe it or not," I smile, "a lot of our clients give it to their pets. And Prozac for dogs."

"Really."

"Yup. When an animal is really stressed or anxious, sometimes they need a boost just to get over that hump."

A moment of silence. "RoseAngel?"

"Yes?"

"Did we meet? Yesterday?"

Damn. He must have recognized my voice the way I did his. I panic and state, "Just the phone call." Did my voice raise an octave? I hope not. I close my suddenly-dry mouth and stare at his name on the computer screen.

"Really?"

I hold my breath, not deigning to answer. "Why?"

He pauses, and I feel my heartbeat revving so fast I fear I'll start sweating. I really don't like lying. I sense sadness but he says, "Never mind."

I switch gears in the pause. "How's Pringles today?"

"Still hiding."

"Okay." I settle into my seat, hoping it will settle my racing heart. Focusing on his problem, I hope, will deflect the RoseAngel/ Marie comparison. I take a couple deep breaths and say, "Now, you said yesterday you recently moved. How recently?"

"Three days ago."

At least the stories match. "Okay. Where is your cat?"

"Hiding behind the couch."

I already know that, but say, "Okay, here's the game plan. You ready?"

"Oh, I'm ready." His voice is so sensual and seductive that I can't believe I lied to him, even if it was by omission. I really want to tell him the truth. Maybe Friday night.

I grin. "I want you to keep Pringles in one room, with everything he needs. Food, water, litter, toys. This can be a bathroom, but I really recommend your bedroom. Is this a studio, or do you have a room?"

"I have my own bedroom. It's got a king-sized bed," he tells me, clearly inviting me to join him.

I'm back to thinking he's a cad, which really detracts from my experience with him yesterday. Maybe I was a little too evasive; maybe I should be more evasive. What kind of man flirts with every woman he encounters? What kind of woman wants a man like that?

I already told him I'd meet him tomorrow night; if I back out, I can't tell him the truth, which would mean I'd have to lie to him again.

If I tell him the truth, then I'd have to admit I already lied to him.

I grumble. Did I mention I hate lying?

Oh, the tangled web I weave ...

Back to the conversation. "Good, so Pringles should have plenty of room to curl up with you. Sometimes a scared animal will only come out at night. Having you there where he can have all night to get brave enough to come out should boost his confidence. The drugs should take away his fear. After about a week, he can have supervised outings to the rest of the house."

"Great. More imprisonment," I hear Trevor mutter, and my ears perk up at that.

"I beg your pardon?"

I can sense he hedges and comes out with, "I'm sure we both feel trapped here. Like I said before, neither one of us is really happy about the move. The last thing I want to do is confine him."

I've heard this argument before—although not from someone shrouded in darkness—so I give him my standard reply: "Cats need to feel safe before they venture out into new terrain. Once he feels safe at your side, for the full time you're sleeping, he'll want to explore. You'll merely be granting him time to come to terms with the move at his own pace. Think of it as bowing to his whims." I smile. "He is a cat, after all. We humans are programmed to serve."

He chuckles, and I remember how he put his head down to do that yesterday when I wouldn't give him my real name. I think he's doing that now. "Okay, okay. Just for you, RoseAngel. Just for you."

"No, for Pringles," I counter. "I'm here to help your pet."

"If this works, then I'm going to owe you a dinner anyway."

Back to this, huh? I feel a lopsided smile tugging my mouth. "We'll see. Give me a call in a few days and let me know how he's doing." I don't see any prison bars in his past, but I definitely sense confinement. I'm going to have to really get him talking tomorrow night and delve.

"I'll call you Monday and let you know."

"Okay, good luck. Bye."

We hang up.

I'm going undercover.

I shiver when I realize that has two totally different meanings.

I let my mind wander with that tantalizing prospect so long that I totally miss the next incoming call.

Chapter 5

Darlene agrees to meet me, and we go clothes shopping at our favorite department store. I have a store credit card for here, so if I find something that Darlene says I absolutely must have, then I'll bite. Otherwise, I'm here for advice.

"So, he totally flirted with you on the phone?"

"And in person." I give her a significant look. "When he met me at the grocery store, he didn't know who I was." I bite my lip, meet her eyes, then glance down. "And, I may have lied and told him my name is Marie."

"Wow." She parts me an evil little grin. "Look at you go with your petty lies."

When I look down, she continues, "But you knew who he was." She pulls out top after top, discarding them with a cute little wrinkle of her pert nose. Darlene is adorable at 5'6", blonde hair curling under at her shoulders, light green eyes, and perfect teeth. Those chompers cost her parents a pretty penny in high school, and that twenty/twenty vision she paid for herself a few years ago. She looks great without glasses.

She's a regular knockout, now, and dresses to kill.

All those guys who turned down Bucky Four Eyes in high school tripped over their tongues when they saw her at our last reunion. Darlene, good for her, didn't even acknowledge them.

"Yeah. Right from the start. I recognized his voice." Now, Darlene knows I have psychic abilities, but I think it sometimes creeps her out—unless she needs something, and then I'll do a Tarot card spread for her. Right now, she doesn't want to hear psychic-babble, so I stick to the facts.

She collects three blouses to try on and drapes them over the cart. "He's cute?"

"The trinity," I nod. Oh boy, oh boy is he. I feel something gathering and tightening low in my abdomen and realize it's excitement. I feel like I have a wind-up key sticking out of my horny gene and someone just cranked it a few turns.

"Ooh," she gives me an excited smile. "Tell him who you really are *after* you get some."

"But what about the darkness? And the kid?" She holds up a black blouse against my chest, and I curl my lip at it. I lower my voice. "What if he's a kidnapper?"

She tucks the top back on the rack and grabs a skirt. It's gray/blue and glittery and looks really nice. I like it. She holds it to my hips and nods, and I take the hanger.

"Well," she starts looking for a complementary top for the skirt, "can you do that Madame Voodoo thing and find out?"

I like the gray/white top she finds and holds up for me, so I nod. "I've been trying. It's not always reliable."

She faces me, holds the top and skirt in their respective places against my body and says, "This outfit will either get you the truth, or get you laid. Go try it on."

I groan and roll my eyes, because, well, I have to, but either outcome holds potential.

Unless, of course, he's a serial killer.

I'll have to call Misha when I get home.

• • •

"Are you crazy?" Misha asks me when I confess my crime *du jour*. At five foot nothing, with short black hair, eyebrow and lip piercings and a large black throat tattoo, people always expect her to be a sullen, despondent, moody Goth.

Misha turns their preconceptions on their ear. She's loud, unconventional, feisty, and the most logical thinker I know. She looks at a scenario and sees it through to the end.

Apparently, my end spells "disaster."

My mouth's still draping and gaping when I clarify, "Not even to find out about the kid?"

I can see her wagging her cautionary finger at me. "Don't go involving an unknown imaginary child as a means to get to know him. You're grasping, Rosie, and you know it."

"No fair," I pout. "I saw the kid way before he started flirting with me. The more I talk to him, the more the kid shows up." I'm pacing in my living room, I realize, but I pause long enough to kick a clump of fur on the rug.

"You don't know this guy, and he's got a bodyguard. What if he's not *famous*, but *dangerous*. Did you ever consider that?"

I hang my head. The fur clump has thwarted me.

My silence apparently condemns me. She barrels on with, "Are you going to cancel tomorrow night?"

And have to return my killer outfit? "No. It's just dinner at the grocery store café. Plenty of witnesses."

"Are you going to tell him the truth?"

I'm still not sure. Darlene wants me to wait until afterward, but then it's more deception. The pain of my teeth on my lip makes me let go. "I ... I don't know."

"The guilt will eat you alive, and we both know it. You need to come clean, sooner rather than later, or this will all blow up in your face."

I crack a rueful grin as I wander around my townhouse. It's small but tidy, with white carpets (whoever decided that should be shot), white walls, a white kitchen. The only color is my brown tattered couch, my dark square table and four black chairs, and whatever other items I could use to inject color into this space, since painting is *verboten*.

I'm finding myself dusting and washing the counters like I might have some sexy overnight company and wonder what the hell I'm doing. "You make it sound like there's a future between us."

"Nothing is for certain. I just know that you're starting off with: A. A dangerous man; B. Lying; and C. Unreliable psychic impressions. I know you're good at this, but there's no science behind it. Nothing can be proven outright. You don't know what you're getting into. Unless you know everything right up front, I say scram while the scramming is good."

I put away the last of my cleaned dishes and stare at the sink. It's eleven o'clock, and I should be in bed, but I'm so jacked I just don't feel tired. Tomorrow will be a full moon, and all the crazies will be ringing in with their problems.

Luckily, they are usually the same people, so I know what to expect.

The down side is that they are usually the same people, so I know what to expect. I close the cupboard and lean against my slippery-shiny counter. "You're right. I should just come clean. But, he needs to come clean, too."

"Amen."

Titan sees me standing there doing nothing, so he goes and waits by the back door. I clip his leash and put him out for his potty time.

She takes a breath. "How are you going to get the truth out of him?"

I chuckle. "How does any woman get a man to speak?"

I sense her wry grin. "Wear your pushup. Make sure your boobs are busting out."

I laugh and pin my phone to my shoulder to mash my breasts together. "Does that mean cleavage equals tales from the tit? Or do we call that tit for chat?"

Chapter 6

On lunch, I hop online and do a little research. I dig around to see if Travis Mattison is a real person. I find an old link to Myspace but it's obsolete.

By about three years.

Hmm.

All the photos have been deleted.

So I snoop on Facebook. No luck.

He doesn't call me at work, but I didn't think he would. After all, I told him to give my suggestion a few days and report back on Monday.

I shuffle through the stack of callbacks, holding off on the ones who are truly loco. Since it's the same problem from twenty-eight days ago (conveniently, the last full moon), I figure they can wait until the waning side of this one for a return call, as my after-hours phone message list is phenomenal today, filled with new clients that I know I can truly help. Like they say: Insanity is doing the same thing over and over again and expecting different results.

No effort on their end equals no change.

I start working through my messages. I talk a first-time puppy owner into keeping her dog, explaining that housebreaking is no different than potty training a child. Since she wants to have kids, she realizes this is a critical training point. I stress that and make her feel like a good mommy.

She signs up for puppy classes, and I now know that dog will have a lifelong home. People who go to class almost never relinquish their pets. They bond and develop skills there that they never would learn elsewhere, and it pays off. Big time.

I suggest, since she's so receptive, that when she has children to sign up for another class so her kids can learn how to be positive role models. She likes that idea a lot. I've planted a seed that will keep growing generation after generation.

I take a moment to rest on my laurels.

And then Charlie appears to me again, reminding me that the dead never rest, and I find myself grumbling with disquiet.

I'm not at my best when I make my next call, but I mentally tell Charlie I'll help him when I'm off the clock, and I focus on dialing my next client. When the woman with the crazy kitten answers, I listen to her concerns, and afterwards I tell her she needs to get it a friend. She's not struggling financially, but believes two kittens will cause twice the damage. So when I inform her that two kittens will tire each other out, she sees and understands my logic.

She's coming in tomorrow to shop for a friend for her rambunctious little boy.

I feel really good about that one, too. Not only did I keep one cat *out* of the shelter, but a currently homeless one will also now be freed.

Which makes me think of imprisonment.

Which makes me think of Travis/Trevor/Opie.

I'll be seeing him in four hours.

My mouth dries.

I think of being bent backward with that kiss.

Lord help me, if I wind up in his arms, all bets are off. I have no idea what my game plan is going to be. I have no idea if I'm telling him who I really am or not.

I've never been one for subterfuge.

Starting at seven, only the magic skirt and top will have the answer.

Chapter 7

The bus comes in with a full load of senior citizens. Wigs, canes, glasses, and BenGay foretell of the geriatric invasion in the cat room. Word spreads quickly in a shelter like ours: Gold Haven Nursing Home has just changed its pet policy.

Seventeen seniors are here to find a new friend.

I am eager to help out up front, something I haven't done since I was first hired, before I moved into Pearls. I take a stooped old woman by the elbow and lead her back to my desk area. Although six of us work here, we can close the door and pretend we're an adoption meeting room for her.

Her name is Agnes, she's eighty-two, and her beloved Bichon Frise died last year at home after a long battle with kidney disease. The nursing home will now allow cats and pocket pets, so I think a fluffy, white, longhair kitty might be a nice second for her late beloved dog.

I ask, "What did you like best about your departed Honey?"

"Oh," she melts, and her rheumy eyes go all moist and make her blink, "she just loved to be petted. I could hold her all day." She tips her head and gives me a shy smile. "She wasn't very dog-like in that regard, was she?"

I chuckle so she thinks I'm agreeing with her. I've met plenty of dogs that desire nothing grander than substituting for a handbag, but Honey was special to her, so I honor that bond. "Now, I know Honey is your standard, but was there anything at all that you didn't like about her?"

I want to make the best possible match, so I figure it's going to be the health issues the dog suffered.

Almost begrudgingly, like Honey would come back from the dead and haunt her (something an animal would never do to its beloved human), the words tear from her over-painted lips, "The grooming. It was so hard to brush her, and the groomer charged so much. I'm on a fixed income … " She meets my eyes with her own lovelorn, love-lost ones, begging me to understand.

I sense how difficult the void has been for her and try to convey that in my own eyes. I look off to my left, thinking, my pinky brushing along my bottom lip. Maybe a longhair cat would not be the best choice for her. My mouth pops open—an idea in my head. "Agnes, do you like surprises?"

She claps her hands and smiles like her youngest grandchild just performed on stage. "Oh, terribly, my dear."

I adore this woman and can't help but laugh at her joy. I rest my hands over her thin wrists. "Do you have any allergies?"

"No."

I give her my best wait-'til-you-see-what-I've-got-in-store grin and say, "I think I have just the pet for you."

I leave her in my office and scoot down the long beige hallway, back into the adoption center. I lift the heavy white wooden hood on one of the built-in cages and pick a guinea pig from its nest. Not just any guinea pig, but Mort. He's seven months old, salt-and-pepper colored, and a staff favorite. Most of his formative months have been spent here, with the parades of volunteers and school kids taming and gentling him.

He's a regular snuggler, and he's already been reliable about using his litter box.

Although skeptical, Agnes accepts my handful of love, and Mort does what he does best: he chirps, he whistles, he purrs in little guinea pig fashion, then settles in for a long snuggle.

Hook, line, and little stinker.

"How much to adopt him?"

• • •

Agnes now sits happily in the lobby, Mort dozing on her lap, and I come out and see Harry Provost's application on top; he is next in line to adopt his new best friend. I glance out at the main desk and see ...

Him.

Travis. Trevor. Opie.

What the hell is he doing here?

I take Harry's application and duck into a cubicle to page, "Tina, dial 281. Tina, 281." My phone rings two seconds later.

"Tina?" My heart is racing, and I'm panting like a Great Dane just dragged me Marmaduke-style around the compound.

"Yeah?"

I grip the desk, wondering when my knuckles turned white. Were they always so pale? I think I'm having a low blood sugar episode, because I notice my hands are shaking despite having locked onto the faux wood top. And I'm not ready to rule out the slight possibility I'm coming down with full-blown end-stage malaria. "Okay, so, you remember that phone call from the flirt?"

"Cellar-dweller?"

I want to laugh, but I'm not sure the sound that comes out of my throat qualifies. "Yeah. Only, he's not, and he's here."

She scoffs. "So, why are you calling me?"

"Look ..." I'm completely panicky, and I recognize this, but I'm not ready to meet him and come clean. I grab the front of my shirt and twist the material into my fist. If anything, it helps dry off my suddenly damp palm. "If the front desk pages me, will you be me? Will you come out and meet him?"

She hesitates. "Why? Is he missing limbs or something?"

"No, and he's hot." Tina is really pretty, too, the female equivalent of tall, dark, and gorgeous. The fact that I'm sending stellar competition to the hottest guy I've ever met speaks volumes for my mental state. I release my shirt and wipe the back of my wrist across my forehead.

"You don't want him?"

I can't even justify that with an answer. "Look, he just moved. I told him to isolate Pringles in his bedroom. The cat's on ami, and it's hiding. That's all you really need to know."

I sense her raising a brow at me over the phone. The loudspeaker calls out, "RoseAngel to the front desk. RoseAngel, you have a visitor at the front desk."

"He's hot?"

I gulp, but it doesn't help me breathe. "Yup. You heard the first tape, so you know all the rest."

I envision her gathering up her "girls" in preparation for meeting my impromptu visitor. "I'd say you owe me, but maybe, after this, I'll owe you."

I so did not want to hear that. I mumble, "Thanks, Tina."

The loudspeaker again calls for me, and I ease close and peer around the corner to watch Tina figuratively purr and roll around like a hussy at the feet of the man of my dreams.

• • •

Harry adopts a senior cat, a gruff old white-and-black former tomcat with a notch out of one ear depicting his glorified youthful days of adding kittens to our intake numbers. But old Butch is calmer now, wiser, neutered and settled and really sick of living in a two-foot-squared cage these last six weeks. Harry likes how Butch head-butts him and then gives him a feeble swat to back off.

They're a couple of regular crotchety old bachelors, and I feel they'll get along just fine.

I'm feeling rather crotchety myself, and wonder if it's safe to return from the dog meeting area (where I had to hide) and head back to my desk.

I'm afraid to go back. My overactive imagination has Trevor sitting in Tina's chair, her sprawled on his lap, while he dangles grapes into her mouth. Or is she feeding him? I imagine Disney-style music and cartoon animals dancing around them, confetti sprinkling down into their hair as little birds drop flower-laden leis around their shoulders.

Damn. What the hell was I thinking? Introducing them?

The senior train chugs out fifty-five minutes after parking at our door. I powered through four back-to-back adoptions in that time, which is really great. No tire kickers today! Over the loudspeaker, Margie, our shelter manager, announces thirty-four animals just got adopted in one hour, and the shelter staff cheers. It's a record we are ecstatic to have.

(Not all thirty-four left on the bus, by the way; we aren't that desperate! The seventeen seniors adopted twenty-two pets, including finches, cats, a lizard, two guinea pigs, a rabbit, two turtles, and a hamster; Two foster homes had finalized their adoptions of a no-longer-heartworm-positive dog and a three-legged hit-by-car cat. The rest were daily adoptions, most being picked up after their spay/neuter surgeries were complete.)

The staff now has a lot of empty cages to clean; I volunteer to help in the kitchen and laundry room, as it's farthest away from both my desk and the front door, and therefore the least likely place to be found by hot men with ghostly side-kicks.

Besides, I'm now feeling a little surly, and the Disney movie in my head has Tina in a yellow feather wedding gown with a peacock train, and she and Trevor ride elephants to the door of their private jet, then take off on a two-month-long honeymoon to exotic places like Greece, Egypt, and Rio de Janiero.

My life sucks, and I'm totally to blame.

I scrub finch cages, guinea pig cages, water bottles, bird dishes, cat dishes, twelve litter pans, dog toys, and after that I toss in a load of laundry and fold the one coming out of the dryer.

Another hour has now passed, and I'm assuming my unexpected visitor has left, along with my sanity. It's almost four. I reach for a hallway phone and ring Tina.

She answers, and I try to be nonchalant when I tell her, "I'll be right back. Hope it wasn't too busy." I am positive my voice wavered, and I cringe as I wait for her to tell me the wedding was beautiful.

I can tell she leans over the phone when she says, "Oh, my God, he was hot! Why didn't you want to come out and meet him?"

He's gone. I mean, really, did I expect him to move in? I feel my shoulders slump but I'm not sure why. "What did he want?"

"Just to say hi, to thank me, well, you, in person. I paged you right after he left. Why didn't you call?"

I frown and pick at some peeling paint on the walls. It takes me a second to ask, "When did he leave?"

"A few minutes later. Oh, my God, if you don't want him, I'm totally going after him. Do you want him?"

I turn at the awful noise behind me, ignoring the question I can't answer and focusing on the one I can. "I was in an adoption room. You can't hear the phone in there." I take a deep breath and hug the wall as a vicious dog on two catch poles is guided down the hallway by two kennel staff. The dog is muzzled (how they managed that, I'll never know) and growling and lunging, and only those stiff metal leash rods are keeping everyone safe.

The two kennel staff guys meet my eyes. One says, "Owner wants him back," and shakes his head in utter disbelief.

"There goes the neighborhood," the other one says.

"Well, I did try to call you," Tina reiterates.

I exhale in relief that the dog didn't lunge and try to eat me and tell Tina, "I've been helping clean up after the adoption rush. I'm done, and I'll be right back."

She leaps back in with, "He was in a suit, too. How can you not like a guy who dresses up for work? And he smelled *so nice.* Oh, my God, please tell me you don't want him."

I don't look after the dog. Sometimes, like my love life, it's better not looking back.

Chapter 8

When I get back to my office, I see no signs of a wedding, no confetti or leftover cake, no deflated balloons or flower petals and think maybe, just perhaps, my overactive imagination could benefit from a shot of rum.

I sit down and manage three more callbacks, focusing on ones that were really in need and not crazy. I make sure that Twitter, the kitten, is no longer harassing Grumpy, the thirteen-year-old cat who ruled the roost until three weeks ago. I find out Max the Shepherd is doing well in his mandatory obedience classes and is getting over his fear of people, and that Beatle the bunny did not have ringworm, as the owner feared, and would be able to stay in his home.

All in all, a good day at Lucky Clover … until I glimpse Tina's dark eyes, all dreamy as she stares off into space. "He was so incredibly hot. He's like a bad boy. Did you see his leather jacket?"

I don't like the look she's giving me, mostly because I see a naked Trevor covering her in it. I brave a smile and force myself to ask, "Did he flirt with you?"

"Well, yes and no." She faces me and gives me a secretive grin. "He gave me something. Told me not to tell anyone." She unwraps a Tootsie Roll Pop and slurps it in her mouth, a Cheshire grin on her face.

A sucker. He gave "me" a sucker. Well, at least *RoseAngel*, played today by Tina.

I try not to read into that.

She says, "He asked if I had any other advice for Cheetos, and I said to cuddle on the floor with him, try some interactive games. Catnip."

I catch the slip. "Did he call the cat Cheetos, or did you?"

Blank expression.

I press, "The cat's name is Pringles. So, was he testing you, or did you just forget the cat's name?"

Emptiness. "I … don't remember."

Tina and I don't sound the same, and I'm wondering if Dr. Doom noticed I sent in a pinch-hitter.

The loudspeaker announces closing time in five minutes.

I click my pen a few times and finish logging my calls.

Tina whispers, "Did I screw it all up?"

I shrug. "I have a date with him. Tonight. At seven."

Her eyes widen that I neglected that crucial detail, but now I'm too nervous to elucidate. I grab my purse and head out.

Chapter 9

Titan is by far the oddest dog I have ever seen. He has a Pekingese face, long legs like a Sheltie, a long shaggy black-and-white coat with brown feet, and two mismatched ears. He is also the most stubborn, thick-headed, brain-oxygen-deprived dog I've ever met.

Which is why, at almost three years of age, he's still not fully housebroken.

I get the irony of my situation. I know what I would say to any caller with this issue, but my dog is not their dog. I know him too well; I can *see* and read him too well.

I mumble this to myself as I gather up a plastic grocery-store bag and clean up his mess with wads of paper toweling and enzyme cleaner.

Titan stands by, clearly smiling at me, because he knows I'm going to take him for a walk when I'm done cleaning up after him.

Maybe today I won't. Maybe today I'll soak in a bubbly tub and listen to love songs and think of Trevor.

Titan barks and dances at the door, acting like he's got to go. I point at the cleanest spot on the floor and say, "Yeah, I doubt it. Not after that deposit."

He barks again and does some more soft shoe.

I tie the bag shut and grab his leash.

The walk gives me time to assimilate all the events of the last few days. I vacillate about calling my mom, and immediately discard the idea. She'll only want to ask when she should book the wedding. I swear the woman has lost her gourd. I pull out my cell and call Darlene instead.

She answers right away with, "You're not cancelling, are you?"

"No," I grin. "But," I trip over Titan's leash and auto-correct before I fall, "I think you should know he came into the shelter today to introduce himself."

I hear her mouse-like squeak. "He didn't!"

I extract my ankle from the nylon loop and grumble out, "Oh, yes, he did."

"What did you do?" I think she's holding her breath.

I wait while Titan sniffs the lamppost for every nuance of his incoming p-mail and say, "What every self-respecting liar does: I sent in a body-double." I close my eyes and pretend I never did anything as stupid as that.

"Who?"

Titan lifts his leg to add his own tweet. I grimace and say, "Tina?" Like I didn't know who I sent in. Or that saying it gently might not earn me a reprisal.

A gasp. "You didn't! Not her."

I blink like I'm being pelted by blinding snow. "Why?"

"She's gorgeous—not that you aren't, but, why her? What if he starts dating her? What if he comes parading around your desk and sees you there?"

Oops, didn't think that far in advance. My mouth and eyes all drop open, the pelting snow gone. "Uh ... "

"Yeah. I thought so."

Titan yanks me to another lamppost and skids to another stop. It takes a moment to find my voice, and Darlene is kind enough to let me stew in my own pot of confusion while I find my tongue. "So, now what?"

I hear her expel her breath through clenched teeth. "I'm changing my mind. You have to tell him the truth right from the get-go. Don't wait until the morning after, no matter how cute he is. Hot guys don't handle being lied to."

The truth? As in, who I really am? My hand wipes up my face, into my hair, and I feel my fingers grabbing a fistful of skin at my nape. "Shit, what am I going to say?"

"I don't know," I hear her complain. "Think up something. Tell him you were in the bathroom, for cripes' sake."

I worry my lip. "That might work. I could tell him that Tina heard me flirting with him on the phone, so she came down to the front desk and saw a hunky guy and just assumed it was him."

"Lame, but might work."

"While I was in the bathroom?" I add, crouching like a wayward servant girl getting caught with a crust of bread.

"Now you're getting somewhere."

Another tug on my leash, and Titan barrels me down the sidewalk again. For eighteen pounds, he sure knows how to pull.

I am a slave to my dog.

Darlene asks, "Are you going to wear the outfit?"

I'm feeling a little more in control of my life now … at least, this moment. "Yeah, after I shower."

She makes a clucking sound with her tongue, like I'll look smokin' hot or something. I smile at her confidence in my abilities to wow a man.

"Pushup?"

It must be a dating necessity among my friends. I sigh and say, "Yes, mother, I'll be wearing it."

I sense her grin when she adds, "Make sure the girls are mounding and ready to come out and play."

I look at the clock on my phone. It's almost six. "Hey, I've got to go. I'll text you tonight, okay?" I tug Titan the way he tugs me, only I respond better. I drag him away from a dead toad on the asphalt and head home.

She laughs and replies, "Here's hoping your hands are too busy to type."

Chapter 10

My clock says six-fifty-five when I pull into the grocery store lot, and I park and wipe my damp hands on my skirt. I fear the glitter will stick to them and that I'll touch my face and they'll stick there and then I'll go down forever in history as Sparkles the Blunder Babe. I double-check my makeup in the rearview and flip down my visor to check my hair, then angle the mirror lower to make sure my blouse is ever-so-slightly revealing.

I've never been so nervous in my life.

I gulp down a lump of dry nothing as I try to get out of the car. It's summer, school is nearing an end, and I've been seeing so many stretch limos that it seems like the Academy Awards are being hosted here, instead of a school full of seniors out for a prom night of glitz and glam.

The sound of my car door slamming seems final.

I look down and see that I have on display a small line of cleavage; it's all I have, so it'll have to do. My heart necklace dips right into the top vee of my blouse, and I'm feeling very self-conscious about my attire.

It's been eleven months since I broke up with Jacob, and this is the closest I've now come to dipping my toes into the proverbial dating waters. No matter how much I thought I knew him, the fact was I didn't.

I focus on my heels clicking across the asphalt as I step under the glowing red letters of the grocery store sign. Being pragmatic, I stuffed my grocery list in my purse, along with some coupons. I figure after this date crashes and burns, I'll be the best-dressed shopper in the place.

It's payday, after all. I'll probably splurge on some Woe Is Me ice cream—three different varieties—as well as another chunk of God-loves-calories Godiva.

My lips will love me. My thighs will hate me.

Trevor stands when I near the dining area, and his smile is so warm and amazed I figure Charlize Theron is sauntering up behind me. But no, as I round the oranges and enter the seating area, he takes my hand and kisses my knuckles. "Hello ... Marie."

Again with the piercing gaze. He dares me to reveal my name, and I feel my stomach flutter. "Hi, Tra—, um, Trevor." When I look at him, I see a Travis, and the name just kind of slipped out.

A shadow crosses his face, and I can tell I hit a raw nerve. "It's Trevor."

Another case of jitters makes me flush, and I'm afraid he might figure out I'm trying to delve into his mystery. "I'm sorry. It was a nervous slip." And how.

He's still staring at me, a distrustful move that makes me think of a cat on a fence eyeing a hungry stray dog. "Why would you call me Travis?"

Well, this was a crappy start to a first date. I stammer, "You, you look like a Travis to me. I'm sorry, Trevor. I didn't mean it." I hold his eyes, wondering if I should just leave now and come back tomorrow to do my shopping.

Or move out of state.

He's still staring at me, like he doesn't believe it was a nervous slip on my part. "You sure we've never met? Another time, another place?"

I shake my head no. "Unless we met in New York City."

He shakes his head as well. "Never been." He rubs the back of his neck. "It's just, of all names," he meets my eyes. "Never mind."

Now would be a fantastic time for a mindreading ability to fully manifest. I wait a few seconds, holding my breath, but the mystics are unkind.

He almost smiles as he tugs me in and leans forward as if to kiss my cheek, but he whispers, "Although I'd much rather be called Travis."

There it was again. He really was a Travis, and was hiding it. But why? Did he have a name change? Is he on the lam? I meet his eyes and ask, "Why?"

He leans back and holds my gaze. "Perhaps, like you, I prefer a different name than the one I shared. Unless, of course, you have something you're hiding?"

I think my face flushes, and I find myself taking a step back. I open my mouth, but nothing comes out.

His expression changes, softens, like he was merely teasing me and not expecting a reply. Instead, he looks at me like I'm the gentler sex in full need of his reverence. I get another image of me limp in his arms, this time naked, and I know it's totally from him; I'm way too nervous to be envisioning myself *au naturél*.

I'm no Charlize Theron, but dang if the boy doesn't make me feel like a million bucks. "Beautiful," he whispers. His lips brush my earlobe, gently, and I hear him take a deep, appreciative sniff of my perfume. "Pretty. I like it."

I'm still rattled, and I babble out, "It's an essential oil I bought at a festival last year, the kind you can also burn in one of those room diffusers. It's called Rain Goddess."

His eyes darken with promise, and he asks, "Do you need worshipping?"

My body is responding to him on a level I never knew it could achieve. As a kid, I used to lock hands and ankles with my brother, and we'd spin and spin and spin around so fast that the world became a blur of green and blue, and when we'd let go, we'd fall backwards and laugh and try to stand and bump into each other and fall back down and giggle at the kaleidoscope encircling us.

I'm feeling like that right now, but with a dash of horny tossed in for good measure, and Trevor's eyes seem to tell me he knows exactly what he's doing to my frazzled nerves.

He scoops my shoulders and guides me before him into line, and when I stand there, he places both his hands on my shoulders and leans over me to whisper, "Whatever you want is my treat."

I'd like *him* as my treat, but I feel my face flame and merely nod. I realize he's fully able to look down my shirt, standing where he is, and I smile that I'm so interesting to him. I do, however, want to lean back against him and feel his arms loop around my stomach. I know if I do, he'll gladly humor me, so I fight it and stand perfectly still while I order a vegetarian burger and mac salad and green tea.

He orders chicken pot pie with a salad and soda and takes the tray to our table. I like that he pulls out my seat for me and tucks me in.

I clutch my hands in my lap, afraid to touch anything for fear I'll drop it down my gaping shirt. I'm withholding my name, my job, I'm dressed way too provocatively, and now I've even gone and ordered an identity stand-in, and the man doesn't even know what I've been up to.

Or does he? Is that why he seems to have this amused expression regarding my middle name? Why he thinks we've met? What about how he looked so cornered when I called him "Travis?" What did I stumble upon? Is Travis related to Charlie? If I Googled it, what would I come up with? A missing child? Runaway dad? Top Ten Most Wanted? Or simply nothing?

It is the full moon, and I've gone completely loco.

He points his fork at my plate. "Eat. Or tell me about yourself." A wink.

I make a mental note to not poke the dragon as I take a bite of my burger and moan at the sheer volume of visible veggies. I'm not all that reassured to know that I'm a stress eater, for the food tastes amazing, and my stomach is so tight that I figured, if anything, a meal would make me choke.

Not that lucky, I guess.

I notice his eyes dip to my shirt, and I smile into my burger. He takes my avoidance of conversation and clears his throat and runs with it. "What core values do you like in a man?"

I give him the eye, intrigued that he'd start with such a heavy topic and not like, oh, which *Star Wars* trilogy was superior. "Honesty."

He nods and points at me with his fork. "Which you've totally nailed. *Marie*."

I ignore the slight with only the barest of blushes and continue with, "Integrity."

"Which I do have." He smiles when I meet his eyes.

So I start warming to his topic and think of Jacob. "To be accountable for his actions."

He leans back at that one and holds my eyes, and he means his words: "No one has been more accountable than I, especially over the last three years, and for the next four days."

I frown at him. "What does that mean?"

"It means," he leans forward, "that right now, I can only be as honest about my life as you are. Until next Tuesday, at the earliest."

Well, that had some promise. I crack a grin and continue with, "Being financially responsible."

I really like the smirk he's giving me. He seems so wry, so sarcastic, that I'm liking him more and more, even though neither of us seems to be able to let the other one in.

He breaks the crusty top of his pot pie into manageable pieces as he says, "Did I mention I'll be a bank manager starting Monday? I think I've nailed financially responsible."

I counter with, "Doing a job well is not the same as doing life well." I would know. Titan makes sure of it. Daily.

His head is tipped when he looks up at me, mirth in his gaze, and I feel that little flutter trip across my stomach again. I clear my throat and continue with, "Being open and communicative. A good listener."

He reaches for his drink, takes a swig on the straw and sets it back down. "I'm sorry, what were you babbling about?"

I laugh, because he's totally teasing me. His eyes are warm and chocolaty and I'm so not going to be able to wait for that Godiva. I glance at the menu and see they have brownie sundaes for dessert.

Hell, they have an entire bakery here; why limit myself?

"What about loyalty and commitment?" he asks, and I notice his gaze is diverted, his voice low.

"That should definitely go without saying." He hits a nerve with that one. Jacob springs to mind, so I snatch my green tea and shake the bottle before trying to twist off the cap.

"It should," he echoes, but his eyes are on his salad, his thoughts dark and far away. I notice I've stopped giving my tea its last rites and merely study him. His low voice adds, "I've seen far too many cases where it is exactly what someone fears it is."

"Deceit?" I'm trying to divert his attention away from me and my own guilt and focus on what he's saying, hoping my voice didn't shoot up an octave in the process. I can't get the bottle open, but Travis … *Trevor* reaches over and claims it gently from my hands, gives it a good twist, and with the seal break it *pops* open.

He hands it back to me and says, "Deceit, lies, betrayal … it's enough to drag a body down." He's still looking at his salad and jabs a leaf with his fork.

Rationally I know he's not talking about me, but I still can't help but notice the comparison. I'm no better than anyone else he's known in his life, and that leaves a bitter residue in my throat. I lick my lips and mumble thanks, then focus on a word I clued in on: "Cases?"

He meets my eyes. "I can't talk about it. Yet."

So I'm thinking he's a policeman, or FBI agent, out following some bad guy. I don't even feel so weirded out by Mr. Matrix now, who is suspiciously out of sight. I lean forward and ask, "Is that why you have a bodyguard?"

"Lots. Just for now. Soon, hopefully, this will all be over."

"Why do you need bodyguards?"

I'm sensing a deep combat between darkness and light, and know he's really trying to put all this behind him. His eyes flick to mine before looking back down, a mere headshake the only answer I was going to get to my question.

So I whisper, "What's in four days?"

He meets my eyes again, and I really like when he does that. I feel like I can fall into them and wrap myself up in his soul and that everything really will be all right in my life. He exhales a deep breath and says, "I can't tell you. Yet."

I see a blindfolded woman for the barest of seconds, but I'm fuzzy on the meaning. Was she one of his hostage cases? Something spawning from deceit? Lies? Betrayal? Or a Tarot card? Spearing my mac salad helps deflect some of my angst. Some. "I have a question for you: Are you the king of evasion?"

"No." He leans back in his chair, his body open, inviting. "I'm not. This is really hard for me to hold all this in."

Again with the wave of darkness. He looks down and shoves his pot pie pieces around the bowl like a fisherman trying to herd carp with a paddle. Agony squeezes my chest, and I know he's still trying to deal with the death of his wife.

His voice is low when he says, "It's been three years, and I haven't even been able to say goodbye." Now I see the real pain in his eyes, pain hidden behind flirting and joking. "I don't even know where she's buried."

I catch my breath. "That's terrible." I've never been married, but the thought of not knowing where my beloved's remains are buried brings the burn of upcoming tears to my eyes.

He shakes his head and closes down, stabs a chunk of carrot and starts chewing. The topic is closed, and when he next looks up, his eyes are bright and the darkness is receding behind closed doors. "Where do you stand on humor? Curiosity? Creativity?"

I blink away my empathic tears and focus on his question. I smile and lean back and opt for a literal answer. "I've never stood on humor a day in my life. I imagine it would be … rather bumpy."

He laughs, nice and rich, and I like that I made his eyes sparkle.

"As for the other two, I embrace them. Creativity gets me through the day."

It's his turn to eye me. "Answering phones?" I can tell by his look that he's waiting to catch me in another lie. I remember my vague job description and feel my smile collapse. "Answering phones." I recap my tea and give it another shake. Doesn't tea need to be shaken frequently? I pop my straw back in for a swig, since it seems like my tongue is now dry. "What did you do in your last job?" My voice is a bit low.

Trevor turns his head a bit to study me. "Ask me next week. Maybe then I can tell you."

I must have given him a less-than-thrilled expression, because he leans close and asks, "What's a girl like you do for fun, and where can a guy like me take you for it?"

He means it, and I offer him something I haven't done in a few years—the beach. "Well, there's a ferry that goes south out of town, straight down the river to the Hamptons. I haven't been there in a few years. That's always fun."

His smile is one of complete interest. "The Hamptons? Like, on Long Island?"

I nod.

"Are you going to be in a swimsuit?" His brows waggle, and I'm pretty sure I blush.

I think I'm smiling as I pick pieces off my bun. "Well, yeah, it is the beach." My cheeks still feel hot, so I focus on spearing some more mac salad, trying to get one elbow on every tine of my fork. Am I even ready for the bathing suit level?

He raises his index finger, pulls out his Smartphone and does some research. "Weather tomorrow looks great, sunny and eighty."

He frowns and does a little more digging. "Looks like … we can leave at nine tomorrow morning." He looks up. "Want to pack some sandwiches?"

My jaw drops. "To—tomorrow?"

"No time like the present."

His smoldering eyes tell me that *I* am his present.

I find myself nodding just to make him smile.

Chapter 11

Grocery shopping with Trevor for the beach tomorrow comes easily. We debate the merits of sliced watermelon versus cantaloupe, making sandwiches versus packing all the separate ingredients, water versus soda versus sports drinks.

I've never enjoyed shopping as much as I do this moment.

My cart is overflowing with sunscreen, lip balm, a new pair of flip-flops, a towel that Trevor absolutely had to have (he's a Broncos fan—who knew?), snacks (both healthy and not), and I make one last run for ice cream, because it's a known fact that chocolate replicates the feeling of being in love, and I'm totally having a dish before I crawl into my empty bed tonight.

He buys everything that's for tomorrow, leaving me with only thirty dollars of groceries to pay for. He winks and says, "If I ate shredded wheat, soy milk, or hummus, I'd just pay for everything, but you're on your own, there."

I give him a good-natured shove. He's so joyous and playful it's hard to reconcile him with the dark man I first met.

I try not to assume I'm the reason for that change, but it's hard when the man in question keeps laughing like he hasn't done so in years.

It's well after ten by the time we push the cart outside. Trevor leads me to his car, and he gathers up all the goods for tomorrow and puts them in the back of his silver Elantra.

"Do you have a cooler?" I ask him.

He looks at me like I spoke Greek. "Um, no."

With an even regard I ask, "Do you want me to just bring them home and pack them for tomorrow? You know, in my cooler?"

He grins. "Nope. I'll take care of everything." He closes the trunk and leans back on it, his arms not crossed, but on the car at his sides, open. Despite his inability to share details of his life, I find his body language wonderful.

He looks incredibly huggable.

I bop a shrug, and I see his happiness reflecting in his eyes. "My Maserati is over there," I point, and Trevor of course has to ask, "Maserati?"

I veer toward my Honda, the next aisle over, and Trevor joins me. Few cars are in the lot right now, but another drove of prom-night stretch limos are pulling in. I watch a parade of tuxedos and gowns spill out. The girls giggle and mingle while the tuxes head into the store.

"Buying condoms," Trevor says. "Watch and see."

I gasp and face him. "You!"

I notice three limos idling at the far edge of the lots, waiting for their occupants to emerge from the store. I stick my key in the trunk lock and Trevor informs me, "This, um, isn't a Maserati."

I gasp and lunge for my driver's side mirror and cover the glass with my spread palms. "Shh!" I chastise him. "He can hear you!"

We share a chuckle, and I pat my car to assuage the insult placed upon his noble bumper. "Don't listen to him, Figaro. The man knows not of which he speaks." To Trevor I explain, "He hasn't broken down since I changed his make. Don't jinx it."

I can tell I amuse him by his expression, and I like that I can be goofy with him and he plays along. I load up my car with my paltry few bags and Trevor takes my empty cart back to the corral.

I like that he doesn't just leave it for another car to crash into and I wonder, does this qualify as accountability?

He comes back to me as a herd of tuxedos jog out of the store, laughing and jostling one another. I check the bags in their hands and see a few boxes looking suspiciously like Trojans. Trevor gives me the raised eyebrow, the I-told-you-so look, and I smirk at him.

The boys spread out, and they begin trying to pelt each other with grapes. Trevor steps nearer to me, and I'm guessing by the look in his eyes it's for a goodnight kiss.

I hear the boys racing for their limo behind me, but my eyes are on Trevor. He steps near, sees something behind me, and then wide-eyed with fear grabs me and dips me toward the ground.

I'm breathless and limp as a bowl of hot noodles. He yells over his shoulder to them, "Knock it off!" and I hear them gasp and run away. Whatever they did, they think they hurt me, and the tones Trevor barked at them put him totally in control. I sense their fear as a palpable beast as their limo pulls out.

I look into his face, and concern is foremost on his brow. "Are you okay?"

I'm flaccid and placid and the most submissive I've ever been in my life. My feet are somewhere under my buttocks, unable to support me; my shoulders a scant two feet above the ground; a beautiful rogue man is holding me powerless and captive ...

Yup. I'm way better than okay. I manage, "Why? What happened?"

"They threw a tomato. It almost hit you."

"Oh."

He crooks a little-boy grin. "But, with that red hair, I don't think you'd notice."

He's still smiling, so I add, "It's not a very good conditioner, though."

"No?"

"No. Eggs are way better."

I like the way he's scanning my face. He's a Dipper, the extinct subspecies of man gone the way of Clark Gable, William Holden, Gene Kelly, and that famous unnamed sailor in Times Square kissing his nurse as he steps off the WWII battleship.

I upgrade his status from "extinct" to "endangered."

He should breed.

Right now.

He cocks a brow and asks, "You'd rather have been beaned by an egg? Wouldn't that hurt?"

I watch his lips when he speaks. They are perfect lips. Fleetingly—or incessantly—I wonder what they'd feel and taste like. "I didn't say I wanted to get hit by it; I just said eggs are better conditioners."

He's smiling that we're conversing as if this is a perfectly normal position for such. "Are you sure you're okay?"

"I'm fine. Nothing hit me." Shy of, say, Cupid's Arrow. I manage to raise my limp hands to touch his shoulders in the traditional I'm-ready-to-be-kissed position, but he still doesn't relinquish me.

In fact, his brown eyes seem to have darkened over the last millisecond. "I've half a mind to kiss you senseless before I let you up."

I find my lips saying, "Only half?"

I like the warm smile he gives me; it makes my abdomen twist with need. I have an irrepressible desire to make our personal Velcro patches *stick*.

"Will you tell me your real name first?"

Crap. After all the planning, all the reciting, all the promises I made myself today, the fact he pushes me right when I'm the most vulnerable makes me fearful. The twisting sensation in my gut uncurls, my hands falter, my lust … doesn't plunge one iota. But I can tell my smile does. "What if you get mad and drop me and I crack my skull open and die?"

Warm fingers spread across my back and waist, drawing me closer to his lips, closer to telling the truth and pushing him away with it. He's smiling when he asks, "Why would I get mad?"

"Because I lied to you."

"How so?" His expression is one of amusement, and he is really enjoying the fact that we're in this position. A limo drives by and toots its horn. He grins, but his eyes never leave mine.

"I'll tell you tomorrow."

"Promise?" He has a secret, I can tell, but I don't know what it is.

I fall into those brown eyes just like I did two days ago. I'm upside down, but I feel like I've Bungee-jumped off a thousand-foot cliff, the air sucked from my lungs, the wind whipping past my face and tears streaking from my eyes as I reach the bottom for the blessed millisecond of rest and then career straight back up, and then my stomach sinks as I reach the apex and gravity snaps me back down over and over again. "Promise," I breathe.

Slowly he draws me to my feet, his hands finding their way to my head. His fingers nestle into my temples and stroke the length of my hair down to my shoulders. He leans in and places a gentle kiss on my cheek, then another one on my earlobe.

I shiver.

"I'll kiss you when you tell me your name."

His fingers tighten on my nape, his teeth graze my ear, and I hear him inhale deeply of my perfume again and moan with appreciation. His body is hard and tense and holding back by the merest thread. I'd be willing to bet if I brushed my lips to his, he'd bend me backward again, the way he keeps wanting to.

But I don't.

I want him to really kiss *me*.

I'll tell him the truth.

Tomorrow.

Chapter 12

Sleep, when it does come, seems spotty and elusive, teasing me with its allure while dancing further away. Dreams of seashells and crabs remind me I'll be on the beach with Trevor, and I wake up again, excited and nervous.

I text both my friends when I get up to let them know where I'll be, and of course, with whom. Misha tells me I'm crazy, natch, but Darlene is all for it. Frantic typing reassures one that I won't get murdered and the other that I'm not sleeping with him today.

Despite the fact we'll be in the water, I do shower and dress in a filmy beige skirt and gauzy white top. I take Titan for a walk and he doesn't poop, so I know I'll have *that* to look forward to when I get home.

I had given Trevor my phone number and address last night, and he pulls in the drive at eight-twenty. Domesticity drapes from him as he beams and gathers up the grocery bags of snacks to bring. Titan practically trips him at the door, and Trevor smiles wide enough to stop my heart.

"Look at him! He's so cute!" He scans my townhouse with frank appreciation and then two strides bring him into my kitchen, where he drops the goods on the counter. "You look great," he says to me, and I tell him the same. He's wearing a light green t-shirt, which really complements the dark green and navy of his swim trunks. He's got nice legs, firm and muscular, but not too bulky or thin.

He's still smiling as he squats down, asking, "Who's this? Is he friendly?" He claps his hands, and Titan perks up.

"Annoyingly so," and Titan wiggles his little shaggy heinie while he sniffs those camel-brown Birkenstocks. "His name is Titan."

"*Titan*," he repeats in a playful tone, spreading his arms wide and dropping into a play bow. Excitement lights up the dog's eyes, and he yips once and bows in return and spins two or three times before racing off into the living room.

"Now you did it," I intone.

Trevor stands up and steps near to me, mock concern filling his lips and eyes. "Why? What did I do?"

I point to the living room, not even needing to look to know Titan is now bouncing off the furniture. The telltale squeak of his latex pink whale soon follows.

"I did that?" he asks, thumbing the shaggy ping pong ball.

"You did that." I'm so happy to have him standing in my house that I'm afraid all my joy shows on my face. So much for being mysterious and playing it cool. I touch my quivering stomach to quiet the ripples.

He steps even closer and places a lingering kiss on my cheek, then murmurs, "Did I tell you that you smell great, too?"

I whimper, and one hand on my back draws me close—an almost hug. It's my turn to envision myself limp in his arms.

Just as abruptly, he switches gears. "Okay, where's the cooler? Chairs? Beach towels?"

I drag my spinning soul back into my body and point to the living room, where I had pulled all of it from storage in my tiny basement. He gives me a playful swat on my tush as he marches over to the pile.

I gasp, of course, covering my bottom with both hands. He parts me a rogue grin. "Come on, lighten up. Life has far too many serious moments already. Got to grab each day by the horns."

I challenge, "Is that what you were doing? Grabbing?"

He leaves the beach pile and comes near, arms and legs spread wide as he shakes the mamba. "Come on, give me some sugar!"

I squeal and back into my galley kitchen, my back wedged between the trash can and the fridge, but Trevor grabs me and shakes all over me like a two-bit whore.

I can't stop laughing, and I can't push him off.

"Come on, you sexy mama, let's tango." He grabs my hand and stretches out my arm, holds me terribly close and cheek-to-cheek and marches me straight to our supplies, the happy barking of Titan the only accompaniment to our music-less dance.

I let go, laughing. "What the hell are you smoking?"

"Freedom. Fresh air. A day to relax and be me and share it with the prettiest girl I've met in eight years."

I like the time frame reference. That one comment tells me he's never looked at another woman the whole time he was married— or, before that, emotionally involved. "Thank you. You're very sweet."

"My pleasure," he winks while he slings the fold-up canvas chairs and towels over his shoulder and loads up the car.

But then I have a refuting thought: "Is that how long you were imprisoned?" I realize my voice wavers somewhere between serious and sparring, and I'm not sure which way he'll take it.

I'm rewarded with another rogue grin. "Just because they call women 'the ol' ball and chain' doesn't mean it's hard time." His mood turns piquant. "I did, in fact, offer Jasmine a life sentence."

I glance down then back up. "Your late wife?"

He nods, solemn, and I see her then: Curly auburn hair, small green eyes, thin lips, my height. A little like me, but not entirely. I feel a little better knowing that I'm his type, and a lot better knowing I don't really look like the deceased.

Sensing he's finally starting to come to terms with her loss, I exhale and tell him, "I'm sorry. I didn't mean to pry."

"Not at all." He smiles, and it's like the morning sun has painted pinks and reds and oranges all across a navy sky. "I fully intend to find out *your* story today. *Marie.*"

I groan and grab his incredibly strong shoulders and turn him toward the last of our pile to pack up, and he chuckles and takes the last few bags.

I grab gel ice packs from where they were wedged in my freezer and load all the cold foods into my cooler. I see everything—and I mean everything—he brought with him is labeled. When he comes back in, I hold up the baggie of sliced watermelon and ask, "If I put a cantaloupe slice in here, do you re-label the bag, or does your world come crashing to a halt?"

He stops mid-bend of picking up my giant beach umbrella and looks at me, feigning fear. "I hope I never have to find out."

Oh, I'm *so* going to mess with him now. I wait a few seconds for him to hoist the umbrella over his shoulder. While he finagles our cumbersome shady spot into his car, I quickly peel off the masking tape from *Avocado* and move it to the *Doritos* bag, and that label goes to *lettuce*. And so on.

His world might implode.

Someone should be there to witness it.

Chapter 13

"So, why Titan?" Trevor asks me as we drive toward the ferry. A sizable amount of cars are on the road for a Saturday, and since they're also moving southbound, I have to assume word of the sunny weekend got out and people are making their Mecca toward the beaches.

Two clouds hover in a robin's egg blue sky, looking lonely and wispy and not long for this earth. "The name, or the dog?"

"Both," he answers. I notice he pays equal attention to the road, his passenger (that's me), and his GPS.

It's an oft-told story by me, and I dive headlong into it, like I've done a hundred times. "He was a cruelty confiscation. A woman rescued a really sick dog from this," I air-quote, "*breeder*, and for two weeks she couldn't reach the person to return the dog. She went back and saw the place was deserted. Our staff went in and found thirty-eight dead dogs and one barely alive. Titan was the last man standing." I shrug like I had no choice but to foster him, which, in reality, I didn't.

"That's why you kept him?"

I nod and watch the two kids in the SUV ahead of us wrestling in the back seat. "Yup, for four months I fostered him, bringing him back and forth to work to help socialize him and get him healthy. When he was good and ready for adoption, I just didn't have the heart to return him. He really bonded with me and my cat, Grimm, who also helped bring him out of his shell." I part him a half-grin. "We call that 'foster failure,' when the animal never leaves its temporary home, because we're suckers." I make an "L" with my finger and thumb and stick it to my forehead in the traditional "loser" salute.

"So you work for an animal shelter," he states, crooking a secretive little smile while he says it.

Trapped. I never even realized how neatly he walled me in. Shit and shinola, he's onto me! Once I manage a breath, I take a cue from Mr. Evasive and ask, "Does it really matter?" I start playing with the air vents in the car to keep my hands from wiping the sweat from my face. The A/C is blasting, but right now, the heat is on.

He grins wider, like he's glad he caught me in a lie. I'm wondering if he knows my alter ego and therefore my name. Now I'm really torturing myself—if he knows, why isn't he mad? What's the big deal if I prove him right? But if he doesn't know, I'll be stranded on a ritzy island with all my fave belongings in someone else's car, so I clamp up.

He must have figured it out by now, I tell myself. Right? How on the phone 'he thought we met? And then Tina botching the name of his cat? And now I went and flat-out admitted I work in an animal shelter. I should just spill the beans.

"No," he sings his answer, "I guess it doesn't matter at all, except where that whole honesty thing is concerned."

Ugh. I see the two of swords—the Tarot card showing a blindfolded woman holding both blades aloft. I'm indecisive and hating it and the universe is letting me know. I bite my lip. "Yes, I do work at a shelter. Please don't ask me any more."

I realize at this moment that two blindfolded women exist in Tarot; the other is Justice. I'm wondering if there's a court case coming up in, say, three days.

He grins out the windshield, a huge smile that tells me he finally feels like he's getting somewhere with my answer. "I've never met such an evasive woman before. Sheesh, you'd think having employment was a capital offense."

I counter with, "And what did you do before this?"

He pauses, and I see the humor leave his eyes. "I really want to tell you everything, but … " he sighs and his shoulders drop. He follows the barking orders of his GPS and makes the appropriate turns into the ferry parking lot. "I'll tell you Monday, because Tuesday, if things go horribly wrong, I might not have another chance, and I'd like you to know the truth."

Bitter fear crawls up my throat. "Trav?"

He reaches over and squeezes my hand, and I see images of men, well-dressed, with expensive suits. They have the look and feel of powerful CEOs or political figures, but not judges or lawyers. With a sad look he tells me, "As much as I love hearing my name from your lips, you really should call me Trevor."

I like the looks of his fingers lacing with mine. Again, the name just slipped out, but this time he's confirmed it. "It's not your name, though." I can play the statement game, too.

A wry look, followed by a scoff. "I have a Social Security card and a driver's license saying it is."

"And I have you introducing yourself saying it's not." That part was true, and I didn't even have to mention my psychic abilities. Geez, with my hang-up about lying, I had totally forgotten about deceiving him with all my voodoo hoodoo.

I fear I'm going to hell.

His lip curls, and I know it was a slip on his part. He maneuvers the car in line to board the ferry and pays the crossing fee. We drive onto the ship and park and get out.

Trevor offers me his hand, and I willingly give him mine. I repeat his name over and over: Trevor, Trevor, Trevor.

We walk hand-in-hand around the ferry, and I point to the bow. I love seeing the sound stretch before me, the miles of salty water cresting and spraying, the promise of sandy shores just beyond the horizon. Dead fish and algae odors choke the air in puffs as the convection currents carry it up the sides of the boat to our noses, but then a fresh gust of wind wipes it away, leaving only the delightful scent of sunshine and sea spray.

I fill my lungs with it every chance I can.

Trevor guides me before him at the railing and stands behind me, locking me captive between his arms and the rusting steel bars. I feel the warm sun on my face and the heat of Trevor's body behind me and feel content as I haven't in a long time.

His soft voice in my ear says, "You're right; Trevor is not my name." I try to turn to see him over my shoulder, but he comes up closer behind me and holds me tight. I can't help but lean into him. My hair flails in the snap of the summer wind, but he gathers it up and twirls it into a rattail and presses his cheek to my ear. "How'd you know my real name?"

I look back at him. "I told you, you look like a Travis to me. I have to force myself to remember to call you Trevor." I shrug. "That, and I've never met anyone who botched up their own name before."

"Hm," he says, and presses his lips to my nape, holding us still in the summer sun. "I think I now believe you when you said we've never met. I don't think I would have forgotten you."

I'm falling, and I never want to get up.

"Is this the ocean?"

I smile and close my eyes, hearing the gulls cry on the pier, the waves lapping at the shoreline, and the chug of boats taxiing close. "It's Long Island Sound. The ocean is over there," I flap half-heartedly to the East with my left hand.

His low moan and chuckle tickles the hair by my ears. "I've never seen the ocean before. Does the sound have dolphins and sharks and things, too, like the rest of the ocean?"

No one—and I mean no one—in Connecticut would ever claim to have never seen the ocean, so I have to spin and stare at him. "You're kidding."

A solemn head shake. "I grew up in a landlocked state." I watch the awe and reverence in his eyes as he tries to fathom that sheer expanse of water.

I remember the first time I saw the ocean; I was four and felt amazed and alone and awed—kind of what I'm seeing in his eyes now. "Where?" I'm thinking the Broncos might be my answer.

He tears his gaze from the salty stretch and looks down at me. "Monday." He winks and turns me back around and wraps his arm across my shoulder. "Have you ever seen dolphins out here?"

"Once," I tell him. "I was seven or eight. We were on a speedboat, rounding the island, and a pod of three or four raced us. It was pretty neat."

"I'll bet."

I can practically watch the negative ions sucking the darkness from his soul; he is now a being of light and joy and happiness, the bad in his life never happened, his world is full of possibilities, and the Fool card shows me he sees his life as one of wondrous imaginings, with no harm, no sadness, and no preconceived fears.

I'm really liking what I'm seeing, and I tell him so.

He thinks I'm enjoying watching him experience his first ocean, so I let him think that.

I tease, "Are Travises more fun than Trevors?"

"Infinitely," he vows, with a hint of promise in his eyes.

I really like that I'm part of his change, his future.

His joy.

Well, at least *Marie* is.

Chapter 14

We're only a mile or so away from the Connecticut dock, but I know I can't lead him on any longer. I want to get past this before years fly by and my name on the wedding invitation says "Marie Dobson" and my entire family either mocks me or throws them out.

I'm already visualizing a whopping eight people at our ceremony, when my mother's invite list topped one hundred thirty, and that was two years ago.

Who knows how many others she's added to the list this past year that I've been single?

I spin in his arms and lean against the scorching hot railing. "Trevor, I ..."

"Travis, please."

I hold his dark gaze, searching his soul for the name he deserves. "If you want me to call you by your birth name, then I'd really like you to call me by mine."

His eyes alight with interest, and he angles closer. I open my mouth, but a nearby tugboat blows its horn, startling and interrupting me. I glare over the railing at it, angry that I finally braved this hurtle, only to be thwarted. When I open my mouth to try again, our boat toots a deep, lung-rocking reply. "Seriously?" I yell out to the heavens, but Travis stands there, waiting, smiling that secretive smile.

His eyebrows raise a bit, silently asking me to continue.

I take a deep breath, look around while I wait for a third horn, then tell him, "My name is RoseAngel. RoseAngel Marie Dobson."

"It's about friggin' time," he replies.

My jaw drops; I can only stare at him. "You're not mad?"

"Only that you made me wait so long to kiss you." And he does. He grabs my head and plants a long, lingering one on my lips. I close my eyes and feel my head swirl like the top of a custard ice cream cone, complete with brain freeze.

He takes his kissing seriously, and, I have to say, I like the way he kisses. We are in perfect harmony, mouth-wise. He nibbles my lips and alternates from soft to demanding and his tongue dares me to explore his mouth the way he does mine.

The wind at my back pushes me into his chest, a chest that I'm very eager to place my hands upon. I like the hardness of his pectorals under my fingers, and his own fingers grip my waist and tug me closer. I feel my hair dancing along our cheeks, obliterating our kiss from the general public's view.

Eventually he pulls away, and when I eventually drag open my eyes to meet his, I have to ask. "But, I lied to you. Why aren't you mad? When did you know it was me?" Our boat has picked up speed, and my hair whips and flails around my face. I shiver, but I'm not sure if it's from internal or external forces.

I like the warmth in his eyes, and Travis cups my cheek when he says, "The very first moment you spoke to me, at the deli counter. I'm incredibly adept at recognizing voices; that's why I asked you if we had met the next day when I called the humane society, where you work as a, what did you call it? Your desk job? Receptionist? Not glamorous?"

I feel my lips curl in a smirk to match my groan, and he places another gentle kiss there.

I gasp in realization and swat him on his amazingly-hard chest. "Why didn't you just tell me you knew my name? I've been sweating it out!"

"Yeah," he crooks a grin. "It's been fun watching."

I swat him again, and he chuckles and grabs my hand. "I was trying to—" he meets my eyes. "It's part of what I can't yet tell you. I needed to know more about you, what you knew about me. The rest was just me having fun watching you crack under pressure."

I groan and mumble under my breath.

He asks, "The question I have for you is this: What made you come up and speak to me?" He leans back, a tease in his eyes. "Are you always such a saucy little vixen? Picking up men?"

I think fast and tell him, "I'd never seen you before, and, well, truth be told, I thought you were pretty cute."

"Cute?" The word repulses him; he looks nauseous. "I've never once since high school thought of myself as *cute.*"

I cock my head at him. "Huh. Never once? Not at all?"

He smiles and leans in, and I find my head tipping back in preparation for another kiss.

I can feel his breath tickle my lips, and his hands spread out on my waist. "I prefer manly, or hubba-hubba, or maybe even smokin' hot tango dancer, but no, cute is not in my repertoire."

I spare a scoff-smile; my eyes flutter closed and ready. This time when he kisses me, the strangest thing happens: I see a blur of motion, like a movie in fast-forward, with flickers of light just like the old black-and-white films, and I race into what I assume is a kitchen. It slows from fast forward to play, and I find myself in a metal-walled box, blinded by darkness, but by squinting I can see through the slats in the door. I'm in a closet, the broom closet, wedged in, and the shadows just beyond skulk past on determined boots. Gunshots ring out, and two bodies hit the floor. I hear cupboards being tossed open, and I taste and smell my own fear.

I'm hiding for my life, and the killers are only feet away.

Travis angles over me, his tongue toying along my lips, and I wrap my arm around his neck to draw him closer. I'm having my first honest-to-God premonition, and I can't let it end.

Never mind that I'm having it on the ferry while being kissed senseless.

That's a complete bonus I'm not willing to concede.

The shadows move away, and I ease out of my confined space. I see a rustic kitchen, pine cupboards, a discarded bake-at-home pizza box on the counter. I step further into the kitchen and find myself framed in the wide doorway between that room and the living room. Two bodies, both agents, are on the ground, dead.

I see the deadly assailant, dressed completely in black, from ski mask to gloves, standing in the middle of the room, his back to me.

I recognize the place from the first time Travis called; it's his log cabin, the one he hates. I see the tan couch and soft yellow lamp. I see the moving boxes still unpacked.

I freeze, rooted in fear. The man's head dashes up, once, twice, three times, and then the sneezes begin. He's allergic to Pringles, and his allergies send forth a battery of sinus attack.

I take the distraction and slide out the side door at the far side of the kitchen and duck down beside the trash cans. I see an agent in the shadows at two o'clock. I wave, and he runs over in crouched fashion and guides me to the gate in the barbed-wire-topped eight-foot-high military fence, where he takes a ring of keys off his right hip and waves me through.

Travis tries to pull away, to end the kiss, but the vision isn't over. I wrap my arms around his back and renew efforts on my end.

I'd hate for him to think I'm not paying attention.

I'm shoved through the gate at my keeper's behest and can make out a line of four parked cars in the dark. The second one is unlocked, the keys in the ignition for a quick getaway.

More shots fire out behind me; I jump in and take off, keeping my lights off so they can't see me. I go left down the road, and after exactly two point one miles, I pull off onto a dirt road on the right, angling up a sharp hill. Trees shelter the entrance, and anyone barreling down the road would blast past and not even see it. I hide there, and a minute later the other three cars blow by underneath me in hot pursuit.

I back out, relieved, and feel myself jump ahead a few miles to a gas station, the lonely kind that sells everything from fuel to food to novelties, and I pull in back and hide.

I'm safe here.

It's over, I'm still alive, and I release my death grip on Travis's back and lips.

A few people onboard clap at my performance. I feel myself blushing at my wantonness, when in reality so much more just transpired.

I look at Travis, and he looks beyond pleased, but with a touch of confusion sprinkled in. His lips are red and swollen from my attack.

I feel sweat break out on my forehead and neck, even though I'm shivering, this time with fear. I wipe my head with my wrist and find myself panting as I gaze fearfully out at the sound. My mouth is dry despite the millions of gallons of water just feet away, and I'm afraid to swallow. I don't know why.

My hands and arms are shaking.

Someone's out to kill the man I think I could one day love.

I take off at a run.

Chapter 15

"Getting married?" the bartender asks me as I sip my glass of red.

I look up at him, dazed and getting my earliest buzz ever. "What?"

He's an older man, about fifty-three, with slicked black hair and a giant nose that bespeaks his addiction to the liquid elements of his job. He indicates the front bow with what might be a jeer. "I saw you out there and just wondered if you were getting cold feet."

My performance, as it was, is gathering some attention on board. I don't answer, but down a good mouthful of cabernet sauvignon. It goes straight to my head.

I'm beginning to understand why psychics turn to alcohol to dull their visions. I'm terrified and don't even know how to proceed. As my blood pressure drops, I realize the vision played out at night. I don't know when, but I sense soon.

Travis yanks open the door, relieved to finally find me. "There you are. I've been looking everywhere."

I'm not myself, but I'm glad he can tell that, too. He joins my side, facing me and not the bartender. "Are you all right?"

I manage the world's smallest headshake while I stare at my wine. The shaking resumes, and I spread my palms on the counter.

His gentle hand lands on my shoulder. "I didn't mean to embarrass you," he whispers, then leans closer, "I was trying to pull away, you know. I'm not totally to blame, here."

His touch soothes me. My lips move in what I hope passes as a smile while I spin the stem of my glass. "I'm not blaming you." I do manage to glance up at him for that, but then take another sip and pin the base to the counter with both hands.

"RoseAngel?"

I love hearing him call me by name. I suck my lip again, feeling how swollen it is from my ardor. God, I've never thrown myself into a man's arms like that. I'm not even sure what my limbs were doing then; who's to say I hadn't wrapped my legs around his hips and gone to town?

The heat on my cheeks this time is from the wine; I'm glad I'm sipping more to help hide my shame.

"Rosie?"

I shake my head once, still looking into my drink. "People are trying to kill you, aren't they?"

I feel his fingers twitch on my shoulder, an involuntary gesture he didn't mean to let happen. "What are you talking about?"

En vino audacia, for my dose of courage makes me face him. "Are they or aren't they? It's a yes or no question."

He holds my eyes, looking from one to the other, the way people do when they search for lies. "You got all that from a kiss?"

I slow-blink a yes, and a parade of red flags starts waving before my third eye. What the hell is it with this man? I find myself angling away from him, and the words tumble out of my mouth before I can stop them: "Are you dangerous?"

"Only to the bad guys, RoseAngel. I truly hope you're not one of them."

Great. What's his definition of a bad guy? Do I qualify as one? And if so, what? He'd toss me overboard? Buy me some concrete shoes? Plop a horse head in my bed? Perhaps my alarm is displayed in my widening peepers, for his warm hand falls from my shoulder. "I told you I'll tell you everything Monday. For today, I really just want to enjoy a day off from worrying. Can we please do that? Hm?"

I push away my glass, noting I've downed two-thirds of it. I'm buzzing and flying and it's barely nine-thirty and logical thought is not my friend. I want to believe and trust him so much it physically hurts my chest. I want to trust my instincts that tell me he's a wonderful man, but then the darkness and Charlie and men shooting at him make me wonder if the full moon has sapped my brain dry and turned me into a doddering biddy.

I turn on my stool to face him and say, "I haven't had wine in over six months, and never before seven at night. FYI."

He waves over the bartender and orders me a tall water, which I gratefully down. Same with the second.

I can tell Travis waits for the bartender to busy himself at the other end before asking, "What happened out there? You seemed, I don't know, beyond desperate to keep kissing me." He gives me a rogue grin. "I promise you, there are lots more where that one came from."

I'm not ready to talk psychic abilities to him, and I'm not ready to concoct another lie. I hold his eyes. "I don't want to talk about it right now." But then I have to grin and scoff and say, "Monday. I'll tell you Monday."

He chuckles. "*Touché.*" I like how he takes my elbow and guides me to a nearby table, like I might be unsteady on my feet and he refuses to let me fall. A few couples and families are in here, although I set-up the bar for drinking on the morning run. "Are you sure you're okay? You look like you've seen a ghost."

I look up at him at that. Am I looking at one right now? Dead man walking? Is Mr. Perfect on borrowed time? I sweep my gaze back to my third water and chug another mouthful, replaying the vision once more. He—I—had escaped and hidden at the gas station. I don't know what will happen after that. I touch my hot face, then press my fingers to both my cheeks. I brave a smile and face him, knowing I've got at least ten hours to figure out what to do, how to handle it.

How to enjoy every moment with this amazing man.

I take a deep breath and say, "Let's go back outside. Maybe we'll see some dolphins."

He can tell I'm trying to forget, and I like that he's willing to overlook my embarrassing moment.

I mean, really, he can't abandon me on a boat, right?

Chapter 16

"Let's talk about a new subject, shall we?" Travis asks, and I wobble a grateful look at his words.

"Yes. Let's." The sun is streaming through my hair, and I hope I'll get some nice raspberry-lemonade highlights today. It's a little chillier out here, with no land to break the wind, but the salty air fills my lungs, the sun glints off the swells, and I even see a few shearwaters diving down from the heavens to pluck stray fish from the waters.

"You saw me stop in to see you yesterday, didn't you?"

He's leaning on the railing beside me, and I look over at him. I'm done lying about Marie/RoseAngel, so I say, "Yeah. We had a busload of senior citizens come in to adopt, and when I was taking my second client, I saw you at the front desk."

He's studying me again, like I'm some fascinating organism under a microscope. "And?"

"I panicked." I shrug. "I hadn't come clean yet, and when I saw you out there, I felt terrified."

His smile is nonjudgmental, only curious. "So, what did you do?"

"I called Tina and begged her to be me."

He shoulder-bumps me. "As soon as she said hello, I knew it wasn't you. But, I gave her the rose, anyway."

Well, that certainly catches my attention. "I thought you gave her a sucker, a Tootsie Roll Pop."

He wrinkles his nose at my proclamation. "A sucker? What man gives a woman a sucker? I specifically said, and I quote, 'This rose is for RoseAngel, for all the help.' And it was pink, which means, 'thank you.'" He winks and confides, "I had to research that, just to make sure I bought the right color."

I lick my lips and look away to tell him, "She's hot for you, just so you know."

His hand lands on his chest. "Not my fault."

I can't help but raise my hand in guilt. "My bad, I know." But I face him and say, "She told me you gave her something in secret and said not to tell anyone. I figured you were trying to trip me up come Monday."

He snaps his fingers. "Darn. I wish I'd thought of that." But he winks. "Well, if you decide you don't like me, at least I know I have a plan B." He waggles his brows to incite me.

I gasp and swat him, and he flinches and chuckles and grabs my hands to stalwart any more abuse. I let him draw me near and hold still for another scorching kiss on my cheek. I have a feeling we're both a little shy about another display onboard, so I'm glad he's being chaste.

"So," he continues when he knows I'm done attacking him, "I really know nothing about you. I should start with the basics: Are you single?"

"Yes." I give him a good-natured shove.

"How long?"

I pause but answer, "Eleven months."

He looks off into the sky, watching the shearwaters dive, and I like how he smiles at their efforts. "Who ended it?"

"I did."

He grumbles and parts me a serious look. "Well, that doesn't bode well for me."

I crack a grin. "Why not?"

"You might get sick of me, too." An innocent shrug.

I watch the bird come up with a bit of seaweed for the nest and consider what he's not saying. "I thought karma stated that you'd break up with *me* next."

"Doubt that," he tells me honestly, complete with a soul-scorching head-to-toe gaze, and I think the wine has been suitably diluted and the blush is genuinely mine to own. "What happened, if you don't mind my asking?"

His curiosity to know me better overwhelms my poor judgment from my past. "Jacob and I were together for four years. He gave me a promise ring, but he never proposed." I try to keep the harshness out of my voice at that and continue with, "That was probably because he was too busy getting high with his friend. Jenny."

"Oh, really."

My thumbnail is able to fleck off pieces of paint on the railing, so I focus on doing that. "He swore they were just friends, and they had been neighbors and schoolmates since the fourth grade, but," I look up to Travis' eyes for a second before returning to my paint stripping, "when I went to collect him from her house so we could get to the arena for the show, I just sensed something was wrong."

My mouth is dry, but I try swallowing anyway, with no benefit. "Jenny wouldn't look at me that day. Jacob was acting funny, too." I had seen an image of the two of them naked on her bed, but my powers were pretty patchy back then, mostly because I didn't want to rely on them, so I blocked them out. That day, though, I opened my eyes and *saw.* "We were going to a concert, and the tickets cost me over a hundred bucks. I remember just standing there, staring at them, and I think I could even smell the sex in the air, you know?"

Travis seems to be reading me the way I read others, but he's quiet and insists I finish with a nod.

"I went without him, stood outside the main gate and hocked the ticket to a cutie and kissed him before the night was over."

Travis nods and asks, "His name?"

I shrug. "Don't know, never got it. Didn't matter. I was done with Jacob the way he was done with me."

Now Travis leans in with a wicked grin and asks, "Did you take him into the ladies' room and have your way with him before you left?"

I glare at him. "Despite the red hair, I'm not an impulsive person. I have my moments, just like anyone else, but I'm not brash or brazen or any of the myriad of other qualities ascribed strictly to redheads."

He merely smiles at me, and, I have to say, it warms me through and through. I ask, "Do you have siblings?"

One nod. "I'm the youngest of three boys."

"Your poor mother," I lament, and he grins.

He looks back over the water, the sunlight fanning down on his chiseled features, and I watch the sweep of his lashes on his cheeks. "My father died in the line of duty, but that didn't stop the rest of us from signing on."

Signing on? "Fireman? Cop? Military?"

He licks his lips then and seems uncomfortable in the way he laces and loosens his fingers. I see a vision of blue uniforms but he says, "I probably shouldn't say."

I have enough of a feeling for what's going on that I don't really need every detail, but I like hearing how he paints the pictures of his life. Like young Opie, Andy Griffith—the father figure—played a cop. I'm only getting the puzzle pieces one by one, but the picture is still coming together. Still, I press with, "Does Opie have anything to do with it?"

I think he sees where I'm going, for I watch his chin drop in a small nod. He's told me without words, and I feel like he really wants to let me in, but can't. Yet.

He cocks one elbow up on the railing and faces me. "Tell me if this helps narrow down my field: You, RoseAngel, are turning twenty-nine next month, you have an older sister named Amantha and a twin brother named Ray. You graduated with honors, got a two-year degree in eighteen months, have worked at Lucky Clover

Animal Shelter for six years, and are getting a really big raise in January."

My jaw drops. "Are you a spy?" Now I'm cautious; how much else does he know about me? Does he know I'm reading images in his mind? What if he exposes my abilities?

A head tilt tells me he believes I wasn't fully paying attention. "Think of what my dad did."

I rack my brain for a second, forcing myself to think despite my paranoia. Cop? "Detective?"

He winks and touches his finger to the tip of his nose. "I made up the raise part."

His joking tells me my secret is still mine. After all, it's not like schools and public records keep track of this sort of thing—not unless the person is outed and wants the publicity. "You!" I swat him, and he crunches me in his arms. I twist to face him, relieved, and I have to stretch up and give him a quick kiss, if only to make sure I can do so and not be assaulted by black-and-white movies again. "Guess there's no point telling you anything about myself, as you've gone and found it all out on your own, despite your prior claim to knowing nothing about me."

"Old habits die hard," he tells me, but then kisses me once more, lightly, like he, too, is being careful. "That's how I knew you were lying to me about your name. That, and your voice."

I heave a put-upon sigh. "Lying has such negative connotations; can't we just say I was actively avoiding the truth?"

The captain comes over the loudspeaker, announcing landfall, and I have to admit I'll be glad to be back on solid ground.

This last half-hour has certainly turned my world upside down, and I can't help but blame it on the waves.

Chapter 17

I take a few moments to program in directions on his GPS to the beach I want to go to, as it's my favorite and I'd love to share it with Travis. I also take out a twenty, as parking is not cheap once we get there.

We're another half-hour from Westhampton Beach, and I'm getting excited. The wine has mostly worn off, and Travis—wonderful, beautiful, tolerant Travis—has forgiven this crazy, undependable, unexplainable side of me, and still wants to hang.

Life is good.

We pull into the park, and I shove the bill into his hand before he sees the sign showing the cost of parking. When he does, he glowers at me, but I smile and put my hands in the air and say, "You drove, and paid for the ferry. This one's on me. Detective."

"P.I.," he replies, and I'm even more impressed.

I open my mouth to ask, but his palm forestalls me. "No more. Not yet." But the light in his eyes tells me he holds no hard feelings.

We pull in and unload and kick sand at each other while we get the chairs and umbrella and cooler set up. He's like a big kid on the beach, and I can't help but laugh when he yanks off his t-shirt and goes running into the waves.

And running out a second later. "It's freezing!"

"Yeah," I drawl out. "It takes a while for a bazillion gallons to warm up."

I take my beach towel and drape it over our snacks, because the gulls are circling, and those little vultures will make off with anything not nailed down.

Travis pulls out a Frisbee from one of his grocery bags. "You play?"

"I can."

I watch him lower it and inform me, deadpan, "Um, the beach is for swim suits, not skirts and blouses."

I'm wearing my suit, so I strip off my clothes and kick off my sandals and hear his breath catch. "Okay, let's go." I like the look on his face. I'm not even scantily clad—just a mix-n-match two piece that mimics a one piece, making me look like I'm in a tank top and short-shorts. My top is pink and yellow stripes, and the bottom piece is plain black.

I'm not even model-thin, just your average homegrown white bread chick.

Travis makes me feel like I'm Miss America, so I crook him a grin and snag the Frisbee and race out onto the white sands.

I whip the disc at him while he runs after me, and he fumbles it off his fingers. I laugh and take off down the shore, my most-handsome P.I. in hot pursuit.

A gal could get used to this.

I think he's throwing the disc way better than I am, because after his seventh or eighth fumble (which I totally tease him about), he charges me, grabs me, and carries me into the ocean.

I'm squealing, kicking, and really liking the feel of his chest against mine, but I know how cold that water is, and he's going to dunk me.

"Geez, this is still cold," he hisses through gritted teeth, but then he drops my legs, and I yelp in protest when I touch down. "Well, I didn't come all this way to look at it," he tells me, and sure enough, he holds his breath and goes under.

When he jolts back up, I tease, "Blue looks good on you."

He grants me a wolfish grin before lunging at me, and I splash him and back up, my laugh bubbling all the way up from my frigid toes. "No, it's too cold."

"Then I'll get to warm you back up."

Well, that sounds great—except for the whole getting cold part—but he does manage to grab me and scoop me up again.

"No, please, drunk women shouldn't go swimming," I explain, hoping my logic will thwart him, but he only chuckles and continues to tease me.

"What if I just dunk your feet?" he asks as he tips my already-dripping toes toward the waves.

"Travis!"

"Or your bottom?"

I can feel the water brushing my butt cheeks, and I clench and arch into his arms, squealing, "No, no!"

"I can be bribed," he offers. His voice is lilting, sing-song-y.

I stop struggling and look up at him. He is so much fun to be with that I expect to see light dancing in his eyes, but instead, he looks hungry.

That kind of hungry.

I feel my lids flutter. "Yeah?"

"Oh, yeah."

I wrap my arm around his neck and melt with his kiss. This time, no vision attacks me, just the sensation of his cold lips on my warm ones, and I'm able to thoroughly enjoy how his hot tongue explores my mouth this time.

I purr and nestle into his strong arms.

He breaks away with a snap, and I can't help but wonder if he was getting turned on, too. "Okay, time for Frisbee. I can't let a girl beat me."

He marches to the shore as fast as the drag of the waves will allow, and I have to laugh. I tell him, "That's funny; that's what my brother always says."

Chapter 18

We play checkers on a tiny board (he wins) and some more Frisbee (I win) and then we spread out the beach blanket to lie on under our umbrella. I like how comfortable I am with him as he stretches out beside me on his stomach, our shoulders touching, the shade offering no break from the heat of the day.

Or from each other.

I know I'm more attracted to him than I've ever been to a man, and know for a fact he feels the same way. Having psychic abilities isn't all bad, I decide in that moment. I've noticed over the last two hours that every image Travis sends me is warm, comfortable. Even the naked ones aren't gratuitous, only those of a man who's really into me.

Not like what I would see in middle school—when I could first see, the boys all wanted threesomes, foursomes, with all the girls (and this included me) servicing them.

Travis wants to service *me,* and the image of him with his head between my thighs, his tongue all up in my business, makes me horny with the possibilities. I look over at him as he opens up a home-improvement magazine he brought with him and realize he really is a great guy.

I can't wait for Monday; I have to know his story.

He taps a picture in his magazine and asks, "You ever want to own your own home, or do you like living in a townhouse?"

I give it some thought, and see he's reading about how to update electrical outlets. "I don't know. I guess I always figured homeownership should go to families. You?"

I see the dreamy look in his eyes as he drifts to either a place in the distant past, or perhaps one in the future. "I'd love my own house. Maybe, after this, when I get settled in my new job, I can find one. I'd like a fixer-upper."

"Really?" I study him, the fervor in his eyes. His excitement, I have to say, is a real turn-on. "I guess I never reconciled a bank manager with being so hands-on."

"Yeah," he says, his voice soft, and I watch him drift off into the past. "My dad used to do a lot of work around the house. I used to help."

That's so sweet, and I touch his forearm. "A way to keep your dad alive." Any man who loves his family gets merits in my book. I was feeling so generous, I even gave him an extra one.

"Yeah, I guess." He flips through a few more pages and shows me an old home with a turret in front. "I'd like an old Victorian, something like this."

The house he shows me is painted in soft purple and navy and yellow, with white trim. I wedge my elbow into the sand and rest on my palm to face him. "Really? You strike me as a more modern-house type of man."

"Nope." He nestles closer and points to the picture, his interest in it evident. "Look at the shingles; they're called fishscale, for obvious reasons. And these corbels, aren't they beautiful? And the decorative scrollwork under the eaves … you just can't find workmanship like that anymore."

I'm thinking I've never met a man who finds so much beauty in the world around him, especially one who hates his home and believes he's shrouded in darkness. "If you like homes like these so much, why did you move to a place you hate?"

"It's just another safe house," he tells me, and he meets my eyes for the barest second before looking down and pushing out his breath between barely-parted lips. "God, I want to just tell you the whole story, but my friggin' keepers told me to keep my yap shut." He closes his eyes for a moment, and I sense his burden as a terrible onus he tires of carrying. "They're letting me out without being tailed, finally, which is great, but I still hate it."

"Are you on probation?"

He turns to face me, mimicking my position. His body is open, his expression is gentle, his chest is … distracting. I want to bury my fingers in his patch of black hair and feel the strength of his muscles underneath. "Probation implies I did something wrong. I didn't." He leans forward and kisses me once more, making me fight the urge to cuddle up despite the heat. "Now, no more questions, because I'm barely holding it all in." A soft smile tells me he's only gently chastising me. "You ever want kids?"

Ah, the Giant Compatibility Question. Men only ask it when they're really into a girl, and I try not to get too excited with this secret knowledge. I temper my voice down from the squeal it threatened to produce and say, "Yeah, just not twins. I don't know how my mother survived us," I shake my head and grin and meet his eyes. "Ray was the very devil incarnate."

He's still focused when he asks, "How many?"

I think for a minute. "I don't know. You?"

"Two or three." I like the warm fuzzy smile he's giving me. And then his voice drops to a seductive, tantalizing tone when he adds, "And I hope they're all redheads."

My insides flutter more than a butterfly conservatory at full capacity. I net up all those errant insects and charge ahead with, "You say that, but a lot of us are downright dangerous. Too many in one house and it might implode."

I can tell he doesn't believe me, because he asks, "Are you two close? You and your brother?"

"I have to be, by twin definition." I reach over and lace my fingers into his. "Now, *he's* the very stereotyped redhead." Mostly because he, like me, has psychic powers, but his premonitions are far stronger, and he's more skilled. Probably because he never spent years trying to pretend his powers didn't exist. "There was

91

one time he walked up and punched a kid he didn't even know," to stop a fight from starting, which would have left the boy with a damaged eye, "and he stole a bike from a neighbor," so the kid didn't get hit by a car, "and when he got into a fight with his best friend, he even knifed his tires," so his best friend didn't die when the train crossing bar didn't lower.

He never told anyone but me, but I'm sure mom suspected, as I came clean with my abilities in middle school, as I thought I was experiencing a nervous breakdown or psychotic episodes.

I feel a little bad painting my brother in dark colors, but for now I'm covering for him. If I ever tell Travis what I can see, I'm pretty sure he'll ask if Ray has the same talents.

I think I could totally confide in him about my abilities, which would be a complete first for me.

"What kind of name is Amantha?" he asks me.

I watch him lift my hand to his lips to kiss. The sensation zings straight down to my toes and then halfway back, settling somewhere in my abdomen. Low abdomen. His kisses on my flesh make me feel wanton and restless. I clear my throat and tell him, "I swear my parents wanted to be hippies, but they were too young. So we're all named after flora and fauna. Amantha and Rose are flowers, and Ray is named after the manta."

He groans. "Are you kidding me?"

I bat my lashes and lean in. "Would I lie about my name?"

He groans even louder and falls back to the blanket.

• • •

I'm waiting for lunch time to roll around, and soon enough, Travis asks if I would like a sandwich. I inwardly grin, wondering what his reaction to my mislabeling adventure will be.

He tugs out the cooler and kneels before it, and I grab the paper plates and napkins and plastic ware. I surreptitiously watch him as he opens the top and halts.

He grabs his chest, falls back on the towels, and starts bucking and convulsing like a man in the electric chair. After a few seconds, his tongue lolls out of his mouth, and he tips his head to the side and lies still.

"Well," I sigh, "that was anticlimactic."

He laughs and grabs my arm and tugs me down to him. We're sharing a good laugh, but then he drags me across his body and rolls me under the umbrella and under his chest. "You have been a naughty, naughty girl," he chides me, and I have to grin. Mostly because I've now got my hands on his very-amazing chest, and the ruse to do so was too great. "So," he kisses my nose, "I'm going to make our sandwiches, based exclusively on what the bags say are in them."

"No," I argue, but he holds me down and says, "Now, which one is labeled 'bread?'"

I laugh as I try to eat what passes as a sandwich under our umbrella. Luckily, I had labeled the cheese as bread, so two slices of American hold celery sticks, Doritos, grapes, a slice of bread, and lettuce. Travis opts to try to-furkey, so he gets carrots as well.

It's the best damned sandwich of my entire life.

Chapter 19

The beach has warmed up, so I suggest we try out the water again. The sun is hotter now, and I haven't been out in it much this year to earn a base tan. I grab my sunscreen, but Travis insists on slathering me in it.

His hands are warm and purposeful as he rubs down my arms and neck and shoulders. He's not using his fingertips like friends or siblings do during such a task; no, his hands rub and smooth and massage every bit of flesh I offer him. It's complete foreplay at its finest, and it's working in a big way.

Then it's my turn. I opt to follow his example, electing to forego the fingertip application as well and go full-palm. I try not to grin too much like an idiot as I cover his back with SPF50. His muscles are taut and firm and his skin is smooth and hot, making me hot as I touch him.

Soon we're slogging out into the ocean. It's still cold, but tolerable now. Lots of people are out wading and swimming, and the lifeguards have rolled their towers closer to the shore.

Now that I know Travis is not as OCD as he depicted himself, I have to comment. "I'm glad to see you didn't have a complete meltdown over my changing the bags."

He laughs and tells me, "In all honesty, I just stretched the masking tape across the counter and made a sticker for everything as I unpacked it, just so I wouldn't forget what we had purchased." He picks up a bit of seaweed and sticks out his tongue at it and flings it away.

I like the *we* part. "So, no OCD?" I tease.

"No, not really, although I am pretty organized."

The water is now up to our torsos, and I take a deep breath. "Okay, you went under; it's only fair that I do the same." I grit my teeth and drop straight down, then shoot up again. "Yeah, it's chilly."

He does the same, and I like that he's being gallant about equal suffering. "Yeah," he makes a brrr sound and shakes it off. "I had no idea the ocean was so cold."

Still, I'm up for a swim, so I go back under, and smile when Travis cuts a neat path at my side. "Nice strokes."

"Thanks," he tells me, meeting my eyes. "I swam for years in high school. Loved it."

I brave the doggy paddle, but Travis' form is smooth and fluid and barely breaks a splash. I put my feet down and stand, just so I can have a better view of his muscles in action.

He does one of those fancy-schmancy turns, like a somersault, and comes swimming back to me. I'm smiling when he reaches my side.

"What?" he asks as he stands before me.

I like his athleticism. "That was … artistic."

He grins and kisses my lips, and I giggle and pluck a strand of kelp from his hair. Head hair. I'm still looking for another excuse to touch his chest. Every option I've entertained just seems faked and gratuitous; his chest is my kryptonite.

"What's over there?" He points toward New York City, so I tell him New York City, which only garners me a spiritless look. "I meant, beach-wise."

I make a quick recovery with, "Want to go explore?"

He offers me his hand, and we slosh across the shoreline, the waves pushing us inland and drawing us out in measured foamy beats. The gulls scream and cry over the beach, and I point to a particularly brave one shaking a plastic bag. "Look at that."

He gasps and laughs, and I chide with, "And you mocked me for covering our stuff. They're vultures, I tell you, vultures."

The bird takes to the air—the carrot sticks visible even from our position on the water—and six other birds lend hungry chase.

Soon more squawking and shrieking fills the air, and the violated people leave their volleyball net to whip their beach towels at the winged rats, to no avail.

The carrot sticks are soon history.

"Don't worry," I tell Travis, "they'll be back for more."

He points to our umbrella and I can tell he's concerned. "Is our stuff safe here?"

I squeeze his hand. "The food is covered. The rest of the stuff … I'm glad to say beach people have an honor system in place. And, the twenty-dollar parking fee tends to be a great deterrent for the crime-prone." I give him a meaningful look.

Knowing this is completely new to him makes me feel so worldly. Until this week, I always felt like I lived in a small-town world with big city customers. Being so close to NYC gives us a wide customer base. Even though we are a different state, a lot of people will commute to our shelter to adopt. I've learned that many of our state citizens even work in the Big Apple and take the train in daily.

We find a tiny creek that cuts into the beach and around another parking lot, and the water is blissfully warm. We find hermit crabs, mussels, a dead crayfish, two shrimp, and a gull feather. Half a clamshell is his prize, and he carries it while we continue our travels.

It's a plain ordinary shell, so I ask, "A keeper?"

"A memento," he tells me, his expression gentle, and I think I'm blushing.

I look back and see we're quite a ways from our spot, so we head back. I have a feeling it's getting late, and as I look at the sun to gauge the time, Travis asks, "Where can we go for supper?"

I tip my head at him and affect a lordly tone. "We're in the Hamptons; not the cheapest place in New York to eat. It would be best to head back."

"No," he says as he comes near, placing his hand on my hip. "I'm not ready to end our day just yet."

• • •

We shower under one of those beach spigots and dry off and dress and pack up our goods. We find a nice family diner halfway back to the ferry, and the salad I order comes on a veritable satellite dish. Travis helps me finish it, even though the fried chicken he ordered fills him up.

We drive back to the ferry and board the next boat and sit at the bar. (I only have a soda this time; one drink per day is my new limit.)

I feel the burn on my skin, and Travis is sporting a nice tan already. I can see the lines of it across his face, where a few smears of sunscreen missed the spot.

About halfway back to Connecticut, a tall, blond, no-neck guy with wide shoulders and narrow hips walks up to me. It's hard to overlook his pectorals; each one is the size of a dinner plate. He's good-looking in a not-my-type, hope-he-doesn't-hit-on-me kind of way. "Rose? RoseAngel? Is … that you?"

I look at him, and it takes a second for the face to register. When it does, I smile. "Matt?"

He smiles as well, clearly relieved that I recognize him from high school, although the man before me is worlds away from the weird-haired, acne-ridden kid I recall. Although he's not my type, he's certainly turned into a handsome man.

"How've you been?" he asks, and I shake his offered hand.

"I'm fine. This is Trevor." (I get it right, just to make him happy.) "Trevor, this is Matt. We went to school together."

I notice the handshake Travis gives Matt is strong, unyielding—a pissing contest that I get the joy to witness.

Matt releases Travis' hand and faces me. His face gets a little red, and he casts a worried look to Trav. "Um … can I … ask you something? In private?"

Travis sits taller and his face turns dark. "Anything you need to say to RoseAngel can be said in front of me."

The man turns redder, and I sense he's embarrassed about something and not trying to hit on me. I pat Travis' arm and say, "It's okay," and as I face Matt I ask, "Is this about me?"

He shakes his head no, so I stand and walk to the end of the bar, never having had a man so protective of me. Travis watches me like I'm a tasty June bug in a hungry hen house. "What's up?" I ask while I lean back against the counter.

Matt glances around himself, clearly self-conscious. His voice and head drop. "Are … you still friends with Darlene?"

I crack a grin. "Yes, very much so."

I notice he's getting red again. "Is … she single?"

Okay, I can't help but smile. If memory serves, he was pretty loopy over her in high school, but he was on the football team and Darlene was in drama class, and ne'er the twain did meet. "Yes, she is."

He dashes a look at Travis and asks, "Do … you think I could have her phone number?"

She's one of my two best friends, so I still have to protect her from weirdoes, but that also means making sure she doesn't pass up a great thing when he begs for her number. "Why now?"

I can tell he knows I'll need a great answer in order to ante up the goods, so he stands tall, even though his head is bowed. "I'm … moving back here from Texas. I was on the college football team, heading up, but … I tore my ACL and, well, I … just don't want to do it anymore. I'm … buying a gym in town and … well … I'm … looking to catch up with her."

I like his answer, and say, "Wow, sorry about the injury. Are you going to be okay?"

"Yeah," he touches his knee. "I was off my leg for almost three months, but … I'm better now." He points to a few guys in the corner and says, "I … was killing time with some old pals today and saw you. I … didn't want to let the chance slip by."

I look over and recognize two of the four guys he's hanging with, and I wave to them. Three wave back, then the fourth raises his hand as well, proof that peer pressure doesn't end with the diploma. I smile to Matt and pull out my cell. "Tell you what. Let me text Dar and see if I can give you her number, okay?"

He smiles and nods, and I type: football hunk looking 4 ur number okay to give?

A millisecond later she writes back: who?

Me: Matt Tildesky from school. he misses you

Her: football hunk???

Me: oh yeah

Her: yes

I laugh and wave for his cell and type in her number. He beams like he did in school and shakes my hand over and over and over and then puts his hand on my shoulder to guide me back to Travis. He shakes Travis' hand, saying, "Great to meet you, man," and then Matt even waves at us as he heads back to his friends.

Grinning, I show my cell dialogue to Travis.

"Football hunk?" He silently damns me with his eyebrows.

I indulge him and say, "Not my type, but he's certainly Darlene's." I lean forward and say, "He fawned all over her in school, just, not *to* her. I would watch him mooning away in the cafeteria, and she was completely oblivious."

He leans over his soda and to it says, "I'm not the jealous type, just so you know. It's just … " he sighs and crooks me a sorrowful grin. "Monday."

I chuckle and pat his arm. "Who knew that it would soon be my most favorite day of the week?"

Chapter 20

It's obvious that Travis wants to come inside with me, but I know I'll have a mess to clean up, courtesy of Tiny Titan, so I seize my opportunity to place my hand on Travis' chest and tell him, "Hang on. Let me make sure it's safe to enter."

Did I mention how much I like his chest?

Rigid with alarm, Travis stands tall. "What do you mean, safe?" He scans my door and window, and I have the feeling he's looking for signs of forced entry.

I stand closer, my hand fanning out on his delightful pec. "Titan didn't poop outside this morning. I'd like to open up the windows before you come in."

He seems a bit relieved, but I can tell his guard is still high, screaming *Red Alert! Red Alert!,* which really confuses me. What the hell happened to this man? He nods and sets down the cooler and heads back to the car for more unloading while I slip inside and gag at the smell and grab another plastic bag.

I pull Titan to the back door and put him outside while I toss open windows and clean up his mess. I light a match and blow it out, then chase it with three more. A knock, and then Travis eases open the door. "May I come in?"

All I smell is matchstick, so I wave him in while I tie shut the offending bag.

I can tell he's going to tease me, and he emphatically does not disappoint. "Let me get this straight."

I glare at him. "There is nothing you can tell me that I'm not already aware of."

He's grinning like he's truly enjoying my quandary. "Isn't this what you do for your livelihood? Helping people with pet problems? Like, oh, housebreaking?"

Glaring does not stop his smile, but I point at my little monster and say, "I can't crate him. If you recall, he almost died in a cage. Just show him one and he'll absolutely freak out. He's not just one of those dogs that doesn't like being confined; he equates it with death." I think I'm breathing a little hard, but I know my dog. I've *tasted* his terror.

Travis reaches over and takes the bag from my hands and puts it in my kitchen trash can. He sees it's full, so he tugs it out and gathers it up and ties the whole thing closed.

He's taking out my garbage? Now I'm mad at myself for yelling at him.

He informs me, "I have a lot of cop friends, some within the canine division. I watched a lot of them go through housebreaking with their puppies. Have you tried putting his mess outside?"

I stare at him, trying to wrap my head around the fact he's helping me after I just lost my cool. "What?"

He points to the garbage. "Put it outside, where you want him to go, and praise him when he sees it." He brings the garbage to my front door and looks over his shoulder at me. "Maybe use an exercise pen, too, instead of a cage. Just a thought."

I can only stare at him, wondering why I didn't think of this, but he interrupts my moment of self-contempt with, "What would you tell someone like me? If I called in with this problem?"

I crank a shoulder. "That there's more than one way to train any dog, but the point is to be consistent for at least three weeks before trying a new method. Some people hang a bell on the door and teach the pet to jingle it to go out, some teach their dogs to bark, others simply let the dog out every three hours. And then there's crating and clicker training and shock collars and positive reinforcement and aversion tactics and restricted room access; the list goes on and on."

I like the crooked smile he gives me before he tosses his words over his shoulder as he readies to dump my trash. "How many of those have you tried?"

Honestly, one. I watch him walk out with the trash, and then come in a moment later with my chairs and towels. I'm still standing in the living room, staring at him.

"Did I grow another head?"

I sit back on my couch, dazed, still staring at him. "I think it's time I retire."

Chapter 21

Travis heads home to feed his cat, and I find out Pringles did come out to snuggle last night, which makes me feel a little validated that I'm not completely useless at my job (because it's not about housebreaking, I tell myself).

He tells me he'll call tomorrow, and I invite him over for take-out dinner, my treat. (Complete with a whopping dose of snuggling-on-chest for dessert. Yummmm.)

First I call Darlene, because I have to know if Matt contacted her. I sit on my couch, and Grimm jumps up on my lap.

She answers with, "Are you sure he's a hunk now?"

"Dar," I sigh, "you know how rapper DJ's have records that they scratch and play backwards?"

"Uh, yeah?"

I pin the phone to my shoulder and raise both my hands in the air. "I wanted to play his giant chest like two records. *Pudda pudda eek, pudda pudda eck.*" My hands move to the music.

I can tell she's practically drooling by her tone. "Are you serious?"

"Dead. He's totally your type." I pet Grimm, skimming my fingers over the scarred bald patches on his back by sheer rote.

But she gasps and says, "I'm looking at his picture from high school. He was so weird looking! And his hair!"

I gasp, my fingers scrubbing Grimm's butt, making him arch high into my hand. "And you were … ?" I challenge.

Silence.

I press with, "Dar, I love you to pieces, you know that, right?"

"Yeah," she mumbles.

I lean forward on the couch to press my point, forgetting that she can't see me. "When he calls, go meet him. He's a good foot taller than you, and thick. And muscular. And he seems very sweet. I liked him just as much today as I did back then." He was one of those guys that everyone seemed to like. Being on the football team, I'm sure, helped his social circle, but he was always so kind and good-natured.

"Why didn't you ever date him, then?"

I growl in frustration. "Because he liked *you*, you nitwit."

She starts to say something, but her voice cuts out with call waiting. "OMG, it's him."

"Take it. Call me later." And I hang up smiling.

Grimm flops on my lap, and Titan jumps up to my other side and tries to nose the cat away from me. I push the dog down and give him a firm stroke to settle him, thinking about Travis' suggestion. I look Titan in the eye and send him an image of his BMs outside, which has never worked in the past, but tomorrow, when I clean up after him, I'm going to add the outdoor prop.

He jumps down and grabs his latex whale and gives it a good shake, which I take to mean as, "You and what army?"

I dial my brother for totally different advice.

Ray Jasper and I not only had twin language, we maintained it well into grade school and beyond. It used to make our teachers so angry, because we were able to carry on complete conversations to the exclusion of all others.

We were bilingual with a language only two people knew.

The doctors called it cryptophasia. They assured my parents we would outgrow it by age three or four, and that they should just continue to talk and read to us normally.

I remember telling Ray the grownups (dultane) wanted to make sure we couldn't talk to each other anymore, so we tried extra hard to continue our language.

I think me being named after an angel and him being named after quartz really augmented our supernatural powers, by the way. Once we reached twelve, both of our psychic abilities manifested. Our parents split us up into different bedrooms about that time, making it the first time we'd ever been separated. So we compensated by taking turns sending and receiving and eventually blocking messages.

We were damn good by ninth grade.

Amantha, poor thing, was burdened with the middle name of Ernesta, although I truly believe it helped get her through law school. She makes more than both of us, so I really don't think she's complaining these days.

I hadn't talked to Ray all week, but it's only seven at night, so I dial. When he picks up, I cry, "TB! It's TS."

"Hey, Twin Sis, how are ya?"

I sense he's not alone, but I need his input. "Sorry to bother you; do you have a few minutes?"

"For you, of course."

I see him lean over and kiss a naked Italian girl; I avert my face, which, of course, doesn't help, but it's automatic.

I hear a door close and he asks, "Did you see that?"

"Yeah," I mumble. "Sorry. Who is she?"

"My new squeeze, Angie. It's been about two weeks. Yours?"

He totally knows. "Um, since Wednesday. You like him?"

I can tell he's probing me for input, so I remain still, open. I think about the darkness, the flirting, the FBI guys, the beach.

He really didn't like Jacob, but never told me so in words.

"What's up with him? He's keeping a ton of secrets."

I take a deep breath. "I'll find out Monday."

"Hm." I can tell he doesn't like that. For two people who never hid anything from each other, Baby B is not taking this secrecy thing well. "What's on your mind?"

"Okay, so, ow," Grimm digs his claws into my leg, and I grimace and peel him off my flesh. "I think I had my very first premonition."

"Really? That's great!"

"Well," I hedge and lean back into my cushions, holding the cat at bay. "I'm not sure. I think someone's out to kill him."

I can almost see Ray closing his eyes like he does when he reaches out to the Universe for guidance. "Dark his story is," he says in his Yoda voice, making me laugh.

"What can you see?"

I think he's joining me on the couch, but his couch. "The question is: What did you see?"

I relay the black-and-white film, the gunfire, the sneezing attacker, the odometer, everything.

"Okay," Ray says, "this is how my prems come to me: All the elements that stick out are the most important, like the odometer. Numbers are hard to see in dreams, but they're very potent for mystics. Flashes, to me, show time, like it's the sun going down and coming back up. How many flashes did you see?"

I have to think about that one. "Two? Three?"

"When did you have this prem?"

"Today. Kissing Travis." It seems important to share that, otherwise I wouldn't.

"Adrenalin. You go, TS! That's how I got my first one."

I find myself blinking and frowning. "Making out?"

I hear a moan filled with memories. "Second base."

I growl out, "Is that why you're such a dog?"

"Mystic see as mystic do."

I groan at that. "So, the flashes mean … ?"

"Two or three days from now."

I heave a breath. "The prem takes place at night."

"So, two or three nights from now. What about a clock? Did you see a clock?"

I think back and only remember seeing the odometer. "No."

"Always look for a clock. That's the best advice I can give you. When they show up in my visions, they are spot-on."

This means it happens sometime tomorrow or Monday night. I shift into the cushions and say, "If this interferes with me learning his story, I'm going to be pissed."

"Better get it out of him before nightfall then, sis. Do whatever it takes to get more info, to have the prem again."

I love my brother, and I have to laugh. "So, you're saying I should tongue-tango more often?"

"I'm saying," he clarifies, "that when you find a way that makes it work, it's good to exploit it, gain practice."

I like the thought of practicing. A lot. I smile. "Doctor's orders," I say, and TB chuckles, clearly reading my mind.

I hear a door open behind him, and can see Angie stroll toward Ray, naked. She has super long black hair that billows around her ample curves, and she's beckoning Ray forward with a come-hither finger. "Do whatever makes you happy. Speaking of … gotta go."

He hangs up, and I laugh.

Chapter 22

What I think is my alarm clock is really my cell phone ringing; I fumble it off my white nightstand and look at the number. I half sit up and hit the talk button, since it's Travis, and the prem (as my brother likes to call them) still bothers me. "Hi," I say, my voice thick and sloggy.

"Good morning, babe."

"Good morning." I look at my alarm clock and see it's only seven-thirty. "What's wrong?"

He chuckles, and I can't believe how much I've missed his voice, and it's only been a day. "Nothing. I just wanted to be the first person to wish you happy Sunday."

I smile and sigh and snuggle back into my purple sheets. I definitely want this to be the voice I wake up and fall asleep to, and it is absolutely the voice of warmth and joyfulness. "Since I live alone, there really isn't that much competition."

"Good, because I'm not really in a position to fend off all your competitors." I hear the tingling of metal on metal and assume he's in the kitchen making breakfast.

"Mm." I think I'm thinking aloud. "There are so many of them."

His warm chuckle confirms my belief that I belong with him. "There should be. I've seen you in a bathing suit."

I smile and close my eyes and tuck the sheets around my chin. "How do you like your eggs?"

He laughs again and says, "You can hear that?"

"Yup."

I hear more scraping and stirring, and he says, "Today, Benedict. Tomorrow, who knows? You?"

"Omelet, with lots of veggies and cheese." Grimm growls and grumbles and readjusts himself on the bed. I'm speaking and therefore disturbing his eighteen-hour nap and must be punished.

Travis says, "I'll remember that. What kind of cheese?"

"Cheddar, natch," I answer, and Titan comes to my bedside and puts his front paws on the mattress to stand tall. I groan and say, "Hang on, better put the mighty pooper out before he does his thing."

"Were you sleeping?"

I roll upright and toss back the covers. Morning light streams through the blinds into my white-walled bedroom, making Grimm's fur look a little brown from his perch on my lavender comforter. I see I forgot to put away the basket full of clothes, which sits in front of my white dresser. Tons of framed photos of me with my friends and family compete for space on the wooden top. Two windows on the far wall both have lavender curtains, which tint the room in a soft calming haze. A thick purple rug cushions my feet.

I tuck my toes into my slippers and stand up to stretch, still smelling a trace of the incense I burned last night. "Yup, I was. Shocked?"

"Not really. I'm an early riser." I hear the tone of his voice drop to one of seduction. "What do you sleep in?"

"A bed." I laugh and head downstairs to let Titan outside. "Granny flannel."

His cry tells me he's not buying it. "In this weather? What are you, coldblooded?"

I look down and take attire inventory, feeling a little naughty that I'm telling the man what jammies I'm wearing. "I'm in Taz shorts and a Bugs top, all right?" I bought them online and really like them. I unlock the back door and let Titan outside, leashed.

"That's way better," he says, like I had challenged my commander to a duel and then backed down. "When should I be there?"

I watch my dog sniff around the tiny yard like he's never been there and actually stare at my phone. "I don't know, four or five. Dinner time, I guess. I'm going back to bed when Titan's done."

"Ooh," he whispers, "I'll be right over."

Chapter 23

Somehow I'm not surprised when the knock hits my door a half-hour later. I did toss on a t-shirt and shorts, but I'm braless because I fully expected to be in bed another hour. Travis sweeps in with a grocery bag of food and takes one look at me. "Back to bed with you. You look exhausted."

I rub my face, squinting, and ask, "Whose fault is that?"

I like the sultry, seductive look he's giving me. "If it means I get to see you all rumpled straight out of bed, I'll take all the blame." He opens up my fridge and puts about fifteen dollars' worth of eggs and cheese and veggies in there and closes the door. "Now, go back to bed, or I'll carry you."

Oh, tired as I am, that would mean I get to cuddle against his chest again. I stand there and stare at him, and he is good to his word. He scoops me up and carries me upstairs, and I take a moment to snuggle into his warmth.

He smells terrific.

At the top of the stairs I point, and he carries me to my bed and lowers me in. Then he tucks me in and strokes my hair. I realize he's not here to shag me or dupe me or any other colloquial phrase to get me naked, so I look up at him. "If you're tucking me into bed, what are you going to do?"

He presses a kiss to my temple. "I'm going to train your dog."

I look up, but he turns off the light and closes my door.

• • •

About forty minutes later I wake up to the smell of coffee and the unmistakable scent of onions on the fry. My stomach, being ever so cooperative, rumbles immediately. It seems only courteous of me to finger comb my hair and be present at the breakfast table, so I sneak downstairs and look over the railing, watching Travis reinforce "sit" with Titan and practice the "down" command.

When Titan does lie down on his own with no guidance, Travis rewards him with what I think is shaved cheese. The man's voice is so high and pleased with Titan's performance that I have to clap.

"Okay!" he tells Titan, and my dog springs up and wiggles over to me, looking incredibly pleased with his schooling.

I glance into my kitchen and see a pan of fried onions and peppers, another with sliced apples bubbling over low heat, and my cereal bowls hold chopped broccoli, cheddar, mushrooms, and chives. A larger bowl holds shaved potatoes, and I can't believe the man is going to make me hash browns. "Trav?"

"For you," he tells me, and steps close to buzz my lips. "I saw you had frozen orange juice, but couldn't find your pitcher."

"Yeah, Grimm broke it last month. I forgot to buy a new one." The A/C kicks on, and I realize I'm not wearing a bra.

This could definitely work in my favor.

He looks around the living room and points to my cat, who alternates his resting and glaring at this strange male intruder on his turf. "You know I have to ask."

I nod, knowing he's asking about the bald patches. "He got set on fire. No suspects. His wounds were pretty severe; I had to treat them four times a day to help them heal. He was nasty, too, about it, and not deemed adoptable. So, I took him in." I shrug and point to the front door. "There's a reason my welcome sign is Rudolph's Isle of Misfit Toys."

He moves past me and stands in the front doorway and smiles at the sign Misha had created with needlepoint. "You think you're a misfit, too?"

With rue I answer, "You have no idea."

I like how he smiles at me and steps near, wrapping his warm hands around my nape. His kiss is warm and tempting me to nestle into his arms … along his chest …

I can feel my nipples pebbling against my t-shirt, and the way Travis rubs along me, I'm pretty sure he can, too. I can tell he's smiling while he kisses me.

His arms loop my waist, and I rest my fingers on his delightful pecs again, just because I can. Then his hands slide lower and cup my buttocks.

Then he drags me up along his abdomen, and I can tell certain parts of him are more awake than others. I see young Charlie then, suddenly, after being absent for days. I mentally ask him, *Where have you been?* in the hope that he'll answer.

I see the boy beckoning me forward with two hands. I take a deep breath and begrudgingly pull away. I don't know where Charlie wants me to go, but he's obviously reaching out again and wants me to follow.

And then, just when I'm ready to help him, to follow him where he wants me to go, Charlie disappears.

Thankfully, Travis doesn't push. He smiles into my eyes and gives my bottom a squeeze and asks if I'd like breakfast, to which I, of course, say yes. How rude would I be, otherwise?

He guides me to my small square table and I have a seat, smiling happily that Travis is dicing away in my kitchen.

The doorbell rings, and I look at Travis. I sense a bit of apprehension in him, but he bids me to sit while he eases to the front door and sneaks a look through the peephole.

He eases down the hallway to me and whispers, "Two girls, one tall blonde, one short with short black hair."

I groan. "Friend invasion. Get ready," I warn, then rumple up my hair a bit and feebly whip open the door. "Hey, guys."

Darlene and Misha spill inside and freeze and stare at the hunk standing in my kitchen, armed only with a spatula and wooden spoon. "Good morning, ladies," he says, smiling.

I look at them and say, "Trevor just showed up with a bag full of groceries. Anyone up for an omelet?"

• • •

I have to admit, although I can tell they wanted all the chewy details from my date yesterday, having the real deal inside my home at nine a.m. gives them some substantial fodder. I read the shocked expressions and recoveries and then the happy exchange of names as we girls get settled at my kitchen table while Hunko the Handy busies himself with mixing and stirring.

Darlene mouths, "Wow" and Misha gives me a guarded look of being impressed.

Dar glances at her phone and whispers, "Nine a.m., you're barely out of your PJs, and you're probably going to tell me you didn't sleep with him."

"I didn't sleep with him. He just showed up with groceries." I incite a rather large yawn to back up my claim.

Misha takes her turn to slide him a glance. "He's nicer looking than I thought."

Jacob wasn't the hottest pie in the oven, but he wasn't bad looking, either, so I'm wondering what she really thought of *him*, a year later.

From the kitchen, Travis asks, "Am I making a giant one for us to split, or will you ladies like your own small one?"

Misha turns to face him and asks, "How good of a cook are you?"

He rubs that stomach I want to see again and grins in response. "I'm still alive, so it can't be all bad. Look," and he raises his arms and shows off two nicely flexed muscles. "Good food means strong bones and muscles."

"Cripes," I say and flop back into my chair, "He's a living commercial."

They giggle, because they can tell Travis is totally being a goof, but I think he's flirting just a bit with them to make them feel comfortable. I'm beginning to understand that he sees flirting as an icebreaker, because I can clearly tell he wants my friends to like him.

Darlene is happy to offer, "Whatever's easiest for you."

He nods and says to me, "Hon, I'm going to need a bigger pan. Do you have one?"

I feel my face darken as my friends stare at me with his bold endearment, but I nod and go into the kitchen and rummage under the stove for my biggest fry pan.

When he stoops down to collect it, he kisses my cheek.

Loudly. Like a squeaky door hinge on a breezy day.

So loudly I hear them laugh.

Titan comes running, clearly mistaking the kiss as being meant for him. I swat Mr. Loudlips and grumble all the way back to my table, where I drop loudly into my seat and avoid eyes.

Misha smiles then and whispers, "Trevor seems sweet."

"I really like him," Darlene echoes.

From the kitchen, I hear the sizzle of eggs hitting melted butter, and Travis calls out, "Are you talking about me? It got quiet in there."

"Chefs don't sass the customers," I call out, and we all giggle.

I realize we don't have plates or silverware, but when I stand, Travis is already handing them to me, along with some folded up paper towels and mugs for coffee. "Sit, enjoy your friends. I'll bring it all out when I'm done."

A few minutes later has us eating, not only a cheddar veggie omelet, but hash browns and sliced apples in maple syrup. They taste like pie filling.

The whipped topping certainly completes the image.

"Wow," Misha says. "Trevor, this is really good."

"Are you for hire?" Darlene clearly hopes he'll say yes.

"Oh my God," I tell him. "Who taught you to cook?"

He smiles at my compliment and joins us at the table. "Believe it or not, my father. He thought it would help me get laid." He scans each still face at the table for an instant and amends, "All it did was teach me how to induce food comas."

We all laugh.

Misha, the hard sell, alternates her interrogation with chewing, albeit with deep appreciation. "Do you live here?"

"I do now." He jabs into the hash browns and takes a bite. I notice he has a hefty portion of omelet on his plate, despite already having had his egg breakfast not two hours prior.

The man likes his protein, that's for sure.

"Where?" she asks.

He looks at me for a second, and I can tell he wants to answer without giving away too much. "I'm staying with some people I know while I look for a house."

"Aw," Darlene melts, and I see a sharp image of a family—one with him, me, and two faceless children. "Where are you looking?"

He looks over at her and smiles, and I see Darlene's eyes light up when he looks at her. She totally gets what I see in him now that he's speaking to her. "I don't know yet. I just got here, so I'm going to check out the different towns and see about the commutes and whatnot. Where do you recommend?"

She's totally flustered, and I get another image, this one of her and Matt, same house, same faceless children. "I … I don't know. I like my apartment, so I've never looked for a house."

I tease her and say, "Yet. Let's see what dating Matt brings, shall we?"

Two pink lines streak up her cheeks, and fire snaps in her eyes. Misha picks up on it and says, "Whoa, who's Matt?"

Travis replies, "Some hunky football player. Big muscles. Thick neck. Huge crush on Darlene."

I laugh and tell Misha, "Matt Tildesky."

She gasps. "Him?"

Darlene looks like her secret's been ousted, but Travis continues with, "He'd make a good linebacker. The man's a wall."

Now Darlene is really blushing, and I have to hear the news. "Did you meet him?"

She glares at me, her body so still that I know she doesn't want to talk about him with Travis here.

So he gives her a little shove and says, "Go on, you can tell her. I've already watched the man fall to pieces trying to get your phone number."

While I laugh at his interpretation, Misha's mouth drops open, and she fully turns to face Dar. "Oh, you better dish, girl."

Travis puts his chin in his hands and bats his eyes at Darlene. "He thinks you're very dreamy."

Misha hoots, and I'm laughing.

Through clenched teeth Darlene says, "We went out for dinner last night, then a bar, and had a great time, okay?" Her face is red, her eyes are angry, but her aura, if I could see it, shines the exact hue of "ecstatic."

We girls settle down and I ask, "Where did he take you?"

Her shoulders relax the tiniest bit when she looks at me. "To that really nice steak house on the hill."

We gasp. "No way!"

Travis seems to understand, for he says, "Let me guess, it's expensive."

"And really hard to get into," I add.

"Especially on a Saturday night," Darlene adds, trying to save face.

I bite into my omelet and grin at Travis, then ask Darlene, "Well? Are you going to see him again?"

"Well, yeah," she answers, her eyes coy. She licks her lips and says, "I wanted to know if I could borrow your new outfit."

Chapter 24

They leave around eleven A.M.

As I wave goodbye, I see a long, black car with two people in it watching Misha drive off and turn to Trav. "Are you being tailed?"

He looks out the door and grimaces. "Yeah, I didn't want to freak you out, but they insisted on following me. I told them I was coming here and that they would under no circumstances be allowed inside." He half-grins. "I told them they could show up after eleven. You might want to call your friends and tell them they're about to be interrogated by the Feds, but not to worry."

"Yeah," I shoot him a glance. "That'll go over well."

"Sorry about that," he whispers, and I realize he really hates that I'm involved in this miasma.

I'm barely dressed, so I tell Travis, "Um, I'm going to shower, if you don't mind."

Another rogue grin, and this time he steps so close to me I can feel the heat of his skin. "Need company?"

I thrill at those words, and I can only look up at him while I try to determine how far I want to go.

"Ooh," he gives a little shiver, "she's considering it."

So I shove him off with a chuckle. "No, just trying to figure out how to turn you down gently."

He steps close again and lifts my chin up for a soft kiss. "I can be very gentle."

I think about having that glorious chest before me in the shower, hot water trickling down him, and I have to spin away before my resolve goes as weak as my knees. "I'll be down in about fifteen."

He doesn't come after me, but when I mount the stairs, he's just watching me, his expression one of pure longing. I tear my

117

gaze back to the treads, not needing to trip and fall and have him rescue me from my idiocy in my own house. I find myself getting mad. If he really wanted me naked, why did he tuck me into bed and walk away?

Probably afraid of purple bedrooms, I decide.

I try to reach out to the ghost of Charlie, for really, what else could he possibly be? I've realized by now that the boy must be dead, and having him appear to me just when I was at my weakest reinforces my belief that I'm getting too attached to Travis.

I need to know his story, and I need to know it soon.

I cannot—will not—have sex with a man I know nothing about.

The only thing I know for a fact is that I want to have sex with him.

Everything else is an uncertainty.

If Travis hates purple, he's really not going to like my bathroom, I decide, since almost every accoutrement in it is pink. Bubblegum pink. Towels, shower curtain, soap, toothbrush holder, even the rugs. Anything to counteract the overabundance of white white white that permeates my living space.

The fixtures are white, because the complex was built in the 80s and not the 50s, or I'm sure the pink coloring escapade would have continued.

It takes about twenty minutes for me to emerge, but when I do I'm fresh and clean and dry and nicely dressed and curled and have even applied a bit of makeup and perfume. Travis is cleaning the last of my bowls when I reach the landing, and I say, "Wow, you didn't have to clean up, too."

He steps near, armed with a towel and bowl, and kisses me. "Don't worry about it. I made the mess; it was mine to clean up."

I have to refute that. "But, you made four of us breakfast!"

He smiles and winks and puts away the bowl and hangs the towel. "And it was completely my pleasure. Really, RoseAngel, it's been years since I've been able to take care of a woman; let me enjoy it while I can. Now, what do you want to do today?"

I lean against the railing while I study this domestic upgraded version of Sexy Beach Bum. "I really only planned on doing laundry and cleaning today."

He pins me between his arms again, and I realize that railings are great places to be trapped by a hunky man. His voice is low when he asks, "What if we make love, instead?"

I'm not getting a single image of me naked, which I find interesting. Right now, Travis is saying exactly what he's thinking. I hold his eyes, and his are wide, expectant.

Hopeful.

I push him away. "I'm not sleeping with any man I don't know." I step out of his trap and square up with him in the hallway. "Maybe, just maybe, I'll reconsider this topic tomorrow night, after you tell me your story."

The smile he gives me crinkles his eyes. "Why? You still think I'm dangerous or something?"

I can't help but think of those two dead bodyguards and wonder if there's a way I can save their lives. Even though I've decided I'm not telling him my secrets until after he's shared his, I realize that if I do tell him the truth, he'd have to tell the bodyguards that they're in danger, and then they'd want to know how he knows, which would mean he'd tell them I know, and then they'd want to know how I know, which would mean I'd be Person Of Importance Exhibit A at the nearest FBI building.

An ugly chain of events.

I don't want that kind of notoriety.

I answer his question with, "Well, from what you've accidentally told me, you're living in a safe house with armed guards who are finally letting you out without being trailed. Correction, *were* letting you out. So, yeah, I'm thinking you're in a dangerous situation, and I don't want to get shot, no offense."

His eyes crinkle further. "None taken."

I relax my posture and shuffle my feet. I feel like I've attacked him or something, but he chuckles and says, "How about we take your mutt for a walk?"

Titan yips at the suggestion.

• • •

I bring a plastic bag, because I'm hopeful, but it's been forty minutes and Titan still produces nothing. Travis doesn't let him sniff every lamppost and railing and tree and hedge, and I notice my little monster seems to be listening better.

I look up at the man infiltrating my heart and life and tell him, "He really responds to you."

He smiles and squeezes my hand. "I told you, I have a lot of canine cop friends. Or, had," he adds, and I sense his sadness. Warm fingers caress my hand as he tells me, "I've been in the Witness Protection Program for three years, so I've had to cut all ties."

It's like I just got seventy-five of the one hundred puzzle pieces dumped into my lap, and most are already connected. The sudden death of his wife, the bodyguards fifty feet behind us, the imprisonment comments, the isolation, the unplanned move.

And the darkness.

His utter disgust with the way his life has turned.

Until me.

I still like that part.

"All? Even, like, your family?"

He nods and moves to a large rock to let Titan sniff it, and after a moment my dog adds his own liquid scent. "That part's been the worst. We were always close." He smiles at me, gentle and soft, and says, "I testify Tuesday."

I nod, fully understanding what he tried to tell me without telling me. "Which is why you promised to tell me Monday."

He nods and gently guides Titan back to the path. "I will tell you everything tomorrow. I just wanted you to know what's been going on. I don't know if I'll be able to contact you during the trial. Hopefully, with the landfall of evidence, it'll only last a few days." A rueful look. "Hopefully."

Before I get too emotionally involved, I stop and face him. "And after that? Then what? You get moved around again?"

He stops and faces me, too. Three kids on roller skates whip by, so he backs off the concrete path and stops on the grass, waiting for me to draw near, which I do. He says, "Well, then I start my bank manager job here in town and look for a house, and try to make love to you daily." All said with a piercing, no-nonsense gaze.

Another rush of chills sweeps my arms, just like that first phone call. He's totally serious. "Daily? That's rather ambitious."

Now he smiles, and he dips his head to mine, his lips hovering a tantalizing inch over mine. "I told you, I can be a very gentle lover."

His lips deliver on that promise, and I feel his arms gathering me close. He doesn't dip me, but I'm so weak in his grasp than I can't feel my feet.

I get another vision, another prem. This time, Travis is old, wrinkled, long white stringy hair, wheelchair bound. It looks nothing like him, but the black-and-white movie flashes once and I know in my heart it's him.

I'm a little confused and relieved by it, but it ends, so I take it to mean he'll survive the trial and grow old. I focus on wrapping my arms around Travis' neck and deepening the kiss. There might be a handful of spectators here, but I'm in control now and have no problem devoting my energy to this kiss.

After a long moment Travis pulls away. I like the look on his face when he tells me, "That was great."

I don't feel like I've just kissed an octogenarian, so I nuzzle into his arms, and he complies by holding me.

"Ah, RoseAngel, I hope all this crap will be behind me soon. Then, no secrets between us, I swear."

I rest my chin on his chest. "How will your new job like you only being there for one day before taking off?"

He kisses the top of my head. "I'm only shadowing tomorrow. They know I'll be in a trial. I was very upfront about it. Technically, my job starts when I'm done with that, and then I'll be able to start saving." He leans back and meets my eyes. "Then we can start looking at houses together."

Chapter 25

I'm still rattled by his comment two full hours later, so rattled that I can barely focus on sinking my putt. Trav had suggested we go to Puttering Around Miniature Golf after we got back to my place, and I had capitulated.

I've had so many do-overs that my par three is taking eight attempts, but by the time I manage to sink my happy yellow ball, he records it as a three.

His navy ball banks off the flamingo and slides under the whirling windmill and lands only scant inches from the hole. I jot down two before he even taps it in.

"You don't look like you're having fun," he observes.

"You're kicking my butt," I reply, my tone one of complete hopelessness.

He grabs his ball from the hole and comes over and swats my heinie again. "Such a cute butt," he teases, and I raise my club like a mighty sword honed to cut him down. "Okay, okay," he chides, hands up, his own club pressed between arm and rib. "We only have three more holes. What would you like to do next?"

I look up and grin. "Festival."

He smiles, and we finish our game (he creamed me, by the way), and once we're back in his car, Travis picks up his phone and stares at it. "You know, I'd really like to call my mom. I've been thinking about her, what with the trial coming up, and," he heaves a sigh, "I haven't had any contact with her since the night Jasmine died."

"I understand." Frankly, I'm a little curious to see how he speaks with dear ol' ma; I've noticed a lot of correlation between man/mom and man/wife. Just saying.

"They say I'm supposed to cut all ties, but I don't think the goons could plot a full-scale assault in thirty-six hours, do you?"

I look out the window, but the agents are dutifully scanning the area for threats, when the one they should be worrying about is in Travis' hand.

"Besides," he continues—like he didn't expect me to refute him once the air refilled my lungs—"by the time they get here, I'll be back across country."

He grants me an apologetic grin as he dials. I can tell the phone is ringing when he says, "They might be able to triangulate my position if they actually have the tech to do so, but we're in a public place. They'll never find me."

Now I know why the attack happens. I open up my mouth to stop him, but the line picks up, and he says, "Hi, Penny? You may not remember me, but my name is Opie; I was best friends with your son, Travis, years ago?"

I hear the woman on the other end exclaim her joy at hearing him, and watch Travis close his eyes at hearing his mother's voice after so many years. He is content and happy and reconnecting with family, and I don't have the heart to make him hang up the call. So I stare at him, nervous; I bite my nails and start counting.

"Penny, I'm so glad you remembered me. How am I?" He grins at me. "I'm well, actually. It's been a terrible few years, but hopefully things will improve over this next week. Oh, how are Rick and Dillon? Any grandkids for you yet?"

I watch his eyes light up. "Rick has a girl? Oh, that's great. Do you know what Dillon's having?"

A pause, and then he says, "Not me. If it were mine, I'd like to know and start painting. Any news from Travis?"

He looks at me then and says, "Well, he told me he's got that trial coming up. Oh, and he said he's met the most wonderful girl. He hopes someday soon you'll get to meet her."

He's telling his mom about me. I have to smile, although my fingernail is jammed between my teeth. I'm thinking he's been on the phone about a minute now, and those TV shows usually claim they can trace calls after that. I make the hand motion to hang up.

He frowns at me, so I tap my wrist and make the motion again. I make it urgent, and he says, "Penny, it's been great catching up with you. I'll pass along all the good news. Tell your family Opie says hi, and I hope to talk to you soon. Hugs."

I hear her tearful goodbye on the other end, and Travis just stares at me. "What was that for?"

I hold his eyes. "In case they trace the call."

He waves off my concern. "I'm nineteen hundred miles away from where it happened. I'm not terribly concerned."

I have a terrible feeling he should be.

* * *

'Tis the season of weekend festivals, and parking is a bear, but we manage the mile walk from the car into the village and are assaulted by the scents of deep-fried waffle cones, cinnamon nuts, bloomin' onions and fried chicken, and none of those vendors are even in sight. All the usual vendors have pitched their white tents, their goods spilling out into the aisles. Nestled in-between the standards are the newbies, with eye-catching novelties and household goods that draw first-timers and empty-nesters alike.

Travis buys some spices and kitchen gear, and I find a novelty collar for Titan that I have to have. Fudge and cotton candy make their way into our bags, as well as a silk scarf I can't live without.

A movie prop tent is there for the first time, and the walls are decorated in latex masks. We try on a dragon one and Pinhead and a clown and Freddy Kruger and a female vampire. The tent is crowded, because everyone loves Halloween, but Travis sees a blue plastic bin of more masks and pulls out one to show me. He's excited and shares, "I always wanted to dress up as a crotchety old man for Halloween. What do you think?" He tries it on, and his brown eyes sparkle from behind it.

I stare at him and say, "When are you going to put it on?"

He crunches me to his side and says, "It's marked down to twelve dollars. I'm going to get it."

At the end of that row of tents, in a giant display of junkyard art, Travis picks up a scrap-iron horse head made from recycled car parts painted in blue and orange. The mane is made out of bike chain, the jowl is notched like a gear, and I think the mouth is a wrench. He is so enamored of it he buys it.

I have to give him the raised eyebrow look.

"I'm a Broncos fan, remember?" He sticks out the horse. "Looks like their symbol. It's the first item going to my man cave."

I roll my eyes and turn away, but he leans into my ear and says, "Don't worry, I won't put it over our bed."

Now I'm really rolling my eyes, but inside I'm so excited I can barely contain myself. He chuckles and guides me into another booth, this one with beautiful photographs blown up and mounted for display. We rifle through the smaller ones displayed like index cards and croon and exclaim over our favorites.

I'm really drawn to a large hanging one of an red-orange sun setting on a still beach. The sky is streaked with soft purple, lavender and pink clouds that are breathtakingly beautiful. It's so soothing, I feel captivated, relaxed. No palm trees, no coconuts, no blue water. I see what looks like a piper crossing the sand—a small stick-legged bird caught in silhouette, and can't help but think of how great yesterday was. The sand looks soft and white and inviting, with little corrugated ridges created by the waves.

Trav comes up behind me and makes a soft noise in his throat. "Reminds me of yesterday."

"Me, too."

The vendor is asking a whopping one-fifty for the photo, and Travis motions him over and hands him a credit card.

I spin to face him. "You're buying it?"

His smile weakens me more every time I see it. "It reminds me of the first day of the rest of my life. Of course I want it." With a cheeky grin he adds, "*That* one can go over the bed."

I feel my shoulders drop. This man is a catch, and I have a feeling—no matter how awful his story is tomorrow—we're going to get rather unclothed.

• • •

We hop into my car when we get back, and I toss all our goodies in the backseat to deal with them later. I treat him to Korean food for an early dinner, because that's what he wants, but shortly thereafter I kick him out for my own sanity. I'm getting way too attached to a man I know little about, and the more time I spend with him, the more naked I wish to be.

I'm getting really unsettled about that phone call to his mom, too. In fact, the longer I worry over it, the more likely I think my prem will come to light.

He grants me a lengthy goodnight kiss, which I am happy to return. When our lips part, I hold his eyes. "Will you do me one favor?"

"Of course."

I cup his cheek and ask, "Will you sleep with your clothes on until the trial, and keep your phone and shoes by your bed?"

He gets a little wrinkle in his brow at my crazy request and asks, "Why?"

I almost tell him I have a bad feeling, but I have a suspicion he'll wave it off like he did earlier. Instead I say, "Because it will make me feel better. Will you do that for me?"

His shoulders drop when he smirks at me. "Are you one of those overprotective females?"

I grin. "What if I say yes?"

He holds my eyes like he's reading me, and I watch his chest move up and down with his deep breath. "Will it really make you feel better?"

"For tonight and tomorrow night, absolutely."

He shakes his head like he's gone crazy but says, "Okay, but just for you."

I thank him for humoring me and kiss him goodbye.

Once he leaves, I lean against the door until I hear his car start, followed by the agents' car, then sigh and relive every moment of today.

Chapter 26

Tina attacks me at the office door, and I had forgotten that my parting words to her were about my date with Travis.

She has not forgotten.

She's rather angry about it, too. Fire snaps in her eyes and she charges, "Why did you want me to meet that guy if you were going on a date with him, anyway?"

I plunk my purse on my desk and lean onto my chair and look at the photos of Titan and Grimm mounted on the foam board. The other four employees in our shared office glance up at Tina before pretending to ignore our conversation, which I know isn't going to happen. Kathy is the world's biggest gossip, and she's studying the papers in her hand too carefully to worry about whatever is truly next in her Event Planner itinerary. Sarah and Meghan won't get involved but they'll listen in—being animal behavioralists, they'll want to apply this to their own teachings—but they have enough callbacks to do without getting behind eavesdropping on our conversation.

Bob … well … no one really knows what he does, but he does it with aplomb and lots of aftershave and never gives one whit about any inner-office drama.

My voice is low—not only to calm her, but also to show my roommates I'm not the one overreacting. "I told you. I had met him at the grocery store and told him my name was Marie." I hold her eyes. "I didn't want to come out to the desk as RoseAngel until I could tell him the truth."

She's still mad when she asks, "And did you?"

No one is looking at us, but they are all silent as snowflakes. "Yes, on the ferry to Long Island."

"So you were with him all day." Accusation hangs in her tone, and a damning silence follows. Her line rings, but she doesn't answer it. I wait for the second and third rings to see if she does, but it goes to voicemail.

I affect a placating volume and tone. "All weekend, yes." I almost fed Travis to her, and now I'm ready to protect him from the likes of preying misses.

Tina glances at her phone and sees the "Message" memo on the display. Her voice drops, and she asks, "What did you do?"

I balance my smile so that I don't come off as gloating. She did do me a favor, and I don't want to make her feel bad after helping me. "Friday we met for dinner, then we spent all day Saturday on the beach, then yesterday he showed up at nine and made me breakfast. Scared the hell out of my two girlfriends when they walked in and found him in the kitchen, cooking away. After that, we went to the festival, and then had dinner, and then I kicked him out so I could do laundry."

She smiles then, but it's soft and sad, and I realize she really liked him and had been holding out for another opportunity to get to know him better.

Touching her arm makes her look up at me. "He knew you weren't me, Tina. That's why he called the cat Cheetos. When I finally told him who I really was, he told me he recognized me by my voice the second we met at the store."

A wan smile, and Tina looks down. Then, hopeful, she looks up and asks, "Does he have any single friends?"

• • •

I get a call at lunchtime on my cell from a hunky man, and I feel that rush of excitement as I pick up. My voice is a little high when I ask, "How's your first day?"

Travis chuckles and says, "I think it'll be great. I really like the people here. Very nice, relaxed work environment. I'm glad I moved here. It's a friendly town."

I push the German Shepherd mix puppy off the table in the lunchroom. One of my coworkers is fostering this mountain of a beast, and we're trying to help her teach him some basic manners before he goes up for adoption. The only problem is that she, like me, hasn't been able to find the method that works best for him yet. We tell our clients that not every training method is the right one for every dog. Just like people, they all learn differently. Some need motivation, some need rewards, some need punishment.

At sixty-two pounds, this beast needs to be better behaved. I push my tofurky sandwich away from the edge and tell Travis, "We have a dog here that could certainly benefit from your expertise. He's large and unruly, but he is housebroken." I grin at my coworker, Christina, and she bobs her head at the assessment.

"Maybe when I get back," he tells me, laughing.

"I never tried food motivation with Titan," I share. "I guess I was afraid to add ammunition to his daily deposits, but I have to admit, he held it all night long. So I gave him some shaved cheese when he went outside this morning. He seems to really respond to that treat."

"I'm glad I could help," Travis tells me. "I've always loved dogs, and would help train whenever I could. I love teaching them tricks, like balancing a treat on their nose, or jumping through hula hoops. That's always fun to do."

"That sounds like something Titan would love to learn."

"I would love to teach him when I get back."

I noticed a lot of "love" in our conversation and carry a secret smile in my heart. I nibble my sandwich again, keeping an eye on Goliath, and ask, "Do you fly out for this thing on Tuesday?"

"Yeah," he grumbles. "Red eye at five."

"Yeesh. Are you going to stay up all night?" Another coworker has the dog's attention, so I take a bite out of my vegetarian sandwich amidst the distraction.

Travis gives me a sultry laugh and says, "Maybe *we* can stay up all night."

I look around to see if anyone else heard that, but the dog is bounding around the room, a filched apple as his prize, and I'm completely ignored amidst the ruckus of four people trying to grab the fruit from his jaws.

Right now, this is perfect.

I look down to hide my flaming face, fanning my hair over my cheeks and resting my temple on my curled fingers. "Um ..."

He laughs, warm and inviting, and I know he's not teasing me. He's a man on a mission, and I'm it. "You should be excited," he tells me, "because tonight I come clean."

I'm thinking of a totally different type of *come*.

Luckily he can't read my mind, because he continues, "When do you want me there?"

I assume he works until five, and I better run to the drug store for individually-wrapped latex raincoats and anti-tadpole cream for just-in-case protection tonight, so I shrug and say, "Anytime after six-thirty or so."

"When do you get home?" Like my answer wasn't good enough.

I glance at the clock and shrug. How many people will be blocking the "family planning" aisle? "I don't know, five-thirty or so."

I sense his decisiveness when he tells me, "I brought over enough food to make us some dinner tonight. I'll meet you when you get home." Then he says, "Hugs," and hangs up the phone.

Hugs. The same thing he said to his mom. The woman he's loved his whole life. It's hard not to read into that one, and I literally bite my tongue through my smile. Is that "Travis-speak" for *I love you?*

I realize I'm having supper, stories, and sex tonight.

It's about friggin' time.

Chapter 27

I spend the last hour pacing and cleaning my cubicle. I'm feeling antsy, and it actually has nothing to do with seeing Travis at five-thirty.

But it has everything to do with Travis.

Something is wrong. Wrong, wrong, wrong. I can't put my finger on it, but I keep seeing flashes, like the glint off a car when it drives by, and each one feels like a glass shard slipping between my ribs.

I have a horrible feeling the prem happens tonight. I hop online and look up Broncos and see they are from Denver, Colorado. A landlocked state. I Google the mileage from there to here and see it's nineteen hundred miles, just like Trav had said.

Lots of twelve-plus-story apartment buildings there, too.

He called his mom over twenty-four hours ago—plenty of time for the bad guys to launch a coup.

It's almost five. I tell Tina—who has been snappy and moody today—that I'm heading out. She barely waves goodbye. I pick up my cell and text Trav: leaving wrk, b home 20 min CU soon.

He doesn't text me back before I get home from the store.

I let Titan outside and tell him he's a good boy and by five forty-five no Travis.

Right then I get another vision, and I hate this one: My brother puts a gun to my head and shoves me into a room of killers. We are with a handful of men, and everyone is armed and dangerous and on high alert, and a second later gunshots go off all around me.

I know my brother would never do anything to harm me, but I can't for the life of me figure this one out. I don't think I got shot in the vision, but if it was the last moment of my yet-unlived life, would I even get that detail?

I'm a psychic female, not a psycho female, but now I'm really starting to fret. Am I doomed to be betrayed by the two men I like the most?

I trudge upstairs and put my new supplies in my bedside drawer, shoving it closed. I go back downstairs and tug open my fridge and see mozzarella and ricotta and chives and fresh pastry wraps and smile that Travis had plans to make me tortellini or ravioli or something by hand.

Five fifty-eight. I feed Grimm and Titan and pace, which makes both of them watch, er, glare at me with suspicious eyes. Titan even abandons his food bowl to follow me up and down the hallway and living room, and after I step on him for like the third time, he joins Grimm on the couch to supervise—a much safer alternative.

All the rationalization in the world can't shake my sense of doom—i.e. he went out drinking with his new coworkers, car got a flat, he forgot, he's getting cold feet and backing off ...

Nope. I know Trav well enough to believe when he says he'll be there or do something, then he'll be there or do it.

I vacillate calling my brother, but I'm a little too freaked out to share this vision. What if I find out he's been living an alternate lifestyle?

By six-thirty I make a grilled cheese sandwich, but it's not sitting well with me. I barely make it halfway through and toss the rest. I turn on the news to see if any catastrophe has hit us, like car wrecks on the highway, etc, but nothing jumps out. When the phone rings at seven twenty-eight, I assume it's one of my friends, but I don't recognize the number.

I'm a little tentative when I pick up and say, "Hello?"

"Oh, thank God you answered," Travis tells me, and I sit up on the couch and turn down the TV. I sense fear and frustration in his voice, with frustration clearly the stronger of the two. "They won't let me out. A lot of chatter … some situation about the airport, a handful of suspicious men arriving out of Denver. They're worried about me, so they won't let me leave, not even with a guard." He takes a deep breath. "RoseAngel, I'm so sorry."

"Chatter?"

I think he's waving his hand while he tries to come up with the words. "They scan the airwaves, listening for anything that would be flagged. They're concerned enough they won't let me out."

I almost think he's tearing up, his voice is so thick. Hopes crash, and I know my prem will come true tonight. I dig my fingernails into my palm as the TV news shows all the horrors of today playing out in small snippets.

I lick my lips and manage to speak just over a whisper, "Are they doing anything for you to make you safe?"

"Yeah," he tells me, "they're bringing in more guards." I can tell he's looking out the window, for I see four armed men circling the perimeter, and I assume there are more on the other side. "And they took my phone, but gave me this one. Luckily, I had memorized your number before they shattered my other one."

I look at my screen and say, "I'll program this one in."

"Rosie."

I charge ahead with, "Don't forget your promise to me. The phone. Staying dressed." I'm breathing heavy, and I don't like how fast my heart is beating. Fear has taken root, and every beat of my heart makes it twist and grow.

He takes a deep breath, shares a soft chuckle. "I won't."

I bite my lip. "I'm scared for you, Trav." I feel the burn of tears behind my eyes. I've never had a prem before; do they always work exactly the way they present themselves? It's a question I forgot to ask Ray.

"I'll be fine."

If the prem comes true, step-by-step, he will be. "I know."

"Rosie." I can tell he wants to see me, for he's looking hard at a spot on the wall about my eye level. "In case I don't see you before the trial, please know I really wanted to make you dinner tonight. Manicotti is my specialty."

I hear my voice laugh a nervous, "Okay."

Another man in the background is behind him, and when Travis looks at him I see he's another guard. He's tapping his watch like I did, making the same "hang-up" gesture.

And then Travis adds, "And in case I never get to see you again, please know you were the girl I never wanted to let go."

When the connection ends, when the line goes still, I think my heart does as well.

Chapter 28

Crying is the absolute best option at this time, and only one thing can improve upon it. Through the burning haze of my tears, I go into the kitchen and grab my ice cream scoop and a bowl. I open the freezer and pull out the carton of My Life Sucks, then take the bottle of chocolate sauce and pour on a double layer of Love Stinks, followed by some dry-roasted, unsalted He's Just Not That Into Me, and top the whole thing with a hefty dollop of non-dairy I'll Be Single Forever.

I'm *so* glad I'm out of maraschino cherries; that's one final analogy I'm simply not ready to add.

I plop down on the couch, making Grimm growl at me and take off, and pop in the sappiest movie I own: *Message in a Bottle*.

After, I put Titan out earlier than usual and grab another movie from my collection to watch. It's ten, and I should be getting to bed soon, but instead I go back to the freezer for another round of pity, this time with the carton of Did I Chase Him Off? for the base. (All the other toppings remain the same.) I put on my PJs and tug a blanket out of my ottoman and curl up on the couch for a second round of tears, this time with Kate, Leonardo, and Celine Dion's heartfelt theme song about a doomed ship to help augment my soggy tissue mountain on the floor.

Despite Grimm's complaints, he does love me, and he cuddles up half on my stomach, half on my hip, his purring intended to ease my pain. Titan jumps up and snuggles behind my knees, his little chin on my calf.

Titanic, along with the ice cream pity party overload, lulls me to a sobbing sleep.

...

I dream I'm looking down on myself. I'm a little girl, sprawled out on our turquoise shag living room rug, coloring. A rainbow of crayons encircles me because at that age I liked to draw with both hands. The TV is on, and my dad is flipping through the channels from our orange velvet couch.

Someone knocks at the door, and I watch myself get up to answer it. Somehow I now stand at the door as a grown up, the child I was now gone. I open the door and see a woman I faintly recognize. She has curly auburn hair and small green eyes.

"Jasmine," I say, and she nods.

"Wake up," she tells me.

"But I am awake," I say.

"No, you're not. Wake up now."

I shake my head again. I've never sleepwalked, and I'm carrying on a rational conversation, so I can only stare at her. "I'm awake. What do you need?"

"No, you're not awake," she insists. "I need you to wake up. Travis needs you. You've got to help him."

"I'm awake," I argue, getting mad at this delusional woman blocking my door. I grab the handle to shut it. She reaches through the door and grabs me by the arms and shakes me. "I'm not kidding! Wake! Up!"

I feel the burn of her icy hands on my skin. I shake my head, because I'm awake, I'm clearly arguing with her to stop shaking me, but she keeps screaming back at me and treating me like a rag doll in a tiger's pen at the zoo.

She stops suddenly and holds me still. Her eyes bore into mine, scant inches away. Through clenched teeth and unmoving lips I hear, "Go. Get. Travis."

• • •

I sit straight up with a gasp, in my own townhouse, on my tattered old couch, displacing a very grumpy Grimm and making Titan moan and re-adjust himself to avoid falling. Ice fills my lungs and splinters into my brain, and I smash my wrists into my temples and press hard. My arms burn with frostbite, and I'm afraid to cry for fear of icicles spearing through my orbs.

I grab my cell. It's twelve-fifteen in the morning. Kate Winslet tells Leonardo DiCaprio, "I'll never let go, Jack. I'll never let go."

My freezing hands shake as I grab my cell.

Cold movie images flash in my head.

I'm not ready to let go.

I dial Travis.

It's show time.

Chapter 29

My hands still shake as I hold my cell. My breath comes to me in sharp hiccups, and I feel my frosty heart race as I look for my last incoming call to quickly retrieve his number.

His cell rings once, twice, three times before Travis picks up, but he doesn't speak.

"Trav?" Through his eyes I can see the horizontal slats of light angling into the broom closet. I'm standing in my living room, and I find myself crouching slightly to mimic his cramped position, like doing so will help me better connect with him.

"Sh." So soft I can barely hear him.

I think our hearts thump at the same panicked pace. I tell him, "I'm here for you. I'll help you get out." I look upward, begging the universe to please let my words be truthful.

I sense his confusion then his trepidation as someone walks past.

I hope I can recall every detail of my prem. My brain still feels like a cold knife has severed its way through my cerebral hemispheres, and I press my eyelids into my skull to try to think past my fear. I tell him, "Don't move. Give it a few seconds."

Gunshots ring out, and I hear Travis catch his breath at the same moment I cover my mouth and lean forward. Was he shot? But no, a few seconds later I hear the cupboards being yanked open, their contents spilled to the floor. I can hear Travis' breath on the speaker: shaky, hasty.

The sound of the kitchen being tossed apart soon stops.

That's right, they trash the kitchen first. I know he has to leave the cupboard, now. "Okay, you've got to trust me. Get out of the closet."

He whispers, "No, I can't. There's—"

I force myself to sound way more confident than I feel. I know I have to trust my prem. "Travis, you've got to trust me. His back's to you."

"You see him? Where are you?"

Well, I *did* see him, and I remember the prem like the unending nightmare it seems to be. I opt for a version of honesty: "I'm on your side. I'll get you out. Trust me."

I hear his breathing increase, and then I sense his caution as he touches the latch and lowers it to open the door and eases out of the tiny space.

I hear the sneezing in the background and say, "Shit! He's sneezing! Run for the kitchen door. Gogogogogo!"

I can tell he looks into the living room, for his breath catches when he sees the bodies I know are there.

I tell him, "Hide next to the trash cans, right next to you." I'm panting like I'm the one who just ran, and I'm focusing so hard on his safety I feel a migraine threatening.

"Where are you?" he hisses. "How did you find this place?"

I wave off his question and say, "There should be a guard at two o'clock. Wave to him, and he can open the gate and get you out of there."

"You see him? Where are you? Are you with the Feds?"

"You can't see me," I tell him instead of lying, "but I'm trying to save your life."

I hear gunfire, and Travis says, "The guard just got shot."

"He did?" Shit. This is not at all how my prem played out. I feel panic welling in my chest. I spin and circle in my living room, hand at my throat as I shake my head in denial of his words. "He's got the keys. He was supposed to open the gate. Oh my God, Travis, I don't know what happens next."

He hisses, "What the hell does that mean? You think this is some kind of role-playing game?"

I need to calm him down. I take a breath and say, "You ever have a partner, Trav?"

"Of course," he says, and his voice is strained, like he's looking around for safe passage.

"Good, 'cuz right now, I'm your partner. I just don't know how to get you out safely." I think that made him feel better, for his voice is stable when he whispers, "Don't worry. They think I'm still inside."

My head pounds, the migraine moving in with friends, and all I want is wine. Lots of it. "What are you doing?" Whatever he's got in mind I don't like. Even if it's a stellar plan. Just on principle.

I think he's racing to the dead guard, but it's dark out and I can't see. I can tell when he looks into the cabin, for the assailants are in well-lit rooms, and they are tearing the place apart. I can see the sneezing man has worked his way outside, his attack still in progress.

I hear the tinkle of keys and Travis says, "Okay, I'm out. Where are you?"

I think back to the prem and say, "There are four cars to your left. The second one has keys in the ignition. Get in and go left on the road."

More shots fire, and I hear them rip past. Travis says, "I'm going to have to break in."

What? I frown into the phone and say, "Are you sure?"

Another bullet races by—really close, from what I can tell—and then the unmistakable sound of breaking glass. I hear a noise I can't place, and then a spark. The car starts, and I tell Travis, "Keep your lights off until you're on the street."

After a few interminable seconds, he tells me, "I'm on the road. I turned left."

I have to visualize the numbers that came to me. "Okay, in exactly two point one miles, there will be a sharply inclined road on your right. Go up it and turn off your lights. Don't leave your foot on the brake. These guys are going to be right on your heels, but they won't see you here."

I hear the motor scream as Travis rips down the road. His breathing still rivals mine in pace, but he asks, "Where are you? How did you know about all this? How did you even find me?"

I shake my head. "I can't tell you just yet. Are they behind you?" I head to the kitchen for water and chug it.

"No, but I can hear gunfire."

I can see how rural this area is, with thick forests on both sides, lush undergrowth, and gently curving roads. I finish one glass and work on a second. "Are you getting near?"

"Yeah."

My empty glass lands hard on the counter and I cringe that I didn't break it. "Pull in and kill power."

My cell beeps call-waiting, and I look and see it's my brother. I close my eyes and try to send him a psychic message: *I'm okay*. He must have felt my panic; I hope I didn't tear him away from Angie. I remember him holding me at gunpoint in my vision and know I'll have to deal with that shortly, just not now.

"RoseAngel?" A note of fear in Travis' voice pulls me back to the situation at hand.

"Yes?"

"There's a goddamned bear in front of me."

Now I freak. "What?"

"A she-bear. With a cub."

I hear hard pounding from only feet away, and he says, "I pissed her off. She's shoving my car. I can't stay here."

I know the killers still have to be in hot pursuit, and I cry, "You can't leave. They're after you."

"Rosie, there's a goddamned bear out here!"

Thump, thump. I not only hear the car getting beaten, I can *feel* it moving.

"I'm going to shoot her."

I didn't know he had a gun, but I scream, "No! They'll hear you!" Not to mention, I don't want the bear to get shot.

"She's going to kill me, Rosie!"

"The killers are going to do much worse!"

I can tell the car is getting shoved backward down the hill, and I tell him, "Put on the emergency brake. Don't touch the regular brake, or they'll see you."

He screams, "I can't stay here."

"You can't leave."

"Rosie!"

"No! The cars should be coming any second now. Do you see the cars?" Shit! I take a fistful of my hair and start pacing again.

"Yes, three of them."

Thump, thump, crunch. I hear the sound of breaking glass, of metal bending under three hundred pounds of raw power.

"I'm getting out of here."

I try to weigh the options: Mama bear versus homicidal troop of maniacs. The safety glass should hold. "Let the cars go by first."

"Rosieeee." I can tell he's backing up against his will.

I can see them, their headlights, racing around the corner. Travis has kept his lights off, so I can't see the bear. The headlamps below round the bend on cars number one, two ...

His car slides farther down the hill.

Closer, then the second one blasts by underneath.

Travis is twenty feet from the road.

The third car rips past just as Travis pops off the emergency brake and guns it into reverse.

He skids out onto the asphalt and puts the car in reverse, backing up just far enough that mama bear leaves him alone. When she ambles back to her cub, Travis puts the car in gear, trailing his assailants but staying out of view.

"Okay," he gushes. "I'm out."

My pajamas stick to my chest. My hair is plastered to my skull. I'm shaking so hard I have a hard time holding the phone to my ear. "Are you okay?"

"Yeah. But the steering is off. She kicked in the front fender. I think she broke the radiator, too."

I venture a deep, shaky breath. "There's a lonely gas station a few miles up the road on the left. Pull in back. I'll be there soon."

Chapter 30

I call my brother while I drive out, and he answers before it really rings.

"What happened? *Oo ta dosa?"* Are you okay?

I flap the gauzy top I tossed on—fished from my laundry pile—and I'm still sweaty and pasty from witnessing the most terrifying ordeal of my life, as attested by the fact my empathic brother reverted to our first tongue. "I'm okay. It was the prem, TB. None of it went right." I tell him the idealized version versus the improvised one, and he makes a soft moan.

"The timing was off," he tells me.

"I know. How do I make sure it doesn't happen again?"

He chuckles. "You really want to know?"

"Duh. Yeah." I raise my skirt to my face and wipe my brow. Now that the adrenaline rush is receding, I feel cold but no less terrified.

Somehow, I thought wearing the same skirt I wore to the beach would calm me in the aftermath.

Fail.

Epic Fail.

I sense my brother guarding it, this secret he doesn't think I really want to hear. "You have to tell him the truth."

"But I will. I fully intend to tell Travis about my abilities once I know he's safe."

"TS, you've never told a single man in your life about your talent. If you want a man to trust you, you need to let him in."

I argue, "But I was going to today. When he came over. But they put him on lockdown and I didn't see him."

"Jail?" he asks me.

I tell him, "Witness Protection Program."

"Oh." He seems relieved. "That makes so much sense. However, the fact is you didn't tell him, so he has no reason to believe you. You lack credibility, *Kaiya*."

His name for me. I gasp as I look around at the red light where I'm stopped, not sure which way I need to go. Right feels correct, so I turn that way and say, "You mean to tell me you tell all your girlfriends you can read their minds?"

I sense him laughing at me. "Yeah. It gets me laid every time. Coolest trick ever, especially after they've had a few drinks."

I feel my eyes burning but focus on the road. He makes it seem so easy, like being a freak show is cool and not the biggest con or scam in the world. I choke down my saliva and say, "I had a vision about you. It was bad."

"What was it?"

I focus on the curve in the road, granting myself a few seconds to formulate my words. "You had me at gunpoint and shoved me into a room of killers."

He laughs. "I love you, Kaiya, you know that, right? I would never jeopardize your life for anything. You should know that better than anyone."

A tear leaks out. I sniffle and say, "Of course, Kai. *Eo mach oo*, too."

His voice is kind now, the pressing tones gone. "This guy, from what I've seen, is more man than anyone you've ever dated. Let him in. Have fun. And I swear I won't peek again."

I'm feeling a little better that I told Ray. "Gee, thanks." I see the gas station ahead and see no cars on the street. I pull in and head around back. A dark mangled car sits nestled between the two giant green metal trash bins, and I slow the car to an idle.

Travis steps out from behind the trees just beyond the lamplight, and I turn off my headlights and roll down my window. Ray asks, "Are you safe?"

"Yeah, I'm here," I tell him, feeling my stress level plunge just seeing Travis alive and well and not bleeding. He's careful as he eases from his hiding spot, his eyes darting left and right behind the building before he hastens to my car.

I tell Ray, "I'm fine. Travis is fine." I take a calming breath. "I love you, TB."

"*Eo mach oo, sa*. Now, go get some." He disconnects the call, and I drop the phone on the passenger seat.

Survival sex sounds pretty darn good to me.

I motion to the passenger door and ask the man of my dreams, "Want a ride?"

Chapter 31

I expected Travis to be a little confused, maybe evasive, when I picked him up.

What I didn't expect was this downright hostility. He gets in and fastens his seatbelt and glares at me and says, "Let's get out of here." Then he scoots low in the seat, like he doesn't want to be seen with me.

I try assume he's still hiding from the hunters.

I ease around the building and head onto the road, aiming for the city. "We need to get you someplace safe."

He scowls at me and barks, "That's the only line I've heard for the past three years, and look where it got me today."

I look over at his hostility. "Are you okay?"

"What do you think?"

I take a deep breath and focus on the road. This stretch is curvy, and I don't know the area very well. Right now I feel like I'm traveling more by sonar rather than sight. I'm exhausted, both mentally and physically, and emotionally I think I'm slightly more damaged than the bear-ravaged car. "I think you can try to be a little nicer to the woman who just saved your life."

He scoffs and crosses his arms, his mind a cesspool of tar.

My digital clock says it's one-sixteen. Short of my partying days with Misha (I use that term loosely), I've never been up so late when I have to work the next day.

"Why are you so angry with me?" He's a black hole of hatred, sucking everything in. All I can see is pitch.

He's silent for a while, and I'm wondering if Ray had it right; he doesn't trust me, and now I've gone and blown it. In a distracted kind of way, I wonder what flavor *that* translates to. Does Gone and Blown It have candy pieces in it? Or caramel swirls?

Finally, "Who were you on the phone with?"

I look over at him. "My brother."

"In the middle of the night." He clearly doesn't believe me.

"Yes." I hold his eyes. "I was terrified. For you."

He pulls his glaring from the road to study me. "You always tell your brother you love him?"

"Almost all the time."

Again he holds my eyes, and I see nothing in his thoughts, just like when we first spoke. Blackness only. Deep, pure, utter blackness.

The doubt in his words is honey-thick and oily-slick. "I thought your brother's name was Ray."

I frown and nod. "It is."

"You said something like T.D."

"TB," I correct, understanding his confusion. "Twin Brother. I'm TS. We also go by Kai and Kaiya. Childhood names we gave ourselves."

He's still looking at me, but I need to pay attention to the road. We're approaching the city now, and I'm looking for a hotel. He asks me, "May I see your phone?"

I shrug. "If it'll make you feel better." My last outgoing call was to Ray, and his photo is attached to it. I hand it over, and after a minute Trav hands it back.

He still sounds accusing when he says, "Why did Ray call you first?"

I look over at him as I pull into a hotel lot. I find a spot in back and park, and I hear the bag from our festival visit slide to the floor. Once I pull out the keys, I face him and say, "I'll tell you my story when you tell me yours."

Chapter 32

Since the festival bag has a mound of chocolate fudge in it, I grab it to bring into the room. I have a feeling I'm going to need it, either postcoitally or to help recover from an upcoming blowout. I did have the foresight to bring my purse, and as we start to march silently across the parking lot, Trav grabs my arm to halt me.

"I can't put the room under my name."

I know that, so I say, "Well, duh."

I'm sure that didn't help with his fury, but he looks at my bag from the festival. "You bought a silk scarf, right?"

I nod.

He turns me back to my car. "Get your sunglasses. I have an idea." He fishes through my bag for the scarf while I fumble with the lock for my shades. "Put them on," he tells me, and I look at him like he's nuts just before I lock back up.

"What is this, the Blues Brothers? Sunglasses at night? Really?" I put out my hands like I'm blind, because, well, I now am. He wraps half my scarf around my head like some 50s diva and tucks the remainder into my blouse to bubble like some gentleman's cravat.

"All right, superstar, follow me."

Easier said than done in a dark lot at night. We get into the lobby, and he has me wait right in the middle of the room. He whispers, "Act rich and bored. And snobby."

I turn an impassive gaze slowly onto him, lowering my shades down my nose to eyeball him over the rims. He smiles and says, "Perfect. Hold that pose."

I hear him affect some random European accent, too vague to place, and he places a handful of cash on the counter.

I find out I'm a Lithuanian actress en route to *Chick-a-go* for my supporting role in an upcoming film.

Huh. Who knew? Being bored is a terrible burden. I storm up to the desk and try to match his accent. "Vut is di problim?"

The girl is young and flustered. She drops the key card twice before shoving it across the counter. "Here, Miss Fever. I upgraded you to a king."

"Vutever, dahling." I fake a smile—because I'm bored—and snatch the card. "Carry my bag." I shove the festival goodies into Travis' stomach and look out over my rims at the girl. "Elevatiss?"

She flushes and points, and I nod once and march there, head high.

Once the doors close, I question, "Fever?"

His lips twitch. "Miss Scarlet Fever."

"You suck." I tear off my disguise and stuff it in the bag.

Yeah, he is still mad when we get up into the room, but he pushes me away from the doorway and pulls a gun from his back and holds it aloft as he opens the bathroom and closet and even lifts the mattress to check under the boxed-in frame. Next he tugs the heavy drapes closed before turning on the lights. When he determines the room to be safe, he waves me in, but not before looking up and down the hallway.

I'm not sensing any danger, but Travis circles the room, still holding his gun up. He grabs the two chairs by the work table at the window and brings them to the center of the room, just between the foot of the king-sized mattress and the bureau with the TV on top.

I knew when we got this room that we'd either be romancing or pacing.

Now I'm going for door number three: Inquisition.

I ask, "Where'd you get the gun?"

He eyes me like he doesn't want to answer but says, "The fallen guard. I took his gun and the keys to escape." He indicates the chair for me, then goes to the door and double-checks the locks, then peers out the peephole. I sit, and after a minute he joins me, saying, "Now, you seem to know way too much about what's happened here. Who are you, and how did you know what was happening? How did you manage to bribe that guard, to know he was going to let me out?"

He's still mad, but I'm a veritable vault. Ain't nothing getting out of these walls unless he cracks first. I cross my legs and arms and settle into my chair to glare at him.

"Rosie," he cocks a brow, "if that's your name, you are messing with a federal investigation. You need to tell me."

I cock a brow right back at him. "You are one full day late on your promise. I believe you have the floor."

"Are you a spy? Government agent?"

I scoff. "Hardly. The shelter is my only job. You should know that; you visited me there."

"Never saw you there," he refutes.

"But I saw you, and I got the adoption paperwork to prove I was there working when you showed up."

He glares at me, but then his features settle into a resigned frown. "You want to hear mine first?"

I nod once. "Monday's now over."

He holds my eyes, and I watch the anger settle from his features. His voice drops. "You really freaked the shit out of me today."

"I also really saved you. Don't forget that."

Our eyes lock as tight as my pose. I'm not yielding, and he knows it. He braces his hands on his knees and stands up, then uncocks his gun and puts it back into his pants hem. I hold his eyes as his lock on mine, and after a long moment of this he takes a deep breath and resigns himself to the situation. I watch him swallow and blink and settle into his seat. "About six years ago, I left the force to become a P.I.; I was handling a lot of homicide cases, and frankly, I didn't like it." He touches his head with a finger and gets up and paces a bit. "It messed with my mind, gave me nightmares … I hated homicide."

I nod for him to continue.

"I figured taking on private cases for people would be easier, and really, I'm good at sleuthing. Like I told you, I knew it was you, RoseAngel, the first time you spoke to me in the store."

He wipes his fingers along the top of the TV like he's checking after housecleaning, then dusts them off on his jeans. "Most of the cases were unfaithful spouses." He gives me a significant look, and I realize a man used to searching out infidelity would leap that way hearing a woman telling another man she loves him.

I'm not yet forgiving him for his unfounded jealousy, but I'm beginning to see portions of the portrait he's painting.

"After a while, those became my bread and butter. A few missing persons here and there … a stolen dog, which was a fun case, easily solved. But then four years ago, this woman comes to me. She thinks her husband's cheating, got all the classic signs. Of course I'll take her case. He probably is."

Now he sits down and leans forward to hold my eyes. "Only this time, he's not. It's far, far worse. I trail him, and he's going to this abandoned warehouse in the middle of the city.

"Now, no matter how many unfaithful spouses I've trailed, none of them go into the skids. They hit up the swanky hotels, or their partner's place of business for some hanky-panky. Right away I know this is not what it appears."

He stands again and circles the chair. After a minute he places his hands on the back and leans on it. "I climb up some trash cans and see … " he holds my eyes, "crates and crates of guns and arms. Semi-automatics. Things that Joe Husband doesn't need to be boxing and storing after a long day of selling shoes. I take some pictures and get out of there.

"Later, I blow up the pictures and see some faces that look familiar. So I start matching faces and see that Joe Husband is in league with the mayor, the commissioner, and even the governor. I trace the markings on the crates and find out they're coming in from Argentina. Our goddamned city is smuggling millions of dollars' worth of weapons, and the missus merely thinks her husband has a honey on the side."

He drops into the chair and folds his hands, his head low. "I had to go to the FBI. I couldn't even go to the cops, which really irritated my brothers. They wanted a chance to help me, but I couldn't risk their lives. But they went ahead and brought it to the attention of their superior, who apparently was friends with the D.A. Turns out the D.A. was also involved."

He gets up and paces again, and when he hears the elevator open, he takes a minute to press himself against the wall by our door. He peers out the peephole for a moment, then comes back to sit. "*I* was supposed to die, not Jasmine."

Now I reach out and touch his arm. He takes his other hand and covers mine. "I was supposed to go on a ski trip, but I got sick and didn't feel quite up to it. Jas asked if she could go, so as not to waste the ticket. So she did, taking my car, which I had already loaded up with the gear."

His eyes hold a wealth of unshed tears. "The brakes had been perforated. Somewhere in the mountains, they went."

He lowers his head as I catch my breath, and I feel the wave of his sorrow. I give his arm a squeeze, but all he does is take a deep breath. "As they pulled her from the wreckage, my brothers told me the FBI was officially getting involved. Two hours later, I was packed up and headed for Wyoming, in a cottage somewhere in Bighorn National Forest. After that, it was Church Hill, Tennessee, and then a week in Texas until Hurricane Alex kicked us out, then Pennsylvania, now here."

He looks up again, his expression one of exhaustion. "The trial is today. I will give my testimony, and hopefully the city of Denver will be a little cleaner when I'm done."

He leans back and crosses his ankle to his knee. "That is my entire story. You are the only person outside of the FBI who knows it."

I nod, very glad and relieved to get to the bottom of this. I think back to those traumatic words I had psychically heard that first night at the grocery store and ask, "Do you wish you'd never shot him?"

"Of course. That's exactly what I'd been saying all this time. Had I known those pictures would have ruined my life, I would have passed up the entire case. Now, though, seeing how things have transpired," he heaves a sigh and studies me, "it's harder to say. I just hope my life is on the upswing now."

He takes another deep breath and leans forward, and I have to join him, relieved that he didn't "shoot" somebody with a bullet. "Now, RoseAngel, I've risked my life trying to leave, and I'm here in a hotel room where not one of the agents knows where to find me. If you're out to kill me, this is your best chance."

I have to laugh. "You think I lured you away from the killer just so I could have dibs? Do you think me so dangerous?"

Now it's his turn to fold his arms. "I've got my literal life at stake here. I've lost my family, my friends, my wife, and any chance I could hope for of a normal life. If I came across as jealous or wary or jaded, you'll have to forgive me. I already know how many significant others cheat, and I also know what it's like to lose someone I love. I'm not ready to experience either of those ever again."

I'm hoping I'm in the *love* category, by the way. I nod, for I think if I say anything, I'll blubber my undying devotion and really scare him off.

He seems to have settled, for the tar pit of doom seems to have left him. He nudges me with his foot. "Your turn."

I'm psychic should not be that hard to say, but TB is right—I've never actually told my secret to any man. He lowers his head, watching and waiting.

I lick my lips, knowing I'm going to have to be *on* to prove myself, and knowing that the middle of the night is not going to be my most productive time to broadcast my skills. But I have to trust him, as I've never trusted anyone outside of Ray.

"You're not going to believe me, even though it's the truth."

He cocks a brow. "I have to hear it before I can decide."

I glance up to his steady gaze. "This is really hard for me, for the record. I've never told anyone."

"Rosie."

I heave a deep breath and feel my tongue turn to leather. "I'm psychic."

"Ah, shit." He spins out of his chair and whirls to face me. "Is that the best you got? Come on, Rose, who are you working for? How did you get me out of there, and why?"

I hold his eyes. "When we were nearing the ferry, I saw the men you'll be testifying against, but only because you had them foremost in your mind. Then, when we kissed, I got my first full-fledged premonition. That's why I couldn't let you stop kissing me; I had to see if and how you escaped the attack."

He leans back against the dresser, nudging the TV with the motion. His arms are crossed, and I get the exact expression I never wanted to ever see on his face. Anyone's face. "Really."

I force out my breath and say, "But, you didn't do exactly as I said, which is why it didn't play out as smoothly."

"Like the bear?"

I hold his eyes. "In my prem, you were standing directly behind the attacker when he was about to sneeze. I could see your tan couch, the yellow lamp, the moving boxes where Pringles kept hiding ... even the pizza box on the counter."

He did blanch a little at that.

"By the way, Pringles is a longhaired tuxedo cat with yellow eyes. I never asked you for his description, did I?"

I watch his eyes widen as he eases his head in the barest of shakes.

I continue, "I think the five feet or so delay in you leaving the cupboard made all the difference in the smooth escape. That's why the guard got shot before he could let you out." I feel my tears gather. "I couldn't stop the first two from getting killed, but the third one didn't have to die." I wait for my tears to wane before looking up. "The car you drove, though, was not the one I saw. The one I saw was like a hatchback, not a sedan."

"The one ahead of that one was a hatchback."

I look up and envision the cars and nod. "That one was second in line."

He settles onto one hip. "You said the second car. I broke into the second car I came to."

I smile. "Which was the third car in line. You came up from behind. No wonder the confusion on that one."

I can tell he's wavering over believing me. I figure Ray wouldn't mind if I shared his secret as well, since he seemed so adamant on me getting laid. "Ray and I share the same gift, although his is based more on premonitions, and mine is mostly telepathy. That's why he called me, just when you pulled up the hill and saw the bear. He sensed my fear and wanted to make sure I was okay."

Now I'm definitely getting "the look."

"Okay," I challenge. "Envision a picture, and I'll have Ray call you right now and tell you what you're thinking."

"No, I don't want your brother involved right now. This is between you and me."

I sniff out, "You want to test me?"

He tugs the chair closer to himself and sits down, arms crossed while he frowns at me. "How?"

"Picture something. Anything. Whale," I tell him.

An eyebrow flicks up. "You could have guessed that."

"Right. Sure. Ten million nouns and I just happen to stumble on that one. Fine. Keep going."

He stares at me, and I slowly call them out as I see them: "Tree. Mansion. Dog. Horse. Grand Canyon. Model T. Sports car, with a wide white stripe. Your dream car?" I venture.

But he leans forward and concentrates, and I hold his eyes to better see.

"Shark. Boat. Eiffel Tower." I hold an imaginary torch in my hand. "Liberty. Lady Liberty." Then I cup my hands like I'm encompassing a globe. "The Greek remains, the, um, Amphitheater. Leopard ... no, cheetah."

His eyes grow darker, and he even leans a touch closer.

I'm open and on and really picking up every picture he's sending me. "Building. Outhouse. Lamp. Barn. Cow. Chicken. Table. Couch."

He collapses back in his chair, and I do the same. It's hard work concentrating that intently, but I crook a grin and ask, "Do you think I really guessed all those?"

His eyes have softened, like he believes me and thinks that was pretty cool. "How long have you had this ability?"

"Puberty. Once I saw what was really on boys' minds, I was a little too afraid to date them."

"I'm sure." But then he looks upset and bothered. "Were you reading my mind this week?"

"I can't always stop it." I shrug. "It's why I'm so good at my job; I can see what is wrong with their situation and can help them."

Tentative, he asks, "What did you see with me?"

"Darkness," I tell him. "Tons of it. And your tan couch. And me, naked. A lot." He grins a wolfish smile at that, but I have to ask, "Who is Charlie?"

He frowns. "I thought that was your pickup line."

I shake my head at him and shift in my chair. "I've been seeing him since that first phone call." And then I have a horrible thought, and my fingers fly to my lips. I whisper, "Was your wife pregnant when she died?"

He seems upset by that, so in apology I put out my other hand to rest on his arm. "My God, I'm so sorry, that was terribly insensitive of me."

But he shakes it off. "She couldn't have been. She had cystic ovaries. The doctors said she would never be able to have kids. We were actually looking at surgery, then adoption."

I hang my head. "He must be your guardian, or one of them. He was so active those first two days, but now, nothing." I look up at him. "He appeared to me when I walked by you in the store. That's why I had to come over. I only saw the child when you first called, and then again that night."

I can tell I hit a nerve, so I touch his hand. "I'm really sorry. I didn't know it was such a sensitive subject, and I'm slaphappy and not thinking very well right now."

But his eyes slide to mine. "What were those boys in school thinking?"

"Threesomes, foursomes, oral sex on them." I smirk. "The usual. So I started dating the real nerds, the potheads, the stoners. Guys with little brain space."

He considers me in that moment. "You *wanted* to date them?"

I shake in firm negation. "I wanted to not be seen as some slut in their eyes. I almost lost my virginity at fifteen, then again at sixteen, but I hated the images they kept sending me. Once I started dating the guys in chess and drama club, I wasn't so put off." I crook him another tentative grin. "I'm pretty sure I dated a gay guy, too. He always thought of another boy in school when we kissed."

"That would certainly count."

We share a bonding grin.

Travis seems to be accepting me for who I am, for he takes my hands in his. "How many guys managed to not scare you off with their thoughts?"

I'm assuming he means lovers. "Two."

He's considering me again, like I've shocked him. "Only two?"

I nod.

"Why them?"

Instead of answering, I lean forward and ask, "Why do guys always envision sports stats when they're on top of a woman?"

He laughs, really rich and deep, and I smile while I wait for this elusive answer. "So we don't come so fast. To distract ourselves."

I lean back and consider him and this newfound knowledge. "Wow. Had I known that, I could've said twenty." I heave a sigh laden with wasted time. "All those men who panted after me ... "

He smiles and folds his hands on his stomach, and I see the image he's sending me. I frown and say, "Couch. Why?"

"Just play along."

I settle back into my chair. "Another couch. Chair, overstuffed. House. Picket fence. Dog. Child."

He pauses, holding my eyes.

"Flowers. Bouquet. A pink rose. A red rose," I grin at him, "with angel wings and a halo, cute." A perfect visual of my name. "A dozen red roses."

His eyes have darkened, his legs spread a bit. "Four poster bed. That bed," I point to the one beside us.

And then he sends me an image of me naked, my head thrown back in ecstasy as his mouth claims my breast, his hand sliding down my side. I hold his eyes and say, "Third time's a charm."

Chapter 33

He stands up when I do, but I tell him, "I want to wash off first. Be right back." I tuck into the bathroom and grab a washcloth. After sweating so profusely earlier, I just want to wash down my face and neck, and this escape gives me a moment to come to terms with what I've just agreed to. I shiver in delight as chicken skin races my limbs and excitement makes a low heat curdle in my belly; I focus on that last image he sent me.

Apparently Travis has the same idea, for he grabs another washcloth and turns on the tub a bit. I watch him scrub the cloth through his hair and down his neck as I quickly reach under my shirt and wipe off my formerly-sweaty chest.

He turns off the tub while I scour my face over the sink. I reach for the hand towel and dry off, and when I look into the giant mirror, Travis is right behind me, his eyes burning into mine. Soap scent lingers in the air, so delightful and fruity that I know I'm going to forevermore associate this brand with lovemaking.

I don't need images sent to me; I can read him clearly. He gathers up my hair and eases me upright to lean back against his chest. He places a kiss on my neck, then suckles me there. I tip my head and utter a low moan, and soon I feel his hands wrap around my hips. He draws me against him, and he's hard and nestling into my buttocks. One hand slides under my blouse, slowly, and I arch into him when he cups my breast and pinches my nipple with gentle fingers.

"Ooh, no bra," he whispers.

He guides my hands to the sink counter and slides both hands under my shirt. I watch him in the mirror as he fondles me, enjoying the look on his face the same way he seems to be enjoying mine.

One hand slides down my side and leg and hooks my skirt hem, and I shiver as he drags the edge up to my hip.

"No underwear, either?" he observes, and I smile at him in the mirror.

Those fingers nestle into my curls, and with his free hand he guides me to arch my back. I'm not a big fan of doggy style, but I don't think that's what he's doing. Instead, he strokes me over and over, and I feel my body grow slicker and more swollen with his touch.

Soft, firm strokes rub against me, and Travis does slide his erection against my bare backside, but he is clothed and focused on my pleasure.

"Keep your eyes open. I want to watch you when you come," he whispers.

I'm getting closer and closer, and his other hand slides up my back, under my shirt, then plays with my breasts again.

"Trav … " I whisper.

"You can do it."

I feel it, feel myself about to lose it, and when his touch goes a tad harder against my nub, I arch like a cat and grab the counter, my head bowed as I clench his fingers tight between my weakening legs.

He *tsks* me a few times, and when I soon drag myself back into my crumbling, shattered, heaving body, I hold his teasing gaze in the mirror. "You didn't keep your eyes open. Now we're going to have to do it all over again."

I'm so logy I barely understand, but Travis grins and picks me up and eases me out the door and to the bed. He seats me on the edge, his eyes holding mine. I see nothing in his thoughts and have to smile. "No baseball stats?"

"None."

"No play-by-play? No slow motion tackles?"

His eyes drop to my blouse, and he takes the hem and tugs it over my head. When I try to do the same to him, he pulls me to my feet. I tug off his shirt and run my fingers down his chest.

Did I mention I have a thing for his chest? I nestle into the soft black hair and drag my fingers down the bumps of his ribs, then lean forward and press a kiss there, followed by my cheek. Then I lick his nipple, and he groans.

His arms encircle me, and we hug for a long moment, but then his hands dip into the waist of my skirt hem, and I back off so he can remove my last layer. He kneels before me as he pulls it down, and I love the rogue grin when he says, "I see you're a true redhead." He presses a kiss to my flaming curls, and I feel another round of fluid ease out of me.

I grab his shoulder to steady myself, and he looks up at me. "While I'm down here … "

He pushes me gently back onto the bed, and then he eases himself up to my calves. His kisses sear my skin, and I can't help but writhe with his touch.

He gets closer and closer, and soon I have no choice but to arch into some type of yoga bridge pose, and Travis complies by supporting my buttocks with his hands as his tongue brings me to new levels of pleasure.

"I want your eyes open, RoseAngel."

I look down at him and try to comply. I think I breathe my laugh. "Okay."

I watch him, his eyes lock on mine, but he gives me too much pleasure to process with my eyes open. I roll my head back and forth across the mattress as he attends me, and when his finger rubs against my nub, it's too much. I cry out my pleasure, heaving myself to my side, where I lie twitching, riding the Orgasm-Go-Round. Over and over the waves splash me, and soon Travis cuddles up behind me, his warm hand on my hip.

I'm still clenching when his lips land on my neck, my shoulder. He guides me to my back and angles over me. "You still didn't have your eyes open." He shakes his head slowly at me even though he's smiling, like I'm his most trying student. "Okay, one more time." He eases between my legs and teases, "Think you can get it right this time, or are we going to have to practice all night?" I like the waggling eyebrows.

He slides into me, and I gasp. He's a bit larger than my last boyfriend, and I'm so swollen I don't even know how he even got in, but I release my breath and smile. "I think I might be an *exceptionally* slow learner."

"Perfect." He grins wolfishly and kisses me, and I'm grateful he sends me no images. We are doing exactly what we wish to be doing, and Travis has accepted me, freak show and all. His kiss is gentle but coaxing, and when I arch into him he deepens it.

I love the way he kisses. I realize he sees women as a thing of worship and attribute it to having no sisters to beat up as a child.

My brother learned young that girls can take and give a walloping punch, but Travis has been blissfully devoid of such knowledge. I grip him harder and draw him deeper into me, and he responds by digging his fingers into my back. I want to feel the passion that I've never experienced, the passion of a man with a fully-functioning brain, and Travis is eager to comply.

I see Charlie now, and I mentally tell him to butt out. This is adult business and none of *his*. He scampers off, giggling, and I moan and wrap my arms around the love machine pumping me into the mattress.

His breathing is hard and raspy. "Rose, I don't know how much longer ... it's been a long time ... "

"Don't stop." I feel the next wave ready to crash, and I arch into him. "I'm almost—"

"Rose, I'm going to—"

I wrap my legs around him, holding him in. If he pulls out now I won't climax.

"Rose."

I arch, and his heat spills into me. "Don't stop, don't."

A few more strokes and I'm a being wrought of golden light. I feel every cell in my body glisten and shine, and the rocketing waves course through me from head to toe and back again, like the ocean waves we just met, sucking us in and pushing us back, over and over, letting us know we are mere mortals and slaves to the whims of Mother Nature.

Charlie appears to me once more, laughing and jumping in circles, his hands fisted high in the air, mouthing the word, *"Yes! Yes! Yes!"*

I study the boy's eyes and coloring and look at Travis.

... *Oh.*

Like I first suspected, the boy is his—or soon will be.

It was just that neither one of us knew it yet.

I should be panting after all the orgasms I just had, but this new revelation steals away my breath. I no longer feel my skin or anything it touches. My thoughts don't materialize. Numbness cloaks me in its silent embrace.

Travis kisses me like his world did not just get turned upside down, and he moans into my lips and chuckles and then flops to his back on the bed. He's panting when he tells me, "I think I'm going to have to give you a pass on this one. Your demanding captain just ran out of oomph."

Some detached part of me—I think my mind—tells me I have to plant my feet back into my body and play dumb. Maybe I'm wrong. Maybe it means nothing.

Yeah. Maybe I'm just misinterpreting everything. Again.

I rally and snuggle under his arm and press a kiss to his sweaty nipple, then blow across his chest. He gasps and covers his skin with a spread palm. He smiles at me, and I can feel his joy. He is not just happy to have gotten laid; he is happy to be alive and well and here with *me*.

I hope he still feels that way in a few weeks, when I tell him I'm late. Oops. So much for misinterpretation.

He turns onto his side and cups my nape and kisses me again, then pulls away and looks at the clock. "We have about an hour to sleep. Let me phone in a wake-up call." He dials the front desk and even sets the timer on the clock, then tugs down the sheets. "Come here. Let's cuddle up and sleep."

I don't foresee sleep in my immediate future. In fact, I'm not seeing sleep for the next few years.

His head touches mine, and I worry about the next giant, unplanned step in our relationship. Am I going to be pregnant by morning? Or is Charlie going to be our child eventually, maybe in a few years?

How will Travis take this news?

I'm freaking that I've been having premonitions for a full week without even knowing it, and I can't forget my earlier wish to hear peoples' thoughts, and how much that one messed me up. I no longer want to see ghosts, and I'm deciding I definitely don't need to find people on a map.

I think Trav is oxygen to my fire, making all these happen before I know what I'm seeing, and frankly I'm a little scared.

I'm thinking my life is going straight to hell.

Chapter 34

By four a.m., I had had the most amazing, relaxing, agonizing, troubling hour of my life. If I had thought for one moment that I would be having sex with Travis after all we went through tonight—not imaginary, cyber-in-my-head sex, but honest-to-God, naked-heaving-bodies in a hotel room sex—I would have packed my goodie bag.

I have never been so irresponsible in my life.

I feel cranky and moody and sated and cherished and a host of other unnamed emotions that follow incredibly awesome, unplanned, unprotected sex. His arm never strayed from my waist this last hour, and I should have cried with joy that the man wanted to cuddle after having sex for the first time.

I just really want to cry.

The alarm clock rouses him, and while he kisses me good morning, the phone rings with the wake up service. Trav picks it up and hangs up, then covers that beautiful chest and steps into his jeans.

I tug on my skirt, but Travis takes a step toward me and stops me from pulling on my top. He frowns and points to my shoulders. "What's this?"

I look down at my arms and see an angry set of red handprints, courtesy of Mrs. Dead Dreamwalker. I look up and wonder how he'll take this bit of knowledge. "You really want to know?"

I can tell he thinks some man abused me, for his firm voice answers, "Yes, I do."

So I take a deep breath and tug on my top and say, "Your late wife woke me up." I finger-comb my hair as he studies me in shocked silence. "She wanted, um, *needed* me to go save you."

He sits down on the bed. No, he falls. I watch that rosy angry color fade to gray. "How ... did you know it was her?"

I study him for a second, realizing my words might have come out as a bit of a shock. *I* was shocked. I sit beside him and lower my voice. "You sent me an image of her. Curly auburn hair, green eyes, about my height."

I see a layer of tears in his eyes and gently touch his forearm. My voice is equally soft when I say, "Trav, before you go thinking too deeply about this, let me tell you something I've learned. Spirits want their loved ones to be safe and happy. It's the purest form of love. The fact that she came to me, shaking me awake, ordering me to save you, should tell you more than I ever could."

I watch him take a few deep breaths. A tear falls, but then he gulps and wipes his cheek and claims my hand. "Thank you for telling me the truth."

"You're welcome. I hate lying, for the record. I don't like it, and I don't think I'm very good at it."

He manages a grin and slides his glance to mine. "You're not." His cell vibrates, and Trav frowns at me. "No one has this number."

It vibrates again, and I have no bad feelings regarding it. "What about the agents who gave it to you?"

He shrugs, and I wave for him to answer it.

When he does, he is visibly relieved. "Yeah, I'm fine. We're okay. You are?" His eyes widen and he tells me, "They're downstairs." He listens to what they say and relays, "This phone has a tracker."

I ask, "You sure it's the FBI?"

He nods. "I know his voice."

Good enough for me. I nod in return.

He frowns and paces to whatever bad news he's hearing, then informs me of some shady characters scouting the downstairs lobby and parking lot.

Suddenly my second prem makes perfect sense. I ask, "Can they bring up a wheelchair?"

He frowns at the suggestion until I hold up my bag. I produce the latex mask, and we share a grin.

He tells the agent, "Have someone deliver a wheelchair to our room. We've got a plan."

We strip the pillows of their cases and use them to pad Travis' stomach. (I had the honor of holding them in place.) When the wheelchair-bearing agent comes, I open the door only as far as the chain will allow. The agent passes me his ID card claiming he is Chad Phillips of the Federal Bureau of Investigation, and Trav shows me how to check his badge for authenticity. When I let Chad in, Travis has already pulled on his mask.

I like his thinking: This agent has no proof of who he's with.

I think he's feeling a little punchy when he introduces us by saying, "RoseAngel, Thug. Thug, RoseAngel."

Chad glares and offers me his hand. "Chad, your Wall Street stockbroker brother." He's certainly dressed for success in that black suit—a great way to explain his FBI attire. I also get an image of money and wonder if he likes the idea of brokering.

"Call me—"

"Marie," Trav interrupts, and I shrug and smile.

Travis plunks into the wheelchair, and I grab the spare blanket from the closet to cover his bloated stomach and legs, just like any old, cold man would need.

My heart hammers in my chest. If anything happens, I don't know how it will turn out.

I really don't want anything to happen.

I move to grab the handlebars, but Trav claims my wrist. "We'll be okay," he tells me.

I force a smile.

"Really," he insists. "I've been in worse scrapes than this."

I hold his eyes, hidden somewhere in the depths of latex. "I haven't."

"Come 'ere." He tugs me down, and my lips find his behind the mouth of the mask. "We'll be okay. Just stick to the script." He looks at the Fed. "You, too."

"Okay," I whisper. A deep breath fortifies me only a little. We just have to cross the lobby and get into the car. Cinch, right?

No one is in the hallway. I push Gramps down the long carpeted stretch and wait for the elevator. As it comes up, I locate my sunglasses and put them on him.

"What are these for?" Gramps asks me.

"Your cataract surgery last week."

Gramps tries out his voice as the doors open. "I thought I was going in for a leaky heart valve."

A groggy man and road-worn woman step out, rolling their luggage in their wobbly wake. "Gramps," I pat his shoulder, "don't you remember your eye surgery last week? The doctor told you to wear sunglasses for a month."

He grumbles out, "Stupid doctors with their orders," and I offer an apologetic shrug to the people squeezing past us.

"Now, Gramps, don't go offending strangers like you did at the hospital."

In a loud tone he argues, "I didn't fart!"

I shove him into the elevator as the poor visitors gasp and turn. When the doors close, we all chuckle.

My heart pounds as the doors open to the lobby. Gramps reaches for my hand, and I grip it. My newest brother takes the handles and pushes Gramps across the wide foyer, heading directly for the outside doors.

The same girl is at the desk, so I try to keep my head behind Chad's. I'm not wearing my diva scarf or shades, but I doubt many torch-tops came in within the last few hours, so I'm afraid she might recognize me. We ease past without comment.

A TV plays a snippet of an old black-and-white movie, and Gramps waves us over to it. He points and says, "I took your mother to see this movie when she was nine years old."

I like that he's keeping to character. I pat his shoulder and say, "That's nice, Gramps, but we have to go."

He continues, "She had the cutest girl crush on William Holden. He was a real romantic, you know."

Oh, I know a Dipper when I see one, but I lean forward and say, "Your surgery starts in an hour, Gramps. We have to go."

I nod for Chad to keep easing toward the door, and I see his eyes flick toward a man reading the news on a nearby couch. I sense he's up to no good; I hear my pulse thrum in my ear.

Gramps continues, "Your mother ordered shoelaces at the concession. Do you remember those? They were her favorite, strawberry. They don't make them anymore."

Chad veers slightly from the rotating doors and eases toward the handicap one. I push the blue pad and it swings open. I see another man loitering on the sidewalk, and when he looks at us Gramps asks, "What did you say you do now, son?"

Chad heaves a breath. "I'm still a stockbroker, Gramps. I still work on Wall Street. It's been over two years now."

"Oh, yes, yes," Gramps mumbles, and I swat Chad like any sister would do in defense of the elderly.

Sidewalk Stalker turns away, but I don't like him.

Not at all.

Gramps angles away from that man and faces Chad. "Where are we going, again?"

I tell him, "Your heart, Gramps. You need a valve. It's causing all this memory loss."

"Oh, dear," he says.

I lower my head and focus on the images being sent from those around me. I don't hear anyone in our wake, so I take a calming breath as I head toward my car.

Chad corrects my aim on the wheelchair and indicates a black van. "We're going in there."

"Not another black van," Travis mumbles, and I wonder what his association is with it, but then I sense confinement and it makes sense. If he's going into a safe house, he can't know where he's headed.

The windowless van pulls out of the parking spot and descends on us, and three more agents grab us and help us in.

I manage to see the shocked expression of Sidewalk Stalker as he realizes he's been duped and know he's reaching for a gun or car keys as the sliding van door blocks my view.

"Sit down," one man orders, and I am pushed into a seat.

Travis tears off his mask and leaps from his wheelchair and grabs me and drives us both to the floor.

Our driver peals out of the parking lot, and I can tell we're being pursued. The van whips and skids around corners, and it's not long before I hear what I assume to be bullets ricocheting off the van. I think my color has slipped a bit when I venture, "Is this thing bulletproof?"

"Mostly," a man replies, and Trav grabs my head and tucks me close. The floor is carpeted, but it is the floor, so I'm not really excited to be lying on boot sludge while being shot at.

I've had more enjoyable mornings.

"Not always," Travis corrects, holding me closer. I like that Travis is willing to take a bullet for me, but I could think of better reasons to be buried underneath him.

I hear a hollow, echo-y female voice in my left ear tell me, "Turn right."

I clench my eyes shut. I really don't want to get that acquainted with Jasmine right now, or to announce her presence, let alone my ability to hear her.

"Turn right," she screams at me, and I'm forced to yell out, "Turn right."

The driver calls out, "We've got to—"

But Jasmine and I both yell, "Turn right," at the same time Travis screams, "Just do it."

The van lurches hard to the right, and Trav and I ram into the metal legs of the car seats. He whispers, "Do you know where we are?"

I shake my head and mouth, "Jasmine." I hold his gaze, wondering what he thinks of this.

He watches me and nods, and I repeat her next words: "Go left." I can tell the driver glares at me even from my lowly position, but he complies with a hard turn.

Trav whispers, "Why?"

My expression tells him I have no idea.

The van picks up speed, and two Feds start shooting, one from the passenger window, and the other from a little hatch that is now open in the back door, like a, "What's the password?" window.

I sense Jasmine waiting in the shadows of my mind, and then the van darts around what I assume to be a car, and then I hear a crash and an explosion. Jasmine smiles and the Feds cheer.

Travis takes a moment for a long, celebratory kiss.

"All right, Romeo, get up." Chad grabs Travis by the nape and drags him off me, and with that sexy rogue grin of his he takes my hand and pulls me up.

We take our seats and ask, "What happened?"

The driver tells us, "A cop came shooting out from the left, and I swerved around it, but Hawk there shot out a front tire on our pursuer, and our trail couldn't swerve around the cop. Took a hard right into the train trestle and exploded."

I nod like all went according to plan; Travis leans into my ear and asks, "You didn't know what was going to happen?"

I shake my head once and he frowns and asks, "She just told you to turn, with no reason why?"

I nod.

I can tell he's having a tough time with trusting my actions, for in a hissing voice he exclaims, "And you believed her?"

He's backed off a touch, but our voices are low. "When I'm getting yelled at, I usually do what I'm told."

He's studying me again, but I hold his eyes. Softly he asks, "Are you ever led astray?"

I shake my head and glance around for listeners. "They don't usually contact me unless it's important."

He nods and wraps his arm around my shoulder, and I press my head to his chest.

Nothing would make me happier than to be out of here, away from this madness. I murmur, "What's a guy like you do for fun, that doesn't involve getting shot at?"

Chapter 35

I am whooshed into the airport lobby, along with Travis, ensconced in a sea of suits, this time without him wearing the pillow or mask. We skip the long line of TSA B.S. and head straight through a special line. Travis is rushed down the concourse to his gate, and there he stops and faces me. We're both winded, but he cups my nape and smoothes my cheeks and places a mind-rocking kiss on me.

When his lips leave mine, his eyes are warm and sad. "I'll call you as soon as I can. Don't forget about me."

"Oh, I won't." And when I start to show, I know I definitely won't forget about him, but I keep that to myself.

He kisses me once more, but the agents pull him away from me after fifteen seconds. His eyes never leave mine as they drag him down the chute, two agents looking ahead for problems and two looking up and down the concourse as they follow.

I wait until the final boarding call is announced, and then one Fed comes back out. He stands by me and waits while I watch the plane taxi out of sight and out of my life.

I don't know if I'll ever see Trav again, and the pain of this ignorance tightens a sickening, sour knot in my stomach.

The Fed drops his heavy hand on my shoulder. I look up at him and he says, "You're coming down to the Federal building with me. You have some questions to answer."

Yup. Definitely going to hell.

Chapter 36

If it weren't for falling asleep to *Titanic*, I would have gotten no sleep this night. Dawn breaks over the horizon, an ominous deep red that foretells more doom than I want to know. The Fed eyes me suspiciously, but I have nothing to say to him, so I lean against the semi-bulletproof glass and doze off.

When a jarring pothole wakes me, I look out the window and read the overhead signs. "I'm in New York City?" I know for a fact that the Apple is over two-and-a-half hours from home, as I've been there, and we usually budgeted for spending the weekend due to the travel involved. I can now tally my sleep total to about four hours—which doesn't help my predicament at all, by the way.

A quiet, assessing glance tells me all I need to know.

"Shit! What time is it? I have to get to work by nine." I fumble for my phone to see, but the agent's voice interrupts me.

"You're not going to work today."

My fingers halt mid-purse-probe. "You have no right to—"

"We have every right to bring you into custody," he interrupts, "as you are interfering with a federal investigation." I can tell he's used to people just rolling over and accepting what he tells them.

I, however, am not *people*. I turn in my seat to glare at him and bite out, "How, exactly, is saving your witness' life an interference? Isn't keeping him alive one of your sole requirements? One your group failed to perform?"

He parts me a scathing glance, but the car and foot traffic is already phenomenal, and he can't take his eyes off the road. A sea of black suits and dresses slithers up and down each side of the street, a veritable undulating wave of ebony, ink, raven, jet, soot, pepper, and tar. Random tourists—denoted by such heinous colors as blue, red, and tan—intermingle with the avant-garde

New Yorkers and stand out like bright autumn leaves on freshly-pressed asphalt.

I'm so far beyond exhausted that I don't know how well I'll be able to handle the interrogation.

I don't want to go to jail for helping an innocent man escape an execution-style death.

"What's your name?" I ask, hoping I can still see my answer.

Nada.

I try again. "I have to let my dog out and feed my cat."

Still no reply from the driving statue.

I pull out my cell and text Dar. I tell her I'm in police custody and to please take care of my pets. I'm really hoping they don't put me in "the Program" like Travis. I think I'd go nuts.

My fingers halt mid-type.

I think my life would be a cesspool of darkness.

My friend texts me back with concern and reassurance and tells me she'll figure it out. I heave a sigh of relief that at least my parents won't be reading the newspaper and find, "Humane Society Worker Starves Pets" anytime soon.

"What are you doing?" Anger flies from his lips.

Now that he's speaking, I get his name. It's Rick O'Hara. I look at him and say, "Oh, you do speak. I'm making sure my pets don't starve."

"Give me that." He puts out his no-nonsense hand.

"No." I tuck it back in my purse and cross my arms.

He glowers at the traffic but tells me, "You are a person of importance to this case, and your phone will be part of evidence."

"Yeah, that's great." I face him. "Doesn't what you're doing count as kidnapping?"

A slow turn of his head, and then he levels a cold blue stare at me. "It's for your own protection."

The noise I make sounds rather refuting.

I watch the road and see that cross-traffic is slowing, so our light should be green in a second. I lick my lips and stare out the window, and when Rick hits the gas, I grab my purse and yank open the door and jump out.

He yells at me, and I stumble and land on my palms, but I am able to scramble to the sidewalk. The onlookers seem very curious and eye the driver, and as he screams at me to come back I yell, "Kidnapper!" and run upstream, against the parting flow of black.

I'm in the lightest clothes I own, and boy do I stand out, even in the early morning glow of the city that never sleeps.

I manage to run a few blocks before tucking into a grocery store. I look out the window and don't see any sign of Rick in pursuit.

I know I'm only buying time. I've got to get home. I see a cab nearing my location, so I race out and raise my arm. He pulls over, and I tuck inside. "I need to get to Grand Central."

"Sure thing. Any bags?"

He's a nice older gentleman of Indian ancestry, and the inside of his cab is pretty posh. I didn't think anyone really decorated their cars, but this man proves me wrong. "No bags."

"Get in."

I buckle up and look for my charge card. It's going to be an expensive morning.

And I don't necessarily mean finances.

Chapter 37

I make it home before ten, an hour after I should be at work, and when the local cab company drops me off, I see two black sedans in my small townhouse parking lot. I groan and pay my second cab fare of the day and pretend the cars don't exist. I've been up all night; I need to call work and tell them I was taken in by the FBI, and then I need to sleep sleep sleep.

I knew I got away too easily.

One black sedan descends upon my stoop, and three men in black suits emerge from it.

"RoseAngel Dobson?" the oldest one of them asks as he flanks my left. The youngest one, about twenty-two, stands on my walkway, and the thirty-something guards my right. One man remains behind the wheel.

I'm feeling a little snarky right now, making my manners plunge. "Why ask who I am if you're standing on my stoop? You obviously know and are here for a reason."

He doesn't answer, this dark-haired man of roughly fifty-five, but I sense his name is Ike or Mike. He looks to me like an Ike. "We need you to answer a few questions."

I hear Titan whining away and say, "I have to let my dog out. Your questions can wait."

He steps toward me, but I stick my key in the lock and slip inside before they can make off with me like Rick did. I'm still groggy from yesterday's ordeal and realize my life has been turned upside down since meeting Trav only six days ago. Was this what it was like for him? Strangers showing up unannounced, hauling him away?

I know indisputably the answer is yes. I don't smell anything foul inside and tell Titan he's wonderful as I lead him out the backdoor. As I put him out on his chain, I see the youngest Fed rounding the corner, his wide eyes telling me they undoubtedly believed I would try to escape. I snort at him and tell Titan to do his business. My dog sees the Fed looming and lets out a warning bark. "You tell him!" I say proudly, then slide the glass door closed.

I head into the kitchen and vacillate: coffee or tea? Although coffee would settle me and not make me want to strangle any of my unwanted callers, I'm also really hoping for a ten-hour nap, so I choose a decaf tea bag and pop the water on the stove and kiss to Grimm for breakfast as I head upstairs to feed him.

He jumps off my bed and follows me down the small hallway into the spare room, and I tip his scoop of kibble into his dish and give him a stroke.

I go back downstairs and let Titan in. He stands still as a brick, eyeing the Fed, who has not moved from his position only fifteen feet from my door. I groan that Titan hasn't taken advantage of his potty time and let him back inside. This time, I think of Travis and clip his leash to his collar to keep him tethered to me.

Seeing the leash gets Titan excited, but I'm not giving him a chance to mess inside the house right now. I'm also not taking him for a walk.

The young Fed watches me bring in the dog, and then I walk to my front door and let the other two inside. "Tea or coffee?"

Immobile doesn't begin to describe them, so I stare at them. "The water is on the stove."

Ike waves me forward and indicates the car with his head. "We need you to come down for questioning."

Titan actually makes a half-moan, half-growl at the man, and I nudge him with my heel to stop his noise. I grab the door handle and push in the lock as I hold their gaze. "See, here's the thing. The last time someone," I air-quote, "'brought me in,' I was halfway to Tacoma before I knew I was actually leaving the state."

"Well," Ike says, taking a cautionary step closer, "we need you in our office to answer a few questions."

I inch the door closed, just a bit, keeping my hidden foot wedged behind it. I'm afraid they're going to nab me and drag me off and stick wires to my forehead and make me turn on lights with my ESP. "Yeah, well, see, here's the great thing about questions: they are mobile. They come to you, you don't go to them. Now, you can come in and ask your questions and write my answers on paper or use your little recorders or any of a number of things the FBI uses these days, but nothing in this world will make me get into that car."

They look at each other, then Ike squares his jaw and asks, "When was the last time you saw Trevor Matthews?"

I take a breath born of exhaustion and longing and hold his eyes. "Six hours ago, on the way to the airport. He was flanked by four agents until he was safely boarded."

They look at each other. "He never reached the safe house."

I drop Titan's leash. "I'll get my purse."

Chapter 38

Since the men in black coerced me prior to breakfast, I make them drive through a doughnut chain for an egg and cheese breakfast sandwich. Then, when he tells me he'll buy, I spring for a jelly-filled donut and bottle of whole milk. I figure if my life is going to hell, I'd rather enjoy my last meal. Plus, I'm going to need some serious energy to go through the hundreds of photos I was told I'll be looking at, trying to ID the perps who made off with my man.

This time we're only going so far as Hartford, not all the way to the Apple, and they give me their names, which makes me feel a little better about the ordeal.

(And I totally nailed Ike. Ike Bronson.) Things 1, 2, and 3 are named Bill Koontz, Jed Smith, and Rod Johnston, the driver.

Interesting: I notice they totally school their thoughts. I get no images from them. At first this frightens me, and I panic, thinking I'm so exhausted I've lost my gift, but then Jed thinks of his baby girl—he's the thirty-something—and I know I'm good.

These men are *focused.*

(I'd rather believe that than "brainless," trust me.)

They brief me while I eat. Trav did board the plane, a big 747, and he was counted by the ticker-taker prior to lift-off. The Feds and he all debarked at Denver, and the fearsome foursome headed off for the safe house, which he never reached.

Apparently, none of the men did.

I tell them, "Stop. Stop the car." Rod doesn't stop, and the men beside me (did I mention I'm squished in the middle?) look at me querulously. I suddenly remember all those buddy-cop action movies, where the kidnapped victim gets bumped off. Panic tightens my chest and I ask, "Do you think they killed him? Why do you need me? What can I do to help him?"

Wouldn't I know if he'd been killed? I tell myself my heart is still beating—albeit frantically—so if Travis was gone, surely I would be dead, too?

Ike answers, his thick jowls jiggling as he speaks, "Simply ID the suspects. You saw the men he went off with; we're hoping you can identify them, in case they were impersonating an agent, however unlikely."

I scoff out a laugh. "Rick O'Hara is one, does that help?"

Four sets of eyes look at me. "He told you his name?"

Oops. "I got it out of him." True, dat. "And Chad Phillips. Oh, and they called one guy in the van Hawk." And now I'm wondering, were there any covert glances I missed? Any "tells" that these guys were up to no good? If so, how could I have missed it? But no, they protected us! They tucked us into the van and raced us into the night and careened around corners to prevent our being shot, to save our lives.

They had to be the good guys.

Right?

Rod leans back in the driver's seat and looks to Ike, then tells me, "My brother Don is their driver for that case."

Ike nods and tells him, "Turn around." To me he says, "Thanks. We'll take you home."

Now I'm mad. "What? No, wait. I want to help. Where do you think they took him? Do you think he's still alive? You don't think they'd kill him, do you? What about the trial?"

The car does a U-turn, and no longer do they deign to answer my questions.

Well, there's more than one way to divine the truth. I send a thought to my brother: *Kai, Eo tamak oo. I need you. Right now.*

Immediately I hear: *Dosa. Okay.*

I add one more: *Pack a bag. We're going to Denver.*

Chapter 39

Ray arrives at my door not a half-hour later with a duffle bag, beating me home by a few minutes. I see the agents studying him with unveiled suspicion as he waits on my stoop, and I smile and say, "Oh, look, my brother's here. Wonder what's wrong?"

"Brother?" Ike asks me.

"Can't you tell? He's my twin." Now, Ray is A. male, B. five inches taller, and C. thirty pounds stronger, but he is undoubtedly my twin. I wait for the living bookends to move out of my way so I can get out and tell the driver, "Give me five minutes before you leave, okay?" I sidle up to Ray and say, "Hey! What's wrong? Trouble with the missus?"

"Is it a day that ends in Y?" he responds, totally playing along and hefting his bag on his shoulder.

I show my five fingers to the entourage and pop inside. "*Grabas,*" *thanks,* I tell him, and he comes in and drops his bag and picks up Titan for a second, then hunts around to find Grimm. He emerges from my room with the cat cradled in his arms. I swear if I tried that, I'd be minced, but this cat loves my brother and suffers all the attention.

Ray's opening line is, "You told him?"

I'm incredulous that he didn't spy. "You don't know?"

He grins and settles on my couch, rubbing Grimm under the jaw until my cat's eyes roll shut. "I told you I wouldn't peek. Did you?"

"Yes. And he believed me, after playing One Hundred Nouns."

Ray smiles at my mention of our childhood game. It was how we learned to communicate telepathically. "So, what's going on?"

I hurriedly tell him everything I know about Travis, right up to being dropped off at my door. I see concern on his face, but better: I sense Ray is really happy for me that I'm finally not in love with a loser.

He frowns while he listens, and then he clarifies, "You need me to help you find your boyfriend. In Denver. Where we've never been."

I take a deep breath, exhausted and weak and grasping for straws I've never seen. "You say that like it's a bad thing." I pace a few steps in front of him. "I have no idea how." The tears are burning the backs of my eyeballs; it won't take much to make them fall. I think of his smile, his laugh, the heat of his lips on mine and know I want that in my life from now until the end of forever, and the thought of losing him leaves me filled with never-ending darkness.

He shakes his head and scratches the back of his neck. I notice his hair is freshly shorn and wonder if he did that prior to asking out Angie. "Neither do I, but we should be able to figure something out."

I find myself wringing my hands. My throat works convulsively, and I think my nose is about to run. I barely whisper, "How do we know if he's even alive?"

"Oh, Kaiya," he says, his shoulders and eyebrows dropping down in empathy.

Ray nods with purpose and sets Grimm down on the couch and goes into the lotus pose, with his fingers touching thumbs on the knees of his crossed legs. I know I only have a few minutes before the Feds get antsy and leave, but I wait quietly, looking and listening out the door for the sound of them pulling out.

"Abe says he's alive."

I swear my brother is the only person on the planet who can claim Abraham Lincoln is his spirit guide, but as his queries always get a good answer, I'm the last person on the planet to challenge him.

"But they're getting ready to interrogate him."

My hand crawls up my throat in fear. I think back to some mob movies—interrogations lead to bullets. "Where is he?"

Ray uncurls and growls a sound of frustration. "He's gone." He shakes his head and says, "He's no less busy in the afterlife than he was here. *Don't* sign me up for that. When I'm dead, I want to rest." He grins.

I rub my cheek and temple, then mush my face, despair and frustration at war within me. "How are we going to find him? And, how are we going to convince the Feds to take us there? I can't let anything happen to him, Ray, I just can't."

And then the tears well, and my throat pinches close.

He squares up on the couch again, feet on the floor and asks, "Do you have something of Travis' that we can use?"

I raise a brow and scoff. "And how, but you can't touch it."

He frowns, totally confused that I'm not willing to help him in this. "Why not?"

I point to my stomach and say, "Because Charlie's not done cooking yet." Yup. I said it. I feel completely preggers right about now, no doubt about it.

He leans back. "Sis? Really? A boy? I get to be an uncle again?"

I flop beside him, and TB wraps his arm around my shoulder. I collapse against him and feel the tears fall. "Ray, Charlie's the boy I saw. I've been having prems all week and didn't know it until we made love, and then I saw Charlie dancing around. He looks just like Trav. Like me. Us." I feel the tears falling and wipe my face, and Ray squeezes me closer. "I don't want to lose him. I mean," I cough out a nervous, terrified laugh, "think of all the wedding money Mom wouldn't know what to do with."

Ray chuckles, crunches me. "She'd spend it all on Charlie."

I think I'm blubbering when I say, "I don't want to be a single mom. I don't want to lose Travis. I can't let him die."

Ray starts to rock me, and then he holds me with both arms. He knows me better than any person on the planet, but I'm really hoping Travis will be around to be a close second. I swallow around a thickened throat, then wipe my drippy nose. I push off and snatch my shoulder bag from my laundry closet and start stuffing some clean clothes into it from the never-ending pile towering before the machines. I stop and toss my cell to Ray and say, "Can you text Dar and ask her to watch the kids again for the next few days? And beg or grovel, I don't care."

Ray scrolls through my phone (he has the same one) and I hear him typing away as I pack. He muses, "It would be so much easier if more people were psychic. No more texter's thumb. No more LOLs and TTYSs. Just normal people talking telepathically." I hear him snap shut the phone when he's done.

I pop into my micro half-bath behind the kitchen and stuff my travel toothbrush into my bag. "You think you're normal?"

He smirks at me. "Catch." He tosses me my phone, and I open my shoulder bag and watch it drop in.

"Okay, I'm packed. Let's go."

Chapter 40

We step out as a united front, the two Fed cars actually waiting. I lean into the driver's window and say, "My brother and I are coming with you to Denver."

Ike laughs and turns to face me. "Listen, sweetheart, I know you're soft on the guy, but—"

I hold up my hand. "Don't 'sweetheart' me, okay? I'm not your girl. The fact of the matter is—" My breath gushes out of me. I turn to Ray, feeling my face flush. I can't do it. I just can't make myself tell the truth to the Feds.

Ray has no problem, though, and tells them, "I'm psychic, and you need us." He closes his eyes as they scoff, but then he points to them, one by one, and says, "You were born March seventeen, you, July eight, you," he looks up, then closes his eyes, "December four, and you," he looks at Rod, "are five minutes after your twin brother, but after midnight, putting your birth date on October … six."

They all look at him. Ike seems flustered, but then glares at me. "You hacked into our system, didn't you? That's why you needed the five minutes."

I feel horror at the very suggestion, but Ray must be completely immune to this by now, for he points to Rod, the driver, and closes his eyes. "You were just talking about the ball game. You lost a hundred on it."

That comment earned my brother a cool gaze. "You bugged the car? Set a wire in here?"

So Ray shakes his head and points to the youngest man in the car, Bill. "You. You met two girls at a bar last night. Date the other one."

That man scoffs. "The blonde was way hotter."

"The dark blonde will light a fire that will never die."

I watched Bill look at the other guys in the car, then shift in his seat.

Ike seemed to reach a decision, for he points at Ray but looks at me. "He can come. Not you."

Ray faces me. He won't betray my secret, and I know it's up to me to risk exposure to save Travis' life. I choke down my saliva. "I'm in touch with his late wife. She's the one who told me where to turn when we were being chased to the airport, and how to avoid getting shot. You need both of us."

"Fine," Ike grumbles and indicates the back seat, not happy with our intervention but seeing our usefulness nonetheless. I move to get in, and the man points to Ray and the other sedan. "You get in that car. We'll see you at the airport."

• • •

I keep in touch with Ray as we zip through traffic. In my fugue I forgot to call into work. It's almost ridiculous how crazy the last two days have been. I pick up my phone and my boss answers. "Hi, Margie, it's RoseAngel. Yeah, I know I'm late. Yes. Yes. I understand." Ooh, she's not happy with me. "Look, I'm with the FBI. I'm flying to Denver. I—" she cuts me off. "But, they're right here. Here." I hand the phone to Ike. "Will you please tell my boss who you are?"

Ike clears his throat and introduces himself and tells Margie my particular skills are needed to locate a key witness for a trial. I hear her laugh, "Why? Is the witness a dog?"

I make a frantic slice-throat gesture, terrified he's going to out me. I don't want the shelter knowing I'm psychic; it would freak people out. He nods and tells her, "That information is classified. I will have my office fax you a letter of intent for her business here, if you like. And, Margie, is it? This is a federal investigation. This is unable to go against her or on her record. Do you understand?"

Relieved with my stay of execution, I crack a grin, and he nods into the phone and hands it back to me. "Peach, that one."

I tuck it into my pocket. "How long to the airport?"

"Helicopter first, in, say, ten minutes?"

I flop back and send to Ray: *My boss is a bitch today.*

He jokingly sends back: *What did you expect in a shelter?*

. . .

They let us sit together on the plane, and I crash on my brother's shoulder, all the way to Colorado. I'm groggy when we hit the tarmac, but I rouse myself and know I've got to be *on*. The stakes are too high.

I had gotten a text message from Darlene when I was just sleeping, telling me she was out on another date with Matt last night and had a great time, and of course she would sit my pets once more, and the fifty bucks would be very helpful. (I didn't know I was paying her, but I guess that falls under the grovel category.) Misha had also dropped me a line saying she was sorry she missed my call, but that she made an incredible incense burner shaped like an alien skull in her pottery class and sent me a picture to prove it.

I smile and wonder what I should tell my friends. I do send them a message that I'm in Denver trying to save Trevor's life (I remembered they only know him as Trevor), and if I never see them again, to please know I love both of them, and my parents, and to please take care of my pets, and say a few nice things at my eulogy.

When we arrive at the airport, I tell Ike I need to know what gate Travis came in on, and he checks his info, and we head to that concourse, Ike leading the way, with Jed sent off to rent us some wheels. Luckily, the concourse wasn't far from the gate we just entered. Right now, no one is seated here, so I stand in the doorway and close my eyes. Ray joins me, and I try to *feel* the correct path.

We both turn right and start walking, leaving the feds to dog our steps, which I can tell earns us sour glances.

Ike has called in a van, and he radios in our position as Ray and I head unerringly down the long concourse. At the split, he hesitates, but I veer left. It feels right, so I head there, and Ray steps to my side. He whispers, "Is his late wife here?"

I shake my head, wondering what game he's playing, since he would definitely be able to see her. "No Jasmine. Going on gut."

And then I realize he was just testing me, of course.

The other men flank us, and people give us curious looks as we march by. I don't see any exit leading to the luggage claim, but I stop and look to my left, making the guys behind me almost crash into me. "Sorry," I tell them, and they glare, but I head to a door. I tug the handle, but it's locked. I touch the door, and I feel this is where we should be. I look to Ike. "Get this opened."

He rolls his eyes and motions to Rod to find security, and I touch the door again. Ray murmurs, "Do you think he's being kept here? In the airport?"

I shake my head at him, wondering his game. Ray is way better at this than I am, no doubt about it. He must still be testing me. "No. But there's something with this door."

He considers me for a moment and touches the handle as he closes his eyes. I can't articulate my thoughts, but Ray nods at my guess. A security guard approaches with Rod, and he tells us, "This is the backroom for luggage. No one goes in or out except staff."

I nod and lick my lips, still staring at the door. Something is very wrong. Ray grabs my shoulder and says, "I feel it, too. They came this way."

Ike and Rod go in before us, with the security guard leading the way, and Bill follows behind. We go down a metal flight of stairs and see a system of chutes and ladders all over the place, with squares of neutrally-colored luggage bumping and spilling from one chute to the next, routed midstream like a manufacturing plant as they make their way through the spaghetti nest to their flights.

The agents mill at the bottom and look around, but I scan the place and something makes me head for eight o'clock. I see one of those laundry push bins that one sees in a hotel, and I look inside.

I gasp and launch backwards, hand flying to my mouth.

Ray waves the agents over, and Ike and Rod move a mound of suitcases off the top while Bill and Ray proceed to pull three agents from the bin.

I don't see any blood, and as the men are lowered to the ground, Ike checks for pulses. "They're all alive."

I heave a deep breath. I've already seen three men die today (through someone else's eyes, but still) and don't wish to see any more. I come near and look at their faces. I nudge the nearest one's leg with my toe. "This was one of the guys in the van. And that one's Hawk."

Rod cradles one man and slaps his face, and I see the replicated family resemblance in their tight curls, thick brows and warm Mediterranean coloring. "Don?" I venture, and Rod nods.

Ray touches Don's head and closes his eyes. "He's been drugged. He's dreaming. He'll be fine."

Rod looks up at him, wanting to believe, and Ray smiles and jabs Rod on the arm. "He'll be fine. Slight hangover. Nothing too serious. He had way worse than this with his gallbladder surgery last year, I promise you."

Rod's eyes snap to his, but Ray is genuine, and Rod heaves a breath and nods and looks down.

I have a feeling we may be on the verge of an ally.

I look at the security guard and Ike and ask, "Can you check security tapes and see how long ago they came down here?"

The guard nods and pulls out a walkie and calls in the request, as well as medical help for the downed agents.

"Who did this?" Ike demands, and his men look to him.

I know. It makes sense now. "Chad Phillips. When I shook his hand, I sensed money." Tears fill my eyes, and I look away. I mutter, "That's the trouble with images—they don't always make sense at the time." I hold Ray's eyes and feel the tears slip out. "I think he's getting paid for Trevor." Now I'm really leaking when I ask, "But is it for his delivery? Or his death?"

The agents exchange looks. Ike mumbles, "He's one of our top covert operatives. It would be easy to make himself disappear."

Bill spears his fingers through his hair. "Shit. He can make himself look like practically anyone: male, female, old, young. We might as well kiss this case goodbye."

Rod points at his brother. "You think I'm going to give up after what he just did to my twin? Not on your life."

I'm going to need to resort to every last trick I have, and hopefully a few I haven't yet learned. With Ray at my side, I think we'll be able to find him in time. I can't let Travis die. I've come too far. He means too much to me. I feel my jaw square up, and I wipe off my cheeks. There was no way I was going to let Chad—our only link—just disappear. I tell them, "We're not giving up. Not on my watch. Come on."

Chapter 41

Okay, so I found the unconscious agents, but now that I'm ready to find the father of my child I'm not having so much luck. Perhaps it's due to the clanging and banging of ten thousand suitcases being chugged up conveyor belts and routed all around our heads, or perhaps my terror overrides my psychic senses, but as I move ten feet from the laundry bin, I feel I've lost my trail.

I'm a psychic bloodhound with a uselessly plugged nose.

I look to my brother, scared. He steps closer and takes my hands. "Feel your way, Sis. He was here, so where did he go?" I think Ray might actually know where we need to go, but for years he's attempted to get me to strengthen my powers, and I have a feeling he's totally abusing this opportunity to make me grow.

He's blocking his thoughts from me, too, which I have to admit is more than a little annoying. I feel frustrated and fearful and angry and more than that, just plain scared.

But I have an idea. I head back to Don and tell Rod, "I want to talk to your brother, ask him which way they went."

Of course he looks at me like I'm nuts, because he reminds me his brother's drugged.

"Just let me ask him," I snap, and he does.

I touch my fingers to Don's temple, hoping I can see his thoughts ... maybe. I squat down and speak to the dozing man. "Don? Can you hear me? I need you to tell me where the man who did this to you went. Can you show me?"

I tell myself that I'm telepathic and can read and receive thoughts. I tell myself that just because it's easier to see them on a conscious person doesn't mean the unconscious are devoid of them.

I remind myself Travis needs me to save him. "Don? Where did they go? Show me what happened to you. I need to know."

I focus hard on my somnambulant ally and see: *The group of men stops at the bottom of the stairs and argues with Chad about why they are in the luggage sorting area. Chad pulls a gun and quickly shoots the other two agents before grabbing Travis to hide behind. Don pulls out his own gun but won't risk shooting Travis, instead trying to talk Chad out of it, even posturing that he'll drop his own gun to negotiate. Chad pulls the trigger and shoots Don, but Don's adrenaline burst allows him to crawl a few feet to escape. He doesn't know yet that he has only been drugged and is not dying.*

In a matter of those few spacey-woozy seconds, Don watches Travis retaliate, punch, and kick Chad and try to wrestle the gun from him, only to get shot with the dart as well.

Chad begins screaming the f-bomb over and over, then sees a wheelchair in the luggage chute and pulls it down, then dumps Travis onto it and proceeds to push him down a hallway.

The vision fades to black.

I feel the stab of a migraine reminding me that I'm no dream-walker. I'm feeling a touch pukey, too. So I collapse into a sit and rub my temples and push my eyeballs into my skull until the dagger's edge slides out of my brain.

Travis.

To Rod I say, "Your brother saw everything. Chad shot the other two, then took Travis hostage so your brother wouldn't shoot him. Don tried to negotiate with Chad, but got shot instead. He was willing to risk his life to protect Travis. He is very heroic."

Rod's eyes mist as he looks down, so briefly that none of the men would have noticed, but when he next meets my gaze, I see pride, appreciation.

I see an ally.

"Chad pushed the bin over here before he ran off. He put Trav in a wheelchair. We need to find where he went." I try to recall everything in the background in Don's memory and turn around to see where they were when this happened. I remember a large barrel and pipes and a stairwell and tell everyone to look for that. They split up to search, and I get up and run some of my own recon. Not really run, actually. The last thing I want after a migraine is the jar of my feet on concrete. Anyway, after a few minutes of following pipelines, I locate a hot water tank that looks like the barrel in the vision, and it's near some stairs. Beyond that, I see the hallway from the dream. I call out to the guys. "This way. Come on."

We hasten down the hallway and I go on gut, making a few turns as I deem necessary. It's weird, for sure, but it's like I have a rope fastened to my stomach, and when I start to make a wrong turn, that rope goes taut, and I snap around like a kite snagged on a tree trunk and correct my course.

I glance at my abdomen as I feel the psychic leash tugging me along my path and have a revelation: perhaps it's not my stomach so much as my womb.

My umbilicus.

The child rooting in my belly is also rooting for me to save his dad. My throat swells and dries in direct opposition to my eyes shrinking and moistening. I try to fill my lungs and marshal my forces even though all I really want to do is cry.

Soon I see a door and stop. Ray touches my arm and I look at him. He frowns and touches the wall by me. "A man leaned up against here, sleeping, sitting down." He closes his eyes and his face turns peaceful. "Tall, dark brown hair, solid."

"That's Travis," I nod.

Then Ray makes a fist and lightly bumps the wall by his head. "Shorter man, light brown hair, hazel eyes."

"Chad."

"Angry," Ray continues. "Punches the wall right here." He rests his fingers on the spot. "Swearing. He didn't mean to drug him.

He's not sure he'll get paid now. He's pissed. A million. That's how much he'll ... they want to question him, and now ..."

I've seen Ray in action enough to know the way psychometry works for him. Items hold energy imparted to them, and a *Sensitive* can read that energy as so many letters on paper. As Chad didn't lean on the wall but rather punched it in his anger, his energy comes through in the staccato bursts that Ray now feels. "LoDo, he keeps saying. Gotta make it to LoDo."

"What's LoDo?"

Ike pipes in. "Lower downtown. Warehouse district." He pulls out his phone and pulls up a map. "Over twenty miles."

Rod bends down and picks up something that looks like beige plastic and holds it up to Ike. "Is this what I think it is?"

Ike's face purples like a ripe pomegranate, complete with divots. "Bastard," he hisses.

"What is it?" I ask.

Rod shows me the piece, pulling us into his confidence. "It's latex, the kind we use for facial masks."

"We don't know that for sure," Bill says, apparently unwilling to let me lead them around any longer.

But Rod champions me. "Like hell it's not. Chad's going to go undercover, like he always does. It'll be a damned miracle if we find him." He faces me, his voice low, his eyes searching. "Can you pull that off? Find him?"

"Then we need to get going." Ray is firm when he holds Ike's eyes, and I'm praying for one giant miracle, to go.

Precious time is ticking by, and the pressure of the moment is crushing my bones. "Won't know if we don't try. I'm all for getting going. Which way to the van?" I indicate the junction ahead.

Ike nods and points that way as well. "We have to move. People will be coming in a few minutes."

Bill huffs out a juvenile breath. "Are we really going to let this chick drag us around by the short and curlies?"

My mouth drops open, but Ike does a sharp about-face to Bill. "If this *chick* can help us find the single most important witness to the largest case of the year, then yes, since I haven't heard one fantastic idea or lead out of your mouth at all today. If you don't like it, I suggest you take a cab back to the office."

I don't look at the shame-faced Bill as we hasten down the hall; I have more important things on my mind than one man's ego. Once at the t-junction, I look left and right while Ray touches the right corner, then the left.

I'm thinking left, and Ray takes his fingers off the left wall and points left. I've never had to rely so heavily on my abilities, but it's good to know they're working.

Ike points to a skid mark on the floor, something I never would have seen. "That's from Chad's shoe. He always scuffs his right heel." And he grants a pointed look to Bill.

Having Ray and Ike and Rod backing up my hunches makes me feel a little relieved, but the effort is downright exhausting.

Ike orders our car, and we race outside and hop in. I'm going strictly on gut and adrenaline right now. Between the kite string pulling me along and all the practice I've gotten this week, I'm thinking I'm *this close* to locating someone on a map.

As exhausting as this adventure has been, I have to admit it's been rather exciting, too.

Too bad the stakes are too high for me to really enjoy it.

As we near our destination, I have Rod slow down. I focus on my invisible string guiding me, hopefully to the man of my dreams. Rod willingly follows my directions as I call them out.

I have him stop at an ugly old warehouse with beautiful architecture. Now the bricks are crumbling away, and most of the windows are boarded, and across the street is being leveled for new construction, but right now I just want into this building.

I shove Bill out of the car and we race around back, where I hoist open the second door and race inside. We hasten down the hallway, and I screech to another halt at a door midway down the stretch.

Ray nods at me, wanting me to lead the way. I growl in frustration but yank open the door and almost trip on the abandoned wheelchair tossed against the wall. "This was Travis'" I say as we race upstairs, the thunder of men at my heels reassuring me that we are united in our purpose. I pass two doors before stopping at the third, then pause as if listening while I sense my way. I pull it open and see more hallways ending in more t-junctions.

I'm winded from the climb, but I muster my forces and head down the right wing and skid to another halt before the intersection. A doorway, facing us smack at the end of the hall, feels like my destination.

The fact that Jasmine now hovers eighteen inches off the ground only confirms this. I flub for Ray's hand, and he reaches and takes it. The look he gives me (I only see it peripherally—I'm too busy gawking at my first physical ghost) seems to ask if I can see her, too. Like I said, Ray's powers way outstrip mine.

Jasmine was very pretty when she was alive. My third eye had already told me of her looks, but my physical eyes confirm the rest. She holds a vibrancy of youth, most likely the age she preferred being. She died at twenty-eight or -nine, which is my age, but here she looks twenty-one or -two.

My gut is that she has taken for eternity the age at which she met Travis.

Can't blame her there.

A forest green sweater with a wide white band and dark denim jeans mark her perpetual attire, and I remember she died coming back from a ski trip.

"What are we waiting for?" Ike asks.

I press my finger to my lips and grant him a cautionary stare. I turn back to Jasmine. "Is he in there?"

She nods.

"How would I know?" Ike growls, thinking I was talking to him and not someone only two of us could see.

I ignore him as I feel the tears welling but choke them down and ask Jasmine, "Is he alive?"

Another nod.

"Who the hell are you talking to?" Bill hisses, and Ray glares at him and swats the air to silence his yapping.

She speaks without moving her lips, and I know I'm hearing her voice in my head: "*Five men guard the outer lobby. The one in back guards the door holding Travis. He won't shoot you, RoseAngel Marie, but the others will if you let them.*"

I nod and try to swallow once more, my eyes blinking furiously. My hand lands on my stomach for a second, but I don't want anyone to notice, so I yank it away.

Ray motions for the men to take a step back as he warns them, "Two men coming up the hallways right now. The one on the left will be much closer, but he'll be distracted trying to get his iPod to work, so take out the one on the right first."

Two of our agents move to flank the walls, and I can tell Ike sees the one coming up the left, but he does as Ray says and waits until Jed shoots first, then Ike fires down the hallway.

I had covered my ears and squinted shut my eyes. I don't want to watch anyone die, but blocking my eyes and ears doesn't always stop me from *seeing*.

Jasmine is gone, but I remember her message. "Okay, five armed guys are inside, with Travis in the room behind them."

"How do you know this?" Bill asks, his eyes hard.

Ray jumps in. "Because she just received a message from Beyond. The witness's late wife is helping Rosie save him. It would be best to do as my sister says."

"Let me guess." Sarcasm drips from Bill's voice. "You saw the dead chick, too."

"What's it like?" Ray asks, his eyes wide and innocent.

"What's what like?"

"Being a prick every single day."

Bill takes an aggressive step toward my brother, but Ike clamps a hand on his shoulder and says, "Save it for whatever's behind that door." He jacks his thumb to drive home the point.

I flick an appreciative yet warning smile at my brother and add, "Don't shoot the one in back." I look to the agents, frantic and eager and, yes, still terrified. What was I thinking? Can I really save Travis' life? And the one I'm terrified to answer: Am I willing to trade my life—and that of our baby's—for his?

Ike draws the men in to huddle. "Okay, here's our plan. I'm going to kick in the door, and you two flank me. Surprise will be on our side."

"They're all armed," I remind them, wondering how many of the feds are about to lose their lives to save Travis. Suddenly the vision regarding my brother makes sense. I look to Ray and see his eyes light up in time with mine. "I have an idea. Can someone give Ray a gun?"

"Your vision," he smiles.

I nod and face the men. "I had a vision that my brother puts a gun to my head and leads me into a room of killers."

"What happens after that?" Rod asks.

I shrug, feigning bravery. "Don't know. But I wouldn't see it if it wasn't important."

"Sure it's not your demise?" a surly Bill taunts.

"You can only hope," I add, praying I'm not suddenly cursed like the Cyclops, who traded one eye for the gift of Sight, only to be tricked into seeing nothing but their upcoming death.

Not an encouraging thought at this moment, I realize belatedly.

They don't like this idea of arming my brother, of course, but after a few hard glances between them they hand him an empty one as a prop, and I lean back against my brother and tell him,

"Put the gun to my head and go directly to the guy in back. That's my vision."

"Wait." Ike holsters his gun and unbuttons his shirt, and I see a black Kevlar vest underneath. "Put this on," he tells me as he hands the protective garment to me.

I'm touched by his chivalry, and thank him before I duck around the corner to do a quickeroo clothing change.

At least my baby will be safe.

I return to my brother, and he wraps his right arm across my ribs up to my neck, which makes me hold my arms in the air. He points the gun at my left temple (he's the leftie of the two of us) and I look to our men. "The rest of you are in charge of keeping us safe, right?"

They don't really nod, but I didn't expect them to. They are in charge of this mission, yet following a newbie and her brother, and not a one of them likes this situation. Not one bit.

My brother's arm across my ribs tightens, and I feel his fear as acutely as my own. Perhaps this was a phenomenally stupid idea. Why the hell am I—unarmed—leading armed men into an attack? But my psychic guardian states they won't shoot a female hostage. My guess is that it'll be so odd for them to be confronted with a helpless girl hostage that the element of surprise will buy us a good three seconds of time. I feel my pulse leap and jump against Ray's hand and gun, and my blood and saliva vacate my skull, leaving me with a dry mouth and lightheaded view of the door before me.

My eyes widen and my heart pounds like a caged monkey as the men move into formation and flock us, and we cross into the open. I think my adrenaline kicks in as Ike kicks down the door, and I'm screaming, "Don't shoot!" like a hostage while our agents kick ass and take out the four flankers with a few eardrum popping rounds of ammunition. My eyes are definitely wide and my ears are ringing as Ray pushes me across the room, and I can't say I hold no small level of fearful reaction from the gunshots that just went off around me.

Like Jasmine predicted, the youngest at the back doesn't shoot me, but I blame that on him not being able to un-holster his gun in time. I get the feeling my blue eyes remind him of the last memory he holds of his mom. "Don't shoot!" I beg him, and he looks at the five armed men and one girl hostage and holds his gun aloft, then tosses it to the side.

I move free of Ray and ease close to the last man standing. "I'm here for my boyfriend."

A shadow crosses his face as he realizes he's been duped. "You'll have to kill me to get in."

I wave for the guys to lower their guns, and Bill scoffs to my face and instead aims for the kid's head. I turn to face him, incredulous. "You going to blow this now? After everything I did to get us in here? Tell me, Bill, would you have found this place without Ray and me helping?"

And then he charges, "You only 'found' it because you're in on the crime."

Well, now, I can't let that comment slide. I grit my teeth and say, "I will do anything to save the life of the man behind those doors. Do not stand in my way."

Perhaps Bill comprehends that mama-bear look in my eyes, for Rod lowers his pistol, and Ike harrumphs at Bill. They all lower their weapons, and I turn back to the lone gatekeeper.

"Look," I tell the remaining guy, me acting cool and oh-so-composed, "you don't want to die, I don't want to die, and I know my boyfriend doesn't want to die. Let's just make this easy, okay?"

"You kill me, and you'll never get the code." He's a bit fearful, and I think I can work with that. I just need him to think it, and I'll be golden.

A keypad mounted to the wall is keeping me from the man I love. I step nearer and ask, "Come on, Joey, what's the code?"

His eyebrows dart up, and then he pales. "Who are you?"

"Joey," I sigh, "tell me the code." I indicate the panel.

Ike pulls back on the gun, doing that thing men do when they want to intimidate someone by showing off their weapon. I toss a glance to Ike but step nearer to Joey. My voice is low when I say, "Caitlin needs her father, Joey. Don't be a martyr. These guys aren't going to compensate your wife when you're dead."

Now he's getting frantic. "How do you know my daughter's name?"

"You just told me," I reply, trying to keep my voice low. If he's too panicked, he might not think clearly, and I won't get the info we need. Right now, all he's thinking about is his family. "You're afraid you'll never see your family again, and really, you're interfering with a federal case. What's the code, Joey?"

Ray steps near the keypad, and I know he'll be able to glean the answers with his own fingertips, but I was hoping I'd be able to—"One, two, eight, nine, three, six, star," I tell Ike, and Joey blanches.

"How did you—?"

Jed aims to shoot, but I tell him, "Don't kill him."

Ike pistol whips him across the temple, and young Joey falls to the floor. We take a deep collective breath as Ike pushes in the code and reaches for the knob.

I have one more thought: "Keep the one in here alive, too."

Chapter 42

Ike takes control at this point, looking at the downed men and our own feds. With two fingers he points at Bill and Rod and the door, and I understand they are to go in first.

He waves Ray and me to stand behind him, along the wall, and Jed goes into the hallway. I think he's calling for backup.

I look around the room for the first time. A wooden table and four mismatched chairs are in the middle, two toppled. A few boxes. Three metal filing cabinets. Pretty Spartan.

Ike eyes the two feds balancing on tiptoes before the locked door and types in the code. When the door unlatches, overcompensating Bill leads the charge.

I hear screaming and yelling as the feds tell Mr. Baddie to drop his weapon, which of course only leads to more yelling. I lock in on Rod—my inside guy—to see if I can see through him.

I can. I see Travis—poor, beat-up, beautifully alive Travis—tied to a wooden chair. Beside him stands a lackey in a brown suit, leveling a gun at Travis' head.

He smiles and indicates his hostage. "You think I didn't hear the gunfire? You think I'm not going to pull this trigger?"

I have to see for myself. I look at the back of Ike's head, then turn to meet Ray's eyes. I quietly slip away to the middle of the room, then crawl under the table until I'm within Travis' line of sight. I need him to know I'm alive, that I'm here for him, but when his eyes flick to mine, I decide that was a phenomenally stupid move. I can practically smell the fear on Travis, not so much for his life, but for mine. The fact that I came here to rescue him terrifies him. I see images of Jasmine in the car wreck over and over again and know he's having a terrible time dealing with my presence here.

The men are negotiating the release of Travis, and the perp is getting loud. I watch Rod do the same pacifying thing his brother did to Chad, and hope for a better outcome this time.

While they're distracted, I pass a message to Travis. With my hand I make a falling over gesture.

He looks at his wooden arm chair and then tosses a glance over his shoulder, then gives me a questioning look.

I barely nod and repeat the gesture, indicating with one finger to wait for our signal.

He plants his feet on the floor, ready to kick off.

Now I just need to decide what my signal is.

But I nod, mission accomplished, and crawl backwards. When Ike sees me peripherally, I get the image of him wringing my neck.

Funny, I always thought that was just an expression.

I ease back to my position on the wall, and he glares hard. "What the hell do you think you were doing?" he hisses.

"Running recon. Sending Trav a message."

"I could kill you."

I size him up. "You could, yes," I agree.

He detests insubordination. He's livid when he says, "I can't have you distracting my men. Get behind me and stay there." But as an afterthought he demands, "Where is he?"

I opt for tactical speech. "Perp is at nine o'clock. Feds at three. Trav at ten."

He nods once, his jaw tight, before he returns to his primary target, which is not me, thankfully. And then I realize: I was a distraction, when I need to be the diversion.

The baddie yells, "That's it! I'm sick of talking. Drop your weapons, or the star witness gets it."

Rod's angry voice replies, "You think he's got any bit of evidence in his possession? Don't you think we have that all saved in multiple spots, you little prick?"

I tap Ike once on the shoulder, then I leap in front of the doorway and yelp as I land on my hands and knees, like some poor helpless girl just tripped on a dead body.

All eyes in that room focus on me.

Travis launches backward and crashes to the floor.

Ike rounds the doorway; gunshots ring out. I curl into the fetal position and pray.

I open my eyes and see the bad guy screaming in a puddle of blood, grabbing his gushing shoulder with both hands. That went well, I reason, so I scramble to Travis, this time feeling the blood and saliva and tears race to my skull, and in relief I let the tears fall where they may.

"Sis."

I turn, and Ray tosses me his pocket knife. I pull out a blade and cut through the ties on the nearest hand, then move to the other side. Ray unties his feet.

I help Trav to his feet, feeling his exhaustion rivaling mine. He groans and grabs his side, and by the bruises on his face I'm guessing his ribs have fared no better.

We stand, and Travis grabs my head and kisses me, hard. I feel the split of his lip as our kiss breaks it back open, but I lean into his body and he tips me back and we are so glad to be alive and reunited that for a moment everyone else in the room disappears.

I don't know what I'd do without this man.

Except, perhaps, sleep at night, instead of gallivanting around the globe and getting shot at.

We break apart, and he shakes his head at me. I see his own tears brimming, and he licks his bloody lip and tugs me in to hug. "You never should have come here. It was too dangerous."

I shake my head against his chest, feeling the tears pool on the material. "They were going to kill you."

He blows off my concern. "Nah, I would have been fine."

"No you wouldn't," Ray and I both answer.

He looks at both of us, then reaches out and offers a hand to Ray. "You must be Ray."

"Nice to meet you, Travis." They shake hands, and I like the look in my brother's eyes when they touch. The old song, "Good Vibrations" comes to me, and I know Ray is sending me confirmation that my crush is one heckuva great guy.

But Travis isn't done chastising me. "They could have killed you."

I wave off his concern with an exaggerated wrist flip, the song still in my head … *excitations*. "Nah, I was fine."

"No you weren't." This from Ray again. I turn to face him, and he says, "Another ten seconds and things would have gone a completely different direction."

I look at him, not having foreseen my future. I wobble a grin at them both. "Guess it's a good thing I went with my gut."

Ray gives me a raised eyebrow and crooks a grin, but I watch his eyes drop for a millisecond to my stomach. Luckily, Trav doesn't notice. "I knew you had it in you, Sis."

Ike looks at his watch. "The trial started fifteen minutes ago. We've got to get you to the courthouse."

Travis manages a painful nod, and I sigh. Another day without sleep. But as I look up to the beautiful man who looks down at me, I realize I'll forego a month of sleep if it means he's safe by my side.

As I hold him, I realize my personal hell would be an eternity without him.

I'll take a broken Travis any day, as long as I can take him. I hook his arm over my shoulder, and together we make our way to the van.

Chapter 43

No time to stop and pretty ourselves up for the courtroom, so we go straight from the most horrifying ordeal of our lives to the quiet, damning interrogation room of terror. Ike had radioed in to his office, and they took care of the rest, for a veritable army of suits pours out of the courthouse doors and surrounds us while we go inside.

This might be the exposé of the century, and for a second I'm fearful that another weasel might be mixed in with the men, but once we're inside, the following dwindles straight down until it's just our cozy little group again.

We stop outside the courtroom doors, and the police there open them for us. The oiled hinges give a tiny squeak, and the sound bores straight to my marrow.

It's not the fingernails-on-the-blackboard noise; it's the every-face-in-the-room-sees-you-sneak-in noise. Ike points to a seat in back, so I sit with Ray and Jed and Bill, and Ike and Rod take Travis up to the second row.

The judge's eyebrows move only incrementally when he sees how damaged his star witness is. I think the prosecution is giving opening statements, informing the jury that the witness will be presenting evidence that will horrify them. The bailiff steps up to the judge with a letter from Ike, explaining that we just rescued Travis from the clutches of death, we have a bleeding lackey in the hospital under constant surveillance, and one more recovering from a pistol punch to the temple.

(I know what it says; I watched him write it.)

We hear the rambling of the defense about how people should think for themselves and not listen to the blathering of a former cop.

The quiet of the warm room, my brother's supportive shoulder under my cheek, and the adrenaline crash from the last day of my life comes to a head.

This shames me, but I nod off.

Deep, blissful, uninterrupted sleep.

Ray jars me when they get to Travis. I suck in my breath and sit upright, and I hear him whisper, "Thank God," as he grabs his shoulder and rotates it. I pat his arm and wipe down my face. I send him an, *I'm sorry,* and he smiles at me.

"Your Honor," the prosecutor stands and addresses the Court, "at this time, I would like to ask our key witness, Travis Mattison, to the stand."

Travis rises from his spot near the front of the assembly and makes his way to the chair. I can tell he's stiff and sore as he takes his vows on the Bible and sits down.

The man paces back and forth, and I can tell he's smiling. "Cut yourself shaving this morning?"

Travis tries to smile, but his fingers fly to his lip as the bleeding starts. He grabs the nearby tissue box and dabs his wound. "I don't shave with someone else's fists."

A few people chuckle. I have to smile. I know this man will try to get everyone settled with his humor, and I admire his tenacity to do so.

"Mr. Mattison, what did you do for a living?"

He sits taller, and I can tell he really enjoyed being a P.I. Some part of me wonders if he will sit tall telling people he's a bank manager. "I was a private investigator, and before that, a cop for six years."

"What kind of cases did you have?"

"Mostly cheating spouses."

"But you didn't find a cheating spouse that day, did you."

Travis shakes his head. "No, sir, I did not."

The attorney walks back to his table and picks up a bunch of papers. He hands them to Travis and asks, "Do you recognize these photos?"

"Yes, sir, I took them."

"And can you please tell the Court who the people are in these photos?"

Travis holds up each photo, pointing out the mayor in all of them, the commissioner, Mr. Heins (aka Joe Husband) bringing up a case of missiles, and even a photo of a police cruiser scoping the building tops where Travis had been hiding, like they suspected someone was on to them. He then identifies them in the courtroom, where they pretend they're merely watching an interactive play and not defending their lives.

I get the feeling the attorney's name is Elliot. I like Elliots. "In your own words, can you tell me what you saw the day you looked into that warehouse window?"

Travis recaps everything he had told me about that case, leaving nothing out. He paints his uncertainty of so many political figures being involved, his fear of going to his police brothers, then finding out the D.A. was also complicit.

Then the attorney asks, "How would you describe your life since then?"

"Hell," he answers honestly. "Three years of it."

"Why hell?"

I see Jasmine appear then, hovering at his side, her ghostly hand resting on his shoulder for support. I find myself averting my eyes for a second, but when I look back up, I see she is still there, her attention focused totally on Travis. He takes a swig of his ice water and leans back in the chair. At least it looks more comfy than the hard bench I'm relegated to, but I know how hard this question will be for him. "After they killed my wife—"

"Objection," cries the defense attorney.

"Sustained," interjects the Judge.

Travis' jaw hardens, and I know his gears crank away. His expression turns grim. "After my wife died in a car crash where the brakes had been deliberately perforated, I was—"

"Objection, calls for speculation."

The Judge announces, "Objection overruled." He shuffles some papers, his meaty finger scanning down the documents. "Official police report confirms tampering of the brake lines."

Travis picks right up where he left off. "I was packed up in the middle of the night, with only one bag of clothes and my cat. No photos, no memories. I was not allowed anything personal that could link my new identity to my old one. In effect, Travis Mattison ceased to exist that day."

"You were given a new identity," Elliot confirms.

Travis nods. "I was. I was not allowed to contact any of my friends, my brothers, my own mom. I couldn't even attend my wife's funeral." I watch him pause here, and Jasmine's mouth displays her sadness. "I spent four months stuck inside a house, with only supervised outings into the backyard. I couldn't go to an amusement park, or a ballgame, or even a movie. I had the same rights as a criminal, yet I didn't commit any crime."

"What happened after those four months?"

"I got moved to another safe house, in another state. Slightly bigger. Had a pool. Then another safe house. Then another."

I have to admit, the prosecutor does a great job of bringing Travis' exploits to light. Then he asks, "Can you tell me about the last twenty-four hours?"

Now Jasmine kneels before him, like a dutiful wife telling her husband he can do this. I watch her hands resting on his thighs, her eyes riveted to his.

I get the feeling she cheered him on a lot in life.

Travis nods and reaches for his ice water and downs a gulp. "I had to break my date when the agents guarding me heard a lot of chatter over the airwaves about a group of men coming in from

Denver. They had some concern that the men were related to the figures in this case, and I was put back on lockdown. I called her, and, for the first time, I was afraid. I knew it was real because I had broken one of their cardinal rules: I had contacted my mother. I hadn't talked to her since Jasmine died, and, with the trial coming up, and meeting R—, my girlfriend, I just really wanted to hear my mom's voice again."

I think my ears perk up. Am I his girlfriend? Really? I notice Jasmine looks at me then, and I feel like I've just been identified as *the other woman.* I find myself shifting on the bench and avoiding her gaze, but I do think she's smiling.

Oblivious to my torment, Travis continues with, "I think that was how they traced me. I was really uneasy that night, and went to bed with my clothes on. About midnight, Monday morning, five men broke into the safe house, shooting at least three guards outside before breaking in. One agent outside my bedroom door came in and got me. He led me downstairs and opened a secret compartment in the kitchen for me. I then heard two more men get shot." He pauses and takes another drink.

The prosecutor prompts him with, "And then what?"

Travis looks up and holds my eyes. I take a deep breath and blink and give him a slight nod.

"My girlfriend called my cell and told me she could get me out of there."

Yes, my heart flutters that I'm his girlfriend, and I try not to gloat with Jasmine hovering nearby, but then I brace for what inevitably follows.

"She did? How's that?"

I can tell Travis doesn't want to out me. He knows it's my secret, but I nod once more. "She had a ... " he waves his hand, "premonition. She knew the shooter was going to sneeze, and when he did, she told me to run outside. Another guard outside was also shot, but I grabbed his keys and got out of there. My safety had already been compromised."

Elliot sits on his table, facing Travis. "And then what?"

Travis relays leaving the hotel and being chased and shot at, the escort to the plane, then being rerouted down to the luggage sorter, where he confirms what Don showed me in his sleepy memories.

I have to smile that I picked all that up, and send a blessing to Don and the others that they are awake and well and getting some vacation time after what they went through.

Then Travis says, "I recall being dragged over somebody's shoulder like a drunk, and I saw Chad getting a briefcase from my captors and leaving. Then they tied me to a chair, and some guy tried to," he cracks a grin, "*shave* my chin with his fist. I don't know how long I was out before the 'shaving' started again."

I watch Jasmine reach up her delicate hand to stroke that very chin, and feel a surge of something rivaling jealousy, then immediately chastise myself. She loved the man in life, I tell myself, or she wouldn't be here helping in death.

Doesn't make me feel one iota better, though.

Elliot is curious when he asks, "Should I assume your interrogator asked you some questions?"

"Between punches, yes. He wanted to know what else I knew of the mayor." Trav shrugs. "I mean, I took photos with him inspecting a few million dollars' worth of assault rifles and deadly weapons, missiles, grenades. I thought that was enough. I didn't know what else he could possibly be concerned about, and I told him as much. He didn't believe me, of course, and that's where all the bruises came from. Plus, I was still groggy from being drugged, and it took quite a while before I could even focus on his questions."

He takes a moment to process this, like he's watching Jasmine cluck over her husband, then, "You were a cop for six years?"

"Correct."

"What do you think was in the briefcase?"

"Objection, calls for speculation." Defense, of course.

Elliot stands and faces the judge. "Your Honor, my client made his living on supposition and speculation. I feel he, of all people, should be qualified to hazard a guess as to what was in the briefcase."

The judge studies him for a second. "Overruled."

I can tell Travis is pleased when he looks down, then he meets Elliot's eyes. "Money would be my first guess. A lot of money, in unmarked, non-sequential bills. The man's an FBI agent, for cripe's sake. I'd bet my handgun he has multiple IDs and can readily hide in plain sight."

Elliot leans forward, then stands to pace. "If it pleases the Court, I'd like you, Mr. Mattison, to venture what else you think they tried to glean from you."

"Objection, calls for speculation."

"Overruled."

Jasmine smiles, and Trav shakes his head and shrugs. "I've no idea. He gave me no clue, only kept punching. However, weapons and drugs and prostitution are all friends, so I'd guess it might be one of those."

The prosecution nods sympathetically. "How did you get out of there? Did they let you go?"

A head shake, and Travis looks at me, his expression one of wonder and amazement. "All I know is I heard gunshots in the next room, and suddenly my brave girlfriend and her brother and some more Feds broke in and saved me."

Now I'm his brave girlfriend. I'm feeling rather humble, actually, and my head feels heavy as it dips from my shoulders. I dart my glance at the curious who gawk at me, knowing it's because of Travis' accolades and not that they think I'm a freak show. Yet. I know I'm going to be up there, under the microscope, before this trial is over.

"One last question." The attorney graces Trav with a gentle smile. "Have you had a chance to see a doctor about your numerous wounds?"

"No, sir. I came straight here from being rescued."

Elliot taps the table and faces the judge. "No further questions, Your Honor."

Travis nods and takes another drink of water. Now it's time for the cross.

Chapter 44

I have to hate the defense on principal. Luckily, the man in charge of cross-examination is not very likeable. I see him as smarmy, greasy, and lecherous. He's probably a real nice guy, but I can't go there. He paces a few minutes in front of Travis, obviously deciding where to start. This is not like the courtroom scenes on TV, filled with drama and shouting matches. This is calm, measured. Each question must be carefully worded, and each subsequent one must damn the witness further into being discredited.

After a questionable start, where even Jasmine grew annoyed with him, Council asks, "Did you know who you were photographing at the warehouse?"

"Only my target, Mr. Heins. His wife suspected him of adultery, so he was the man I followed."

The defense slides Travis a look. "Do you know how to Photoshop, Mr. Mattison?"

"Objection, leading," Elliot says.

The judge assesses Travis for a second, then, "Overruled. The witness will answer the question."

Travis looks from the judge to the defense. "I've seen it used, but have never tried to work the program. Frankly, in my line of business, I get enough evidence without resorting to making my own."

I smile.

"Plus," Travis adds, "I get paid for answers, regardless of outcome. People just want to know if they're right or wrong."

"Who is your girlfriend, Mr. Mattison?"

He smiles, his eyes so warm I wish we were alone. "That beautiful redhead in the back row." I'm smiling as he points, but then I catch Jasmine's eyes and struggle to keep my grin.

The defense doesn't comment, but asks, "How long have you two been seeing each other?"

"A week."

Now I sense the man's mood change, like a crocodile ready to launch out of the water for its prey. He crowds close to Trav, so close I can no longer see him around Counsel's looming form, and he charges, "A woman you've been dating a week tells you to run through a house where agents are getting shot, dying to protect you, and you believe her?"

Trav takes a deep breath as he obviously considers the question, and although I can't see him, I doubt he's even squirming. "Well, no, not at first, of course not."

"Of course not." Counsel backs away one step.

Travis eyes him hard for a second, but then says, "But she kept telling me she'd get me out of there. And when the man started sneezing, she said something like, 'He's already sneezing, go!' so I ran, and she seemed to know exactly where I needed to be." He shrugs like he had no choice, and really, he didn't.

The defense backs up one more step and crosses his arms. "And you just blindly did what a woman you had known for a few days told you to do, and you did it on complete faith."

Travis crosses his arms as well. "You ever been shot at?"

"Yes or no, Mr. Mattison?"

He grins, like no matter what this attorney says, Travis is incapable of being tripped up. I have to say I find his confidence a real turn-on. "That was the second time I'd been shot at," he tells him. "Self-preservation is a pretty high priority in my field, and my partner and I have been in high-stakes shootouts before. When someone tells me she's trying to save my life, I'm willing to listen."

"Hm." The defense looks to the jury when he says that, and I try not to growl. "You mentioned an agent named Chad Phillips. When was the last time you saw that man?"

Another rogue grin from Travis. If anything, my man is unflappable. I get the feeling he's been on the stand before, at least a few times. "He disappeared after delivering me to the man who tried to kill me."

"Motion to strike, Your Honor," his cross said. "The witness is speculating the defense's intent."

Travis scoffs and looks to the judge. "Three broken ribs at gunpoint aren't speculation, Your Honor."

"Overruled, pending a physical exam of the witness."

I can tell the defense doesn't like that, but he goes back to pacing. "Tell me about your girlfriend's 'psychic' abilities. This 'premonition' you mentioned."

Travis looks to me, and I look down, feeling my pulse race at the very thought of my talent being broadcasted to the gathered masses. I don't know what he knows of them, and I know whatever answer he'll give won't be enough. Sooner or later, I'm going to have to go to the head of the classroom and write on that giant chalkboard: *I am a freak show, I am a freak show,* one thousand times for all to see … including the paparazzi. I feel like a cornered animal, leg snared in a trap, hungry and thirsty with seven hunters surrounding me with clubs. I catch Travis' eye, then Jasmine's, then look to the judge and lower my head to try and gauge the distance to the door behind me. Can I make it if I sprint?

I cast a wary sidelong glance back to Trav, and I can tell he really doesn't want to reveal too much, which makes me adore him even more (as if that's remotely possible). He tips his head and says, "She told me she can see images, and that my late wife Jasmine came to her and communicates with her."

Jasmine smiles at this, like she's proud of me or something, which completely confuses me.

"I see." Again the man looks at the jury, trying to discredit Travis, but in reality he's discrediting me.

I'm not very happy with this man.

Jasmine sticks her tongue out at him, and I cough to cover my laugh.

So now he turns to the judge and asks, "Might we enter the witness' girlfriend to testify?"

Dread curls low in my stomach, making me nauseous, and I think sweat just broke out on my lip. I look to Ray for comfort.

The judge looks to the prosecutor for answers. "Counsel?"

Elliot in turn looks back to me. "I wouldn't mind."

The judge points at me. "You. Counsel. My chambers."

Ray squeezes my hand as I stand. The room fuzzes out and turns dark, then it tilts and grows deeper as I look to the stand so very far ahead of me.

Travis is dismissed as a witness.

My heart yammers away clear up in my throat, and I feel the lurch of my pulse choking my neck as I try to swallow around the noose of this decision. I take a few hiccupping breaths, since my lungs decide in that moment that air is in dangerously short supply. A high keening begins to ring in my ears, and I'm not sure if it's inside my head or from the buzz of the assembled masses silently condemning me.

Could be both; can't tell.

For the man I love, I will do this.

Chapter 45

I think of a gentleman's smoking room when I enter the judge's chambers. Tomes upon tomes line the walls, a uniform line of canvas-covered legalese denoting the man has some resources at his fingertips. The judge indicates we sit in the provided chairs while he plunks down at his massive oak desk. "Your name, Miss?" I watch him square up the large calendar on his desk until it is perfectly parallel to the edge.

I look to the prosecution. "I don't want to risk Travis' safety." I look back at the judge, whose gold name plate proudly proclaims he is the Honorable Aros Ames. "If I have to give my name or address to the press and reporters and cameras out there, it will reveal Travis' new location, and all the trauma he endured over the last three years will follow him home."

The judge considers me. "You really care for him."

I hold Aros' eyes. "I risked my life to save his. Yes."

The defense leaves his chair and whirls on me. "I'm not buying this whole psychic bit." His name is Cecil, I now see.

I sigh and turn away, noting Amos is now straightening his pencils in a row. "This is why Travis is the first man I've ever told." I look to my accuser, Cecil. "I hate having to prove myself."

Cecil averts his eyes as he focuses on removing imaginary lint from his sleeve. "That's because you're no mind-reader. If you were, you could tell me: What am I thinking?" he demands as he looks up, invisible hair pinched in his fingers.

I stare at him, but he is a puddle of hatred and anger, and all I see is black. I lean back and cross my ankles. "I can't read you when you're hostile. Let's talk about your hobbies, and then we'll see."

"Hostile?" He scoffs and looks to the other men in the room, invisible lint forgotten. "I'm hostile? Can I call her preemptively as a hostile witness?"

I'm very calm when I say, "I'm not hostile. My voice is rather sedate." And it is. I credit the nap.

That irks him, so I try again. "Come on. What do you do when you're not working? Biking? Golf? Tennis?"

I see a boat in his mind, and I smile. "Ah, you like to boat. Sailboat, I see. It's white, with a red stripe."

He leans away from me, and his color and snarl drop a bit.

"*Sweet Freedom* is her name. She's docked … at a cottage."

Now he's white and gaping. "How did you—?"

I cock my head at him, my expression one of pure innocence. "You wanted me to read you, Counsel. Why are you so upset?"

He shakes his head in denial. "I just bought that boat yesterday as an anniversary gift for my wife. It's at our cottage. She doesn't even know about it yet."

I crook him a grin. "She won't learn it from me."

Ames chuckles. "That is a nice bit of wizardry, Miss. How do I know you aren't reading facial cues, or just good at guessing?"

I pinch the bridge of my nose and look down. "Your Honor, this is why no one at home, short of my two closest friends, knows I can do this. I hate being tested. I hate having to prove myself. The fact is, I can do it, and I never know when or how clearly my gift will present itself."

I look up at the men, and they exchange glances. Elliot asks, "Would you be willing to tell the Court what you saw?"

I nod, but it's hard for me to take a deep breath. I force one in and out of my lungs. "If I have to," I answer honestly, knowing how much I'm going to detest every minute up there, double on the ones beforehand. To allay my fears, I turn to Elliot and smile, goading Cecil. "Get that mayor up there, and I bet I can find out what he didn't want Travis to know."

Right on cue he cries, "I object!"

Chapter 46

Elliot is kind while I'm on the stand, not goading me, gentling his questions so I don't feel intimidated. Cecil, however … not so much. He's like a piranha, darting back and forth, trying to grab that last fleck of meat from the bone.

I told them they may refer to me as Kaiya, my childhood name, and Cecil picks up right where he left off in the chamber, demanding to have answers but being so hostile I can't read him.

Cecil stops his pacing and whirls to face me—I feel like I just tugged a tiger's tail. "Miss Kaiya, you have told the Court that the only reason you could find Mr. Mattison in the warehouse is because his late wife helped you find him."

"Well, she showed me what room he was in; that's true." I also felt the psychic leash yanking me around, but since I don't even understand that one, I'm certainly not going to try to explain or even mention that.

"You expect the Court to believe a dead person helped you?"

"Yes. Truth is often stranger than fact. I can't make people believe what happened." As I sit there, feeling my eyes gloss over during his rant, a whisper comes into my left ear, first as a buzz, then louder. Psychic sounds come in through the left, so I cock my head to listen. It's a woman. Older. And then I really hear her.

It's his late mother. Loud and clear.

Perfect timing.

I smile and cross my knees and lean back. I find my fingers steepling while I study him. Tiger time. "I have a message for you, Cecil, from Kay. She's your late mother, right?"

A wary look, and that man cocks his head, his color dropping.

I lean forward. "She says to check the Bible. Check the Bible. *Check the Bible.*" Now I make claws with my hands to imitate her actions and have the happy thought that maybe dear ol' ma wanted to strangle Cecil, too. "She said you called out to her yesterday, asking about something, very frustrated. She wants to," I snarl like she's doing, pretending to grip his ratty neck in my clawed hands, "blaspheme so badly, but it's in the Bible, so she won't. *Check the bleeping Bible.* She says it's in there. That's why she willed it to you."

Yeah, I made him white again. For a non-believer, he really responds. He kind of falls into his chair and wobbles his eyes to the front. "Your Honor? Might I request a recess?"

Ames looks at the clock. "We will reconvene here in one hour." He pounds his gavel once, and I sprint for the second row.

Travis and I are escorted to our hotel across the street, and we will have just enough time for a light lunch from room service before we have to head back. Since the court has decided that I'm also a key witness, I will be staying at the hotel under protective custody, too. Trav and I are granted connecting rooms (at his insistence), though I'm doubtful we'll be sleeping separately. The agents lead us down the hallway, and one of them enters our double room for safety-checks while the other two guard the doors outside. Thing 1 emerges, gives us the all-clear, and I thank him as we go inside and lock the door.

I look at my dirty clothes, the bed, the tub, and know I won't have time for all of them, but it's been four days since I've seen Travis' wonderful chest ... I give him my most seductive glance and brave a mighty question. "Would you like to join me in the shower?"

His warm eyes scan me up and down, very leisurely, and I feel myself flush under his regard. "Just shower?"

My stomach flutters, and I sigh. "I don't think we'll have time for much else."

"Okay. Would you mind taking a look at my ribs?"

Ooh, inspecting his chest at close range … I pretend I'm not over the moon and say with a wink, "Oh, I suppose I could fit in your request."

"I'll give you something to fit in," he says with a wicked grin, and my stomach feels all liquidy and jiggly again.

I grin in return and get the water going in the tub. Travis strips in the bedroom while I hop under the water, and a few seconds later he joins me.

Yeah, I'm glad we came back to the hotel for lunch. We take turns under the showerhead, then I have him raise his arms and I gently probe his bruises. He flinches (because he's with a girl; I know he'd never flinch with a man doing this) and I don't feel any broken bones, but his ribs might be cracked. His knuckles are bruised, and his eye is puffy and swelling shut, and that lip keeps breaking open every time he tries to smile or kiss me, but he is still the most glorious man I have ever beheld.

He gathers me into his arms, and although he is getting aroused, we both know we don't have time, and I'm frankly too worried about his health and downright exhausted right now to get really frisky. But he turns me around and pours some shampoo into his hand and then proceeds to wash my hair for me.

It is completely, tantalizingly erotic and paradoxically relaxing. I've never felt so pampered as I do this very moment.

His hands follow the bubble trail down my chest, taking time to play with my breasts, but I step away and rinse off.

"I know, I know, we don't have time." He winks and grabs the tiny bar of soap and starts scrubbing himself with the white wash cloth.

I take a moment to fondle him as well, and he predictably responds by growing thicker. "I thought we didn't have time."

"We don't." I take my turn with the soap, and Travis cuddles me from behind. I turn and face him, loving the feel of his lush chest hair against my nipples, his warm arms around my back, the hot water spilling over us.

A girl could get used to this.

We do actually manage to shower and dry off, and I put on some nicer clothes and dry my hair as the knock on the door announces our lunch.

Cheese and crackers and fruit for me, and a ham sandwich and chips for Travis arrive in little silver covered platters, with two colas still in cans. I place them on the table and start stacking my food while he dries off.

He joins me, his hair all tousled and sexy, and holds my eyes. His are filled with depth of sorrow when he says, "I thought they were going to kill you. I really did."

I summon bravado and say, "There's still time."

He groans and takes a bite of his sandwich. "Do you have any idea what the mayor was after from me?"

I take a swig of my soda and say, "I intend to find out. Do you think he'll go on the stand?"

"Probably not. High profile people like that usually don't testify." I frown and stack my cheese-laden crackers four levels high, making Travis laugh and proclaim it, "The Dagwood Tower."

I laugh and bite into it. When I swallow I tell him, "That will make it harder to find out." I nibble on a grape and ask, "How many times have you testified?"

He rolls his eyes. "Twelve? Thirteen?"

I sit back. "Are you serious?"

I love how his eyes light up. "A few times against Cecil Birdwright, there, too. He's really fun to taunt, can you tell?"

I chuckle, tipping my head to study him. "He doesn't get to you?" It blows my mind.

He shakes his head and takes another bite. After a few seconds he continues, "I had to testify all the time. Especially when it goes to divorce court. I have to present evidence. Usually rich people, trying to keep their fortunes from the gold-digger they married, male or female."

"Which is why you're a little jaded when it comes to relationships," I observe, thinking of how freaked he got hearing me tell Ray I loved him.

"Was jaded," he corrects with a wink. "I'm learning rather quickly to trust again." Then he clears his throat and says, "Of course, I've got nothing, so, good luck digging out my gold."

I reach over and rest my hand on his. "I think you've got way more than nothing, at least, to me."

He softens then, reaches across the table to cup my cheek. "I don't ever want to lose you, RoseAngel Marie."

I raise my soda can and say, "A toast, to not losing each other."

He touches his can to mine. "Ever again."

I like the forever thing he's promising, for the record. He makes me want to tell him about little Charlie, but I'm thinking I should wait for a better time … something a little less courtroom-y.

Since she's not here, I ask, "How did you and Jasmine meet?"

He looks up. "She was a kid sister of a classmate in the Academy. She wanted to be a cop but couldn't swim, so she was forced to disenroll." He lowers his sandwich, picks it up, then lowers it again. "Sometimes I think she liked me being a cop more than she liked *me*. She would wait for me to come home and pump me for stories. Half the time, there was nothing to share. That's when she suggested I move to homicide."

"Which you hated." I paid attention to that part.

The mood in the room sours a bit, and Travis seems hesitant when he meets my eyes. "This is weird, but," I see an apology therein when he asks, "Was Jasmine there with me? In the courtroom?"

Damn. My throat swells, but I won't lie. "Yes. Beside you, the whole time you were on the stand."

His eyes sweep down, his dark lashes fanning out along his cheeks. "I smelled vanilla. It was a scent she always wore."

It's not uncommon for ghosts to impart scents. I hear stories of it all the time, so this doesn't surprise me.

He replaces his sandwich on the plate and holds the rim down with both hands. "She's all I had to think of these last three years. All I wanted to do was see the men responsible for her death wind up behind bars. Just knowing she's here, that she's watching—" his voice clogs up on him, and he focuses on his abandoned sandwich.

I smile and pretend my heart didn't just break and change the topic. "Is it weird being home? You are, aren't you?"

"Five miles away," he answers, his eyes sweeping down once more, since I just ladled misery over his sadness.

I perk up, though. "They can enter the courtroom, right? Your family?"

He looks up, silently holds my eyes. I think he's forgotten to breathe as he whispers, "Yes."

"Do they know you're here?"

He doesn't answer, just holds my gaze. His eyes glow before the smile ever reaches his lips. "You amaze me, you know that?"

He pulls me up from my chair and squeezes me tight, and I wrap my arms around his neck—not his chest—and return the hug. I feel an electrical tingle and look over to see a hovering late wife. I don't know what to say to her, and I don't want Travis to know she's here, so I swallow and pretend I'm not the proverbial third wheel in my own life.

"Oh, woman, I am never letting you go."

When I lean back to look at him, he presses a kiss to my lips. His mouth is tender and tentative, but his emotion is rampant in the way his lips angle against mine.

I really wish we had more time to make love.

Not to mention, privacy.

I feel Jasmine disappear and battle my pleasure against her pain. Rationally, I know the deceased always wish well for those they leave behind, but I've never been stuck in the middle.

A very long lip-locked moment passes, and then Travis lifts the receiver, and he smiles once more and kisses my cheek and dials out.

His eyes shine as it rings, but then I hear a voice and a beep, so he says, "Mrs. Mattison, this is Opie. I just thought you would like to know that trial you heard about is going on right now, at the Denver City Courthouse. Hope to see you there. Bye." He hangs up, his expression dark.

"Sorry," I say and touch his shoulder. "I know she'll come when she gets the message."

He nods, and we both turn at the knock on the door. "Five minutes," one of the agents says, and we both sit back down.

The potato chips lure Travis in; he munches and tells me, "I can't believe I didn't even think to make sure she knew I'd be here."

I stack some more cheese on my crackers and say, "You're a horrible son. I mean, it's not like you were in a hostage situation and being shot at or something, where you had no time to call. You're going to hell."

He chuckles and flicks a broken chip at me. "Stinker."

I do look at him in earnest when I ask, "Do you think this case is publicized, or kept under tight wraps?"

"Oh, it should be everywhere."

I nod and take another bite. "What I wouldn't give for a pound of chocolate right now."

"Cravings?" he asks me, and my eyes fly to his.

He can't know already, so I smirk and tell him, "Energy. Only one of us had the luxury of a drugged sleep."

"Ouch. Any battle wounds, Sanctimonious One?"

"*Touché.*" I grin and chug my soda. I realize I'm not going to be able to drink these much longer, and make a mental note to find a suitable backup. I lean back in my chair. "I do like this, you know."

The last of the chips disappears. "What?"

"Sitting down, having lunch, like two normal people on a date. No bullets, no dead people, no lawyers. It's nice."

He seems rueful when he finishes up his soda. "Well, it's not over yet." He takes a deep breath and studies me. "It might be a long trial, too."

Chapter 47

We walk back, hand in hand and surrounded, and Trav squeezes my fingers and looks down to my eyes. "Next time I'm being crossed by Cecil, watch his hand. Did you notice?"

I shake my head, then glance around the street at traffic as we wait for the green to cross. "No, why?" The smell of hot dogs from a corner vendor wafts over only to be choked by the stench of a diesel engine as it chugs past.

He lifts my fingers to his lips to kiss and grins at me. "He makes a fist when he gets frustrated. I've got him up to seven when I've been crossed before. It's fun."

I laugh and ask, "Today?"

"Just once. Don't worry, he'll recall me to the stand, I'm sure." We cross the intersection and climb up the outside steps. I see Ray waiting for us at the top, and my two favorite men shake hands, then we walk in the courtroom together.

I look at Ray, then flick a glance to the mayor's chair, then send him: *Go touch the mayor's chair. See what you learn.*

Ooh, a dare. He strides down the aisle and sits behind the dividing wall and reaches over to rest his hands on the back of the seat. After a moment, he smiles and nods and heads back to sit behind us at our table. *Come get it.*

I send him an image of a ripe melon being smashed to smithereens by a giant sledgehammer, and Ray grins wider. But I probe his brain anyway and tell him he's still a jerk.

The image comes to me: a sleek jaguar or leopard. No, jaguar. Its yellow eyes lock on mine, then turn glassy, faraway. I watch the predator liquefy and get poured into a syringe, then injected into an arm, and the image backs out. That arm is connected to a guy at an intimate party in a skeezy apartment, and when that guy looks up, his eyes turn yellow, and he lets out a gut-curdling roar.

I figure "jaguar" must be a street name for a drug. Okay, so, Trav did say that weapons and drugs and prostitution go hand in hand, but really, in my world, I've never had the honor of such close acquaintance.

It's an honor I'm happy not having.

I ask Ray: *This is what the mayor is up to? Trafficking?*

Yep.

I write a note for Elliot: *I know what he was after* and fold it up and write his name on the outside. I turn around and see an officer at the door. After staring at him for a bit, he senses me, and I jiggle the note for him. He holds my eyes and nods, and when the next witness is dismissed, he takes my note, sees the name, and strides down the aisle to deliver it.

Elliot takes it and reads it and looks back at me, and I give him a small nod.

He calls someone else to the stand.

Chapter 48

Although I certainly don't want to be up there again, I'd really like to get the freak show back on the road and be done with it. I try not to nod off to the plethora of witnesses and character reviews and shouting matches that monopolize the rest of the afternoon.

When the gavel falls at five, I'm more than ready to head back to the hotel. Travis is shaking Elliot's hand when Ames calls for him. The judge points to a bailiff and says, "Make sure this man gets to an urgent care center, or the hospital, right now."

The bailiff nods and marches up, and Travis sighs. I step up to him, and he smiles and waits for me, then kisses me gently and says, "I'll see you back at our room."

I touch his swelling eye with tender fingertips. "I hope nothing's broken."

He crooks a boyish grin at me. "I see X-rays in my future." He puts his hands out and moves them like some deranged mystic. "Ooh, I think I'm becoming psychic."

I swat his hand and we kiss goodbye, him going out the back, and Ray and I out the front. Ray's hungry, so we amble up and down the street until we find an Indian restaurant, where I know I can get vegetarian food. Ray will eat anything, so we have a nice dinner and head back.

Even though I try to shield my thoughts, Ray knows I'm hoping to be alone with Trav soon (which takes no real stretch of the imagination), but as we head back to my room, he comes in anyway and turns on the TV to the latest blockbuster release.

Food coma hits me, and I curl up under the covers, the sounds of Bruce Willis' car screeching around corners with gunshots and explosions as a backdrop to my thoughts.

I pull the comforter to my chin and—

Zonk.

I wake up three hours later. Ray has left, the TV is still on (the sappy rom-com music woke me), but no Travis in sight. I figure if he's at the hospital, he might be another hour or so, so I yank off my shirt and pants and cuddle back in, leaving only my bra and panties on.

For Travis to remove—with his teeth—when he gets back.

• • •

I am awakened by lips fastened to my nipple, while a strong hand slowly runs down my side and lingers at my hip. Wan light filters in around the edges of the heavy hotel drapes, and I can tell by the diffuse sheen of it that it is very early morning.

I moan softly and look at the man who woos me so tenderly. I never felt Travis unclasp my bra, but now it dangles on one arm. I tug it free and drop it to the floor. I notice a butterfly bandage graces Travis' brow, and from this angle, with his eyes closed, I cannot tell if his lid might still be swollen shut.

He pulls my nipple hard into his mouth, drawing my entire breast there until my peak is hard and swollen. His hand traces along the edge of my panties, skimming so lightly I feel my skin quiver. I roll over to face him and reach down to find him hard and taut and ready.

His fingers dip into my panties and slide into my wet depths, stroking me in a way he seems to instinctively know will make my hips arch off the mattress. He seizes the chance and eases off my bottoms, and I kick them free of my ankles as he lowers himself to me. His weight settles upon my body like a soothing blanket, calming me while paradoxically arousing me to new heights.

He meets my eyes, his fingers tracing the line of my jaw. I like how tender he is, how much he holds me in awe. I've never felt so special before—perhaps, because, to someone who never relied heavily on his brain, I never was.

Travis sees me as a marvelous addition to his life, and that makes me so wet I writhe under him. He slides into me over and over, his length sinking flush to the hilt as I hook my feet around his waist and hold him to me.

We make no conversation as our bodies mash frantically against one another, finding all the solace we need in the racing beats of our hearts. Our breathing quickens, sweat slicks our bodies to better slide, and my exploring fingertips find his back to be as gloriously hard and strong as the appendage he unifies us with.

His fingers dig into my shoulders, then one hand grips my waist to hold me still, and his pumping runs harder, faster. Liquid pours from me, and I find my body clenching hard around Travis as he pants and thrusts hard into me, holding himself as deep as he can inside me while he shutters his release.

We collapse.

As our breathing slows, Travis props himself on his elbows and smiles down at me. "Good morning, beautiful."

I smile up at him and point to his bruised temple. "Good morning, Rocky."

He laughs and points to his tiny bandage. "I'm sure this was a six hundred dollar bandage, too."

"Anything broken?"

He sighs. "No cracked ribs—not even a hairline fracture—just lots of bruising. Some bleeding inside my eyeball, which should absorb as the swelling goes down. And, I have one loose tooth. No gum or caramel for two weeks." He seems sad when he says, "Judge may have to strike that comment about my three broken ribs."

I wriggle beneath him, feeling him grow harder the more I clench and squirm. "Well, I can think of one swelling that doesn't need to go down."

He laughs in a manly way, deep and powerful, and lifts off me to stand. One extended hand tells me he wants me to leave the warm bed, too, so I take his hand and get tugged upright. He sits on the corner of the bed and draws me into his lap, and I guide him back into me.

Now I really loop my ankles around his waist, and Travis grips me like he may never see me again. Our lovemaking this time is more primal, more forceful, but no less fulfilling. I find in this position, his shaft touches a different part of me, and I arch my back to gain every benefit I can, even leaning so far back I need Travis to keep me from hitting the floor. He groans and pulls me back up to him. As I bounce faster and harder, I arch more and more, and soon I toss back my head and cry out to the room.

Travis falls back along the bed, cushioning me as I collapse against him. He chuckles and says, "Give me a few minutes, and I'll be ready for more."

I smile down at him, lightly dragging my fingernails into his rogue beard and ask, "Does this mean my pass has expired? My teacher dictates all the lessons, now?"

He guides me to sit astride him, and I wiggle against his patch of dark curls. I look down and note how his Velcro and mine look like lava—his jet black and mine fire red, both hot and wet and swirling together. I feel his member grow and move against my bottom, and I smile with seductive promise. He matches it and says, "Teacher is definitely back in the classroom."

He's hard again. For a man who's been deprived of female companionship for three years, he's come back *en force*. I slide back onto him, and Travis sits up to kiss me long and slow, then lays back down for me to take over.

I lean forward and kiss him slowly, sucking on his good lip while his fingers pinch my nipples. As slowly as possible I raise and lower myself along his shaft, and the way he toys with my breasts drives me wild.

I must be driving him wild, too, for after three or four slow descents on his phallus, Travis grabs my hips and takes over, holding me in place as our bodies pound hard one against the other.

I think we just topped my multiple-climax record. My sex clenches over and over, and the waves of pleasure that rocket through me make me tumble off him and curl into a tight twitching ball.

Travis only gives me a few minutes to recover before he lies upon my body again. I spread my legs, eager to experience more of the passion my life has not known.

It's morning, and Court will soon be in session, but I plan on making love until I can't stand.

Travis, I think, has the exact same idea.

We're in the shower when the room phone rings, and I realize Trav must have set it when he came to bed last night. He hears it too and says, "Guess we should get up soon."

I glance down at his member and say, "Parts of you have been up all morning already."

He cups my cheek and kisses me. "Can't wait to do it again."

My hands fly to my crotch. I tell him, "I might need a rest. I haven't had that much sex since the fifth of Never. I'm a little sore."

Now both of his hands cup my face. "Did I hurt you?"

I love how concerned he is. I smile and say, "You know when you get a new car, and they tell you to drive it carefully for the first two months?"

His eyes narrow to thin brown slits.

I smile and say, "Yesterday was the jump start. Today we just ran the Indy 500."

He sighs and studies me and then tugs me close. I nestle into his arms, my cheek on his chest.

The water starts to chill, so we turn it off and get out. I like watching him dry off. He's so comfortable in his skin, like he was used to a woman watching his mundane movements. Me, this is all new. Perhaps it comes from him being married, this sharing of intimacy, but I'm liking how the very sight of him drops my blood pressure.

Or gets it revving.

I pull on fresh panties and then sit on the toilet lid to put lotion on my feet and pull on socks. "I never got to tell you; Ray found out what the mayor was hiding."

He looks up as he tugs on his pants and zips. "What?"

"Jaguar mean anything to you?"

"Yeah." He tugs his shirt over his head, yanks his arms through. "It's a street drug. New combination of controlled substances, pretty potent; it's supposed to make the user feel powerful. Why?" He tucks in his hem as he looks at me.

"That's what the mayor is trafficking."

He gives a low whistle. "It's not technically illegal, but that's only because the government hasn't 'discovered' it yet. Probably by this time next year it will be." He leans against the wall by the door, one hand on the sink. "You think he's importing drugs?"

"Ray touched the mayor's chair and sent me the image. I saw a jaguar, and then hypodermic needles."

Now Trav crosses his arms, his curious expression exchanged for distrust. "A lot of people sit in those chairs, Rosie. Are you sure it was the mayor, and not another defendant?"

I hadn't thought of that, and I'm sure my widened eyes bespeak as much. "Hang on." I close my eyes and send slowly to Ray, *Are you sure the jaguar impression is from the mayor?*

It takes a few minutes for him to reply, but he says, *Yes. The hand holding the jaguar's leash is wearing a giant class ring.*

I nod to Trav and relay the message.

And a giant key, like a key to the city.

"And a giant key, like a key to the city," I repeat.

Trav merely looks at me and shakes his head. "You seriously just spoke to him? Telepathically?"

I scrub my feet a little harder than I need to for lotion dispersal, feeling my jaw set. "Yes, dear. This is what we do. And it's why I never told any guy I could do it."

He nudges my hands off my feet and my feet to the floor, then he smiles and straddles the toilet to sit on my lap, making me laugh. "You're too big! Get off."

But he holds me and kisses me. "Thank you for all you've done to help me on this case. Seriously, thank you." He hugs me, and I decide I can handle his weight on my lap for a few seconds. He's smiling when he stands, and I can only grin up at him.

"Are you always such a goof?"

Cautious, he asks, "Will it continue to make you laugh?"

I smirk up at him. "Probably."

He stuffs his hands in his pockets to flatten them out. "Then, yes. Definitely."

We finish dressing and head back to the court house, and Travis tugs me to an abrupt stop just outside the courtroom doors. An older woman in a pink dress covers her mouth with her palm, and one of two hovering darkly handsome thirty-something officers smiles broadly as he sees him, then that one slaps the other on the chest, and he looks up and beams, too.

Trav drops my hand. His mouth hangs open. "Mom?"

Tears well in her eyes as she nods, and he dashes over and grabs her, even pulling her to her toes. I hear their joyful cries as they reunite for the first time and watch his brothers both smile and then shake his hand and tug him close for some hearty back pounding.

He is as excited and exhilarated as I've ever seen him as he wipes his eyes and holds out his hand to me. "Mom, obnoxious older brothers, I'd like you to meet my girl."

"Oh," his mom cries, and she walks over and places her palms on my cheeks. "I'm so happy I could cry." She is crying, but it would be rude to point it out. She releases my face and grabs my elbows and says, "I'm sorry, dear, I didn't get your name."

I look to Travis, then look around at all the people milling in the lobby. "Your call," I tell him.

He leans forward to whisper in his mom's ear, and she smiles at me and says, "That's a lovely name. You're going by Kaiya, here?"

"Here, yes. Not at home."

Mrs. M. turns to her sons and introduces me to Rick and Dillon, and I shake their hands as well. I say, "I hear you're both first-time parents?"

The older one, Rick, beams when he pulls out his wallet, and I watch Trav fawn over the pictures of his new niece. He is so excited for his brother, I know it's genuine. "I can't believe I'm an uncle."

Reminds me of what Ray said when I broke the news.

Travis turns the picture to and fro, then shows it to me, as well. He tells Rick, "She's beautiful. Obviously gets that from her mother."

Rick jabs him on the arm.

Dillon, not to be outdone, pulls out his own wallet and shows the photo of his wife's ultrasound. "Here's my little soon-to-be peanut."

I have to lean over and look. "I ... don't think that's a peanut. In fact, I think she's rather peanut-less."

He snatches the wallet back to his chest with a cautionary glare. "We don't know if it's a boy or girl yet."

I shrug, acting rather cheeky. "No peanut."

He kind of smirks at me, and Rick gives him a friendly shove, and Travis crunches me to his side. "You ever look at ultrasounds before?" he asks me.

I shake my head.

"See?" Travis tells his brother. "She's just guessing."

The look I give Travis speaks otherwise, but his firm smile challenges me to refute him. I acquiesce and shrug at Dillon. "Just a guess."

He looks down at the picture and smiles warmly, and I have a feeling he really wants a little girl. Kind of the opposite from what I would expect from a cop.

Maybe he likes the thought of terrorizing her future boyfriends. Just another guess.

Rick assesses me, sizing up the kind of woman his brother would take a hankering to. "Are you the psychic I heard about on the news? Helping out my brother?"

I scoff and give Trav a disdainful full-body scan. "Why would I help him? A big tough guy like Travis doesn't need a little girl getting his back."

"Yeah," Travis points to his cut eyebrow. "You should see the other guy." He crunches me and plants one on my temple.

They like me, I can tell. His mom tugs me out of his arms and faces me. "Is it true you saved his life?"

Ah, shoot, I can't lie to his mom. "Yeah, I guess I did."

His brothers jump all over that one. "Baby brother gets bailed out yet again."

"Does that work? Making the chicks rescue you?"

"Not very manly."

"We called him 'Tragic' for a reason."

They face each other. "At least it wasn't Dad this time."

Rick glances at me. "She's way prettier, you're right."

I watch Travis tip his head back and close his eyes. "Shouldn't you two be working? Mom? Can you make them go away?"

"Now boys," she chastises, and I know she's enjoying this every bit as much as they are, having her family back together again. "Play nice."

"Where's the fun in that?" Dillon cuffs Trav gently upside the head, and he tips away from it, then Trav gives his brother a jab on the chest. Then Rick punches Travis, and Travis punches him, and I grab his mother's hand and say, "For the love of God, let's let the testosterone settle, shall we?"

We go into the courtroom and seat ourselves close to the front, where we have some girl talk while the seats slowly fill. The Trio of Trouble comes in and settles near us, my brother joins my side, and soon the bailiff bids us all rise for the Honorable Judge Ames.

I have a sinking feeling I'll be on the stand.

Elliot calls me up first.

Chapter 49

Yes, it's kind of like public speaking, which rates high on "irratio-nal fears" for most people, so doing this twice in two days thrills me to no end. (Sarcasm. Yes.) But Elliot is kind and smiles and invites me to share.

He pauses before my chair, his body open and relaxed. "Kaiya, welcome back."

I feel my foot tapping a frantic rhythm on the floor and grab my knee to stop it. It doesn't work. "Thank you. I'm so happy to be here again."

A few people smile or chuckle, and Elliot grins at me. I'm pretty sure I hear Trav laugh, which makes me smile. I get it now. Laughter is a good tension breaker. I think I blush a bit and look down, not really meaning to come off as a jokester and wondering how to make my damned foot stop dancing.

"Kaiya, you've already proven to us your psychic abilities. Do you feel you've encountered anything else that may help our case here today?"

I take a deep breath amid the *tap tap tap* and try to focus. "I think the mayor is smuggling a drug known as 'jaguar' into the country. I think that's what he was also concerned with Travis finding out." I look to the mayor and watch his face blanch. I'm hoping the judge notices this as well.

"And, Kaiya, how did you come to this information?"

I go in headfirst. "Psychically. I saw an image of a jaguar being injected into an arm through hypodermic needles."

He nods to me. "Thank you, Kaiya. No more questions, Your Honor."

Cecil marches up to me, and I see his fist clench. I look to Travis, trying not to smile as he looks at the man's hand and waggles his brows. Cecil clears his throat and leans on my wall. "Miss Kaiya, are you familiar with the drug called 'jaguar?'"

I notice his knuckles are really white. He's totally crowding me and I don't like it. I lean back. "Not really, sir."

"Yet you claim to know it's an illegal drug."

My foot has stopped, finally. "Based on the images sent to me, and I've heard that it makes the users feel powerful."

"Hm. Yes. And one of those 'images' was of hypodermic needles?"

I'm still crowded. I think I know where he's going, so I say, "Images are symbolic, and that's what I received."

He leans an increment closer, his eyes alight with fire. "Isn't it true that hypodermic needles can be used for medical reasons?"

I smirk at him, hoping he'll back off. "Yes."

Those fingers flex on my little half-wall. "And that someone in a government role would be in a position to issue needles for medical purposes?"

I'm feeling cornered like an animal, and the only way out is straight ahead. I snarl, "At assault-weapon gunpoint?"

"Motion to strike, Your Honor," Cecil asks as he steps away, granting me a modicum of breathing room.

I lower my head to hide my smile.

"Sustained," the judge says, and I bite my lip. Drat. I could have had fun with that.

"Have you received any more of these so-called 'images' regarding the mayor?"

I look up at him. "No, sir."

"No other 'images,' so the first one must always be right. Isn't that correct?"

I lean back in the chair and feel my limbs tense at his facetiousness. "I only ever get one image. It's like live radio. I can't just replay it. It's not an iPod."

He squares up with me but maintains his space. "Are your images ever wrong?"

I cock my head at him while I consider my answer.

"Yes or no, Miss Kaiya?"

Snarky, I ask, "You tell me. What was in the Bible?"

His face reddens. "Yes or no, Miss Kaiya?"

I inhale a deep breath and the words tumble out of me. "It's not so much that they're wrong as it is that I might misinterpret what they're trying to tell me."

He likes that, and I see the gears chugging away behind those narrowed eyes. "So, by your own words, the image of the jaguar could be about the real animal."

I feel my witticism at an apex. "If he's injecting himself with needles, yes."

That fist clenches. "My client could be sending money and medical supplies to zoos, could he not?"

I cross my feet, angry that he's disputing my vision when I had given him solid proof they work. Hell, *I saved Travis.* What more did he need? "Then he could provide docu—"

"Yes or no?"

I shrug, letting my response hang in the air. "Sure."

"Or my client could be sending money and medical supplies to animal reserves in Africa, by your images, correct?"

I have him there, and he doesn't even know it. I grin and say, "No. Absolutely not."

That hand is open, and I know I'm going to make it clench again. "And why not, Miss Kaiya? You said yourself the images are not always understood."

I glance to Trav and say, "Because jaguars are from South America—the same place most drugs come from."

Yep, it did. Anger colors his words, matching the heat on his cheeks. "Motion to strike, Your Honor. And I would like the court's permission to declare her a hostile witness."

Funny, I never felt hostile before meeting Cecil.

Ames covers the microphone and leans toward me. "Miss Kaiya, I'm going to give you one warning."

I take a deep breath and settle into my chair, looking askance at this grave man. My foot starts *tap tap tapping* away again. "Yes, Your Honor."

He uncovers the mic. "Overruled, Counsel."

Cecil really tries not to glare at me as he starts to pace, vacillating his next strike, er, question. "Is it not true that if you weren't already involved with Mr. Mattison's abduction, you would not have been able to find him in the first place?"

That's a whole lot of negatives, and I try to determine if my answer needs to be positive or negative. Do four negatives equal a positive, or only three? I see Jasmine hovering in the back, just before the swinging doors, pointing at a large woman in the back row.

I frown, trying to listen to her. I can see her lips move, and she channels her mouth like a cheering soccer mom at the final game, but I can't hear her. I shake my head at her.

"Miss Kaiya, yes or no?"

I snap back to Cecil, then look back at Jasmine. She's pointing urgently at this woman. She's large, older, with a three-pound chin bearing more hair than my legs after a month of neglect (I wouldn't know anything about that), her neck slopes to shoulders that are desperately trying to hold up an orange muumuu, and her foot-long mop-head of hair looks like a Shih Tzu fought an epic battle with a bottle of mineral oil and lost.

She's not the kind of person one enjoys looking at overlong.

"Yes or no, Miss Kaiya?"

I'm so confused I can't even answer. Whatever he asked me is gone as I watch Jasmine float over behind this woman and point forcefully with both hands.

"Miss Kaiya, are you even paying attention?"

I look back at Cecil. "Yes, I am, just—" I stop right before saying, "not to you." I stand up and cup my left ear. "I can't hear you."

Now a few people are looking toward the back row. Ames orders me to sit, and Cecil thinks I'm trying to get answers from someone in attendance.

... Which, I sort of am.

Ames pounds his gavel. "Miss Kaiya, I order you to sit."

I plop down and wave for Jasmine to come forward; more people are turning in their seats to see who I'm looking at.

She is so frustrated I feel tears welling. Murmurs start to ripple through the audience, and the gavel pounds the block a few more times. "Order in the court."

And then I hear her: *She's Chad.*

I suck in my breath and whirl on the judge. "Your Honor, might I pass you a note?"

I think I'm pale; I know I'm breathing hard, and tears well in my eyes, but I hold his expectantly, hopefully.

"I already gave you a warning, Miss Kaiya. Am I going to have to hold you in contempt?"

A tear leaks out. "No, Your Honor." I glance back at Jasmine, and the "woman" seems to be getting rather nervous. If the bailiffs at the back don't grab "her," then Chad Phillips, Agent Extraordinaire, would escape. "Please, Your Honor?"

His lips press into a thin line, but he pushes me a pad and pen. I scribble: *Chad. Back row. Lg woman.*

The judge reads this, eyes me over his tiny glasses, and leans over his desk to me. His hand automatically covers the mic. "This is a pretty serious allegation. Are you sure?"

Jasmine waves me forward with both hands, and then she kind of freaks out that I'm not doing anything and flails her hands over the suspect, like she's trying to grab him herself. I whisper, "Travis' late wife has nothing to gain by lying."

He flicks a glance at the person in question. "She's the one telling you this?" He squints like he hopes to see Jasmine.

I nod. "Yes."

The "woman" senses trouble, for now s/he gets up, grabs an overloaded green hobo purse and struggles to reach for something under the bench. Whatever it is must be out of reach, for s/he abandons the quest and heads toward the door. A few people are squished in their seats as s/he tries to get out of the row and into the aisle. I panic and look back at Ames. "Your Honor?"

He points to the back row. "Bailiffs, please detain that person."

Anger snaps in those eyes, and as the bailiffs go to stop Chad, the heavy purse whirls around and thumps one in the head. That man falls, but Chad winds up for another wallop on the second. That man yanks on his free padded arm, and manages to yank the entire limb from Chad's body with a sound like material ripping. Straps of money fall from the limb and tumble to the floor.

The bailiff freaks until he sees the limp limb is part of a fat suit, for Chad has made a fist with his real hand underneath that thick sleeve and punches that bailiff in the jaw. The bailiff uses the fat sleeve as a weapon and swings it with all his might into Chad's head, and he crashes for a second into the bench before recovering. More straps of cash fall out, and the bailiff I see is finding the entire arm is filled with dough.

People scream and hasten out of the way, except for the Trio of Trouble, who race right in. Chad whips his purse around once more, and it looks to me like that, too, is stuffed with bills. Interesting. He tries to bash in another head, but the seam connects with the bench instead, and the purse splits open.

More straps of money tumble to the ground, as well as a few loose Benjamins that flutter in the turbulence of battling men. Ames pounds his gavel and orders the court to remember that all the bills are evidence and they will be arrested for obstruction of justice if they take any.

Travis looks under the bench and grabs the elusive object and holds it aloft like a tribal war prize. "It's a gun, taped to the underside of the bench. Somebody smuggled one in. He was going to shoot somebody!"

Gasps ripple across the courtroom, and I have a moment of concern that the "somebody" might even have been me. Maybe.

Cecil steps nearer to me, kind of collapsing on my cubby as the men in back duke it out. Travis manages a good headlock on Chad, then rips off his greasy mask and flings it away. The pseudo-chin dangles from one ear, looking like a hairy slug, and Travis pounds him a good one on the eye.

Justice, like revenge, is a dish best served cold.

The gavel falls a few more times, and I hear "Order in the court" being yelled over and over. Between the brothers and the bailiffs, Chad is rolled to his massive stomach and detained. Hand and foot cuffs are both used, as the suit would give him too much opportunity to get free. They yank off his other arm sleeve, and thousands of dollars in pretty wrapped stacks spill to the floor.

I'm assuming the entire padded suit is worth about a million bucks, minus his rental fee.

I figure poor ol' Chad must be sweating up a storm in those three-inch fat layers he elected to don.

Amidst the chaos, I tap Cecil on the arm. When he looks at me I ask, "What was in the Bible?"

He studies me for a long second. "Bonds. Mom said she'd will them to me, but they weren't in the paperwork. I ... really needed to find them ... my son just got accepted into Harvard."

I smile. "Congratulations. You're welcome."

He pats my hand as the newest witness is gathered up and brought in for questioning.

All in all, not a bad morning.

Chapter 50

The Bureau is sending Ray and me home on the six-o-seven, and as Travis and I aren't needed as witnesses for the remainder of the day, we, along with two agents, join his family for a few hours. We have lunch at a local restaurant, and his brothers tease me for being vegetarian, making his mom swat them to silence their jaws.

I like this family a lot.

Ray fits right in, too. He takes his role of "brother" just as seriously as the others, by which I mean, not at all. The slights and jabs and slanders fly, and soon I have to add my own, and it's not long before I realize we're the loudest table in the building.

Oops.

By four o'clock, we are escorted back to the hotel, and I pack up my few belongings. We get an actual police escort to the airport, courtesy of Mattison motors, and Travis walks me to the drop-off. I know he's torn between saying goodbye to me—a girl he's known for only a week—and the family he's missed for three years, and I don't have a bunch of time for a long goodbye, thanks to a fender-bender blocking traffic, but dang I wish he wanted to come in with me.

Ike awaits us, his mission to see us safely home, and I feel a bit relieved that we're not just being forgotten at the airport by the men who needed us to be there. Ike stops and faces me and says, "We got a confession out of Chad. Turns out he had a man provide Travis with a GPS-enabled phone that only they could trace. They used the phone call Travis made to his mom as a way to triangulate his position. Then, when Chad got to the safe house, he killed off that man to hide what he did. The next cell phone was encoded so only Chad could locate you, which is how he showed up at the hotel."

So much for relying on those entrusted with saving our lives. I realize Ike has done a great job, and I see a way to both repay that favor and to right a much-needed wrong. "Ike? There's something I need to tell you, a case that needs solving."

He looks at me, curious.

"A local girl, Britni O'Reilly, was murdered. I found her grave only because she led me to it. But I never told the cops that part of it. I mean, it was an obvious grave, so that's all I reported."

He nods once to encourage me to continue.

"Anyway, her clothes are buried in-between the three small shrubs in the same clearing. She told me they were in a plastic bag, along with his DNA. And his name was weird, like Hogwarts, or Hobnail, something like that."

"Hogarth? Hogarth Boyarov?"

I eye him. "Maybe."

He nods once, a hard glint in his eyes. "We suspected him in a double homicide, but had no concrete evidence. He was a suspect in this case, too, but we had nothing to go on outside of the fact he bought gas there that night."

I crook a smile at him. "You do now."

Ike smiles at me—something I didn't know he could do—and takes my hand in both of his. "Never thought I'd like working with a psychic, but you both proved me wrong." He reaches into his jacket breast pocket and hands me a card. "You ever need anything, you call."

I'm touched. "Thank you. This has been the experience of a lifetime. One I hope never to repeat," I laugh, even though I never would have gained as many skills if I hadn't come along.

Ray shakes everyone's hand goodbye, and I hug them all, and after Ray goes inside, I look at Travis. His family tries not to stare, but I know the guys are watching. He touches my cheek, then his fingers pinch my chin. "I'm not done with the trial here, yet; you know this, right?"

I nod.

I watch his head lower until he's meeting my eyes. "I'll come back for you, as soon as this is done. I meant everything I said this week. Everything."

I'm taking that to mean all the way up to house-shopping. I brave a smile despite wanting to cry and nod once. "I know."

He kisses my lips once, then again, and I wrap my arms around his waist as he hugs me. Then he backs off, and I feel the tears burning to fill my eyes, but I hold them off. I don't want to cry when I leave. I just want this to be a see-you-soon, not a goodbye. He kisses me now like he means it, and I ease my hands up his back and his tighten around my waist. Our lips part, and we hold each other close for a moment in a warm hug.

He whispers, "I'll love you forever, Jazzy." Then louder says, "I'll see you very soon."

He walks away without a backward glance.

A thousand stones crush my chest, and my horrified tears drip in fast succession. He called me *Jazzy*. All air leaves my lungs. My body that had been so alive just seconds ago now feels encased in lead. Frozen in mortification, I watch him take two or three steps before he realizes what he just said to me.

He stops, midstride, and whips his head around to me, but I'm shaking my head and backing up.

His features pale. "Rosie, wait."

I shake harder, put up my hand, turn and run into the building. "Rosie!"

I race through the check-in area, looking for my airline. When I find it, I see that Ray, in his old and tattered hoodie, is already twenty people ahead of the end of the line. I shove my way through the people and fall into his arms.

From somewhere behind us I hear, "Rosie!"

I hide behind Ray, and he holds me close while I cry. I don't know if Trav sees me, but I can't talk to him right now. It's too much.

I'll never be Jasmine.

It comes crashing down on me now: the way I look like her, the way she came to me to save him, over and over ...

They are still completely in love.

I'm the outsider.

I don't belong.

I watch Travis race by, and Ray turns me so I'm out of his view from that direction as well.

What happened?

He called me Jasmine.

I feel Ray's shoulders drop as he opens his thin hoodie jacket and wraps me up in it. "I'm sure he didn't mean it," he whispers.

"Except the part where he said he'll love her forever."

Ray squeezes me tight. "Ouch."

Ike sees I'm trying to avoid Travis and actually draws us out of line and takes us to the screening area, where we zip through, courtesy of that gold badge.

Travis races over to us and windmills to a stop. "Rosie, please."

I sadly shake my head at him from the other side of the screening area. Jasmine hovers smack-dab in the middle, looking back and forth between us, her head rotating like a spectator at a champion tennis match. Each word I utter feels like I'm hacking through a lifeline with a chainsaw. "Freudian slip, Travis. You still love her. I get it."

"Rosie, that's not true."

The chasm between us yawns wider and wider, and that chainsaw revs with more vigor. "Isn't it? She saved your life. I was just a means to an end." I feel the last lifeline fray and fall away even as Jasmine reaches out to me.

He shakes his head still, and I have to wipe off my cheeks. Ray wraps his arm around me and tugs me toward our concourse. "Take care, man," Ray waves, and he guides me out of sight.

"Rosie! Rosie!"

I want to puke. I've never felt so dislodged in my life. I think back to *Titanic*, how Rose said she would never let go, yet I'm adrift on an icy sea, alone, abandoned, my one true love slipping beneath the waves, and yet *I'm* to blame—*I'm* the one who severed the lines to the lifeboats.

I'm the one who is frozen and sinking down.

I dodge into the nearest bathroom and hover over the toilet, waiting for the nausea to pass. How could one woman experience such joy, satiation, and utter tragedy in the same day? I feel a tingle of electricity and assume a particular ghost loiters nearby.

I tell Jasmine, "Go away."

She appears before me, standing in the toilet, shaking her head at me. Her eyes are so sad I'm almost tempted to believe she never meant it to go this way.

I hear her: *Please, RoseAngel. Don't do this. Don't leave before I—*

I can't even look at her. "You win, all right? He loves you, you love him. I get it. I'm gone."

I flush, even though my stomach contents stay down, then I wash my hands to rid myself of his scent.

I smell like the hotel soap we both used.

I scrub and scrub, and Jasmine stands behind me in the mirror, one hand extended in supplication. She says: *At least let one of us explain.*

I'm not going to talk to her anymore. I'm not.

I walk out and lean against my brother once more, and his arm draws me close.

He is my support system, and thus far the only man I've ever trusted one hundred percent.

I remind myself there was always a reason for that.

Chapter 51

Nary a word from Denver, and it's been over three weeks since I left. Okay, that's not entirely true. In fact, it's such a complete and utter lie that I should be flogged to death immediately. The first seven days, I listened to forty-seven voice messages on my cell, eighteen at work, and tossed out six bouquets of flowers without reading the notes.

By my third day home, I realized I needed to allow Trav to explain himself, that I was overreacting to his slipup at the airport. And, in truth, I was just about to call him when he phoned me, and I chickened out. I just couldn't talk to him on his terms. I mean, really, what was he going to say, anyway, that I didn't already know?

Now, too much time has passed, and I simply don't know how to apologize. Is there a statute of limitations on freak-outs? I can't find my psychic guidebook and doubt there would be a chapter covering jealousy over departed spouses anyway.

(I don't actually have a psychic guidebook.)

My guilt I carry like a thousand pebbles in my gut, weighing me down. They irritate my stomach, make food taste sour, and make me want to vomit daily. Margie, my boss, interrogated me my first day back, and I told her what little I could without giving away my abilities, stating I had seen the men who kidnapped Trevor Matthews and therefore was a prime witness in the case.

She seemed to buy it.

Tina has been nicer now that the onslaught of Pringles-in-need calls has ebbed, and she even went so far last week as to bring me a muffin from my favorite bakery.

I learned via voicemail that the Feds had brought Pringles to a boarding facility, where he seemed pretty unhappy regarding the entire ordeal and desperately needed some one-on-one, and would I please stop by and introduce myself to him and tell him that his daddy was coming home soon?

Speaking of daddy: my EPT this morning showed *positive*, like I didn't already know.

I seemed to have shut off my abilities, for now the incoming calls at work seem challenging, unpredictable, and my intake numbers are already in the double digits (eleven), which is three times higher than last month.

My life sucks.

I take call after call, my mood anything but helpful. I make it to (almost) five o'clock and head home.

I have noticed that my pets seem to act differently around me now. Titan has been far more reliable about going outside, and I can't help but wonder if the shaved cheese reward was the catalyst. Grimm has taken to cuddling up on the couch with me every evening. It makes me wonder if they know I'm pregnant, depressed, despondent, or all of the above.

I'm just glad to know they love me.

As a woman of modern times, I know I have choices. I flop on my couch and stroke my belly, wondering. In my prems, I adored Charlie. I thought he was the most adorable kid I had ever seen. In my professional life, I endorse spay and neuter. If one can't provide a home for offspring, one shouldn't spawn.

I have no idea what I'm going to do.

I pull out my phone, studying the incoming call icon. Travis has called again, about an hour ago. Damn. The truth is I miss him terribly. I never knew a man could light up my darkness. Here I had thought I was his light, but now I see how dreary my world was before him.

I call Darlene, but no answer. So I call Misha. No answer. It's Monday, so she's at pottery class with Zed. I let the phone drop to my lap.

There's only one person left to call.

Mom.

She answers on the second ring and goes straight into the deluge of trauma she suffers daily. "Oh, thank God you called. I had to throw out four apples today; they had gone soft. Can you believe it?"

I know my role here, so I mumble, "How long were they sitting there on your counter?"

"Only two weeks. You would think for that price they'd have a longer shelf life."

I wipe my fingers into my eyes. "It's fruit, mom. You can't adjust their shelf life based on what you pay for them."

"And then," she continues like my comment had no meaning, "my favorite shirt had a stain on it. I think it was from babysitting your nephew. I think it's grape juice. Do you know the cleaner wants six dollars to remove it?"

"So pay it," I tell her, turning up the TV to better interfere with the sound of negativity.

"Oh, and I ran into Dolly at the store yesterday. Did I tell you? *Her* daughter is getting married, you remember Sidney? She's only twenty-four, and already found the man of her dreams. Quite a catch, Dolly says, but then, what would she know? She married a wallpaper salesman."

I love my mother dearly, but the mention of marriage has just tilted my tolerance meter into the danger zone. "Is Dad there? I need to talk to him."

She huffs and says, "No need to yell, dear. He's sitting in front of the TV, holding the couch in place." And she screams for him.

Dad picks up, and I say, "Hi, Dad."

"Hey, Angel, what's wrong?"

Tears fill my eyes. I think I only ask to speak with Dad when I'm down. Or maybe I only call Mom when I'm down and she drives me to talk to Dad, but the end result is the same. "I don't know."

I can tell he's sitting up and paying attention. "Something happen?"

I lick my lips and turn down the TV. "I met this really great guy, and we saw each other every day, and things were going great … until he called me his late wife's name when he said he loved me. He apologized, of course, but … I don't know. I had gone with him to Denver while he testified in court, and that's when it happened, as I was leaving. I guess I'm a little down about it. I really like him, but I'm not sure he's over his wife."

"Huh." I don't like that. Dad only says that when he doesn't like what he hears. "Sounds like a pickup line to me. You sure he's not still married?"

I shake my head. "No, he's a widow."

"You sure?"

"Positive." Now, I don't know if Mom ever told Dad about Ray and me, but I think he trusts my judgment enough at this stage in the game to not press me.

He kind of catches his breath. "Lots of Mormons out west."

"True, but he's not one of them." With his potency, he could fill the state with babies in two years, provided he had enough willing women.

It wouldn't be too hard to find volunteers, I admit.

"What did he do to need to testify?"

I take a deep breath, my voice low. "Witness a conspiracy involving a lot of political figures. I'm just … worried about him. People were shooting at him."

Now he's alarmed. "How do you know that?"

I should have kept my mouth shut, but now it's too late. "Because I was there, at the airport, sending him off. The Feds killed the shooters, but they were definitely after Tra … Trevor."

"Aw, honey, are you sure he's the right guy for you? This sounds pretty dangerous."

I hear my Mom pick up the extension. "What's going on?"

I take a calming breath and snap my fingers for Grimm to join me. He leaps up and cuddles behind my knees to purr. "Nothing, Mom."

"Still," Dad hedges, "I don't know. It might not be safe for you."

Mom yells, "Dangerous? What's not safe? What's going on?"

I tell her, "A man I was dating is testifying against some dangerous political figures in Denver."

"Dating?" Mom jumps on that word. "How long has this been going on? Should I call your grandmother?"

"No, Mom," and Dad adds, "Francine, calm down. She's not marrying the man." Then to me he asks, "Are you marrying this man?"

I would love to but say, "I haven't talked to him since it happened, so it's kind of a moot point."

"Since what happened?" my mother demands.

"He told me he loved me," I tell her, just to shut her up.

"I'm calling your grandmother," Mom tells me. "She's going to be thrilled," then adds as an afterthought, "I should start pricing out caterers," and she hangs up the extension.

I sigh. "Dad?"

He chuckles. "Do you need me to tackle her?"

"No," I concede, "it's the highlight of her day."

A long chuckling breath. "Are you sure you're okay?"

I shrug and pat the couch for Titan to join me. He curls up by my stomach, and I stroke his silky fur. "Just a bit down."

"I'll be right there."

•••

My Dad is wonderful, in case I'm not highlighting his marvelous qualities enough. He brings a bottle of raspberry wine and a bag of chocolate kisses and *It's a Wonderful Life* and we sit on the couch and watch the movie just like old times.

(Except the wine thing. That's new since I turned legal and something I'm too afraid to indulge in right now.)

We play a game of Scrabble, and by nine I'm ready to get back to bed. He hugs me and kisses my head and tells me how proud he is of me and that everything will work out just the way it is supposed to, which only makes the tears threaten.

Like I said, my Dad is wonderful. I walk him to the door and hug him goodbye, feeling the emptiness of my house gather me in like a wool blanket, blocking out all noises until all I can hear is the lonely sound of my own breathing.

I really don't enjoy living alone anymore. I look longingly to the kitchen, remembering when a sexy beach bum armed himself with a spoon and spatula and made a mean onion and cheddar omelet and proceeded to make me happier than I had been in a long time. Perhaps ever.

I sulk back to the couch to crash.

I pick up the phone, sensing Ray is calling. I answer before it rings.

"TS?"

"Hi."

He takes a deep breath. "Are you okay?"

I sort of laugh and kick out my blanket to cover me as I lie down on the couch. "No."

"I didn't think so."

I snuggle into the pillows, tugging the blanket to my chin, and then tuck my toes under the seams. "How's Angie?"

"Great. She'd like to meet you."

Grimm jumps up and curls up along my stomach, and I pet him, enjoying the sound of his loud purr—a new development. Titan is now relegated to my feet, and he curls up there, keeping my tootsies warm. "I'd like to meet her, too."

He pauses, and I know he wants to challenge me. I reach for my remote and turn the TV on low. Ray asks, "Are you ever going to call him back?"

A tear slips from my lowest eye and pools into the armrest. "I don't know."

"He's the father of your child, Ro, he deserves to know that much."

I nod and flip through the channels.

A few seconds pass, then Ray says, "The trial ended. They got a bunch of convictions. He's probably already home and ready to share his good news."

My mouth automatically forms a word I don't feel. "Great."

He huffs out a breath. "Can I have my twin back?"

I adopt a mechanical voice. "I'm sorry, all twins are busy moping now. Please try your request later."

"Sis, look, I'm ... I'm really sorry. I like Travis. I think he just made a mistake. I mean, Jesus, the woman was hanging around the whole time. Won't you please reconsider, and call him back?"

I turn up the TV. "I've got to go. But I will."

"When?"

"Soon. Bye." I disconnect the call.

Doesn't matter, because Ray sends: *You'd better.*

At least I know my powers aren't completely turned off.

To prove this, Jasmine appears, and I roll my eyes and yank my blanket over my head and say, "Go away. I'm not yours to haunt."

She laughs and says: *I may haunt whoever I choose. It's a benefit of the afterlife. But if you just hear Travis out, I will leave both of you alone. I swear it.*

"Right," I scoff. "And how am I to enforce it if you break your word? Call the cops? Get a restraining order? Go away."

He's worth it, RoseAngel Marie. He was worth dying for, as you yourself were willing to do. Don't let your obstinacy keep you from the one who will make you whole. Love him, and love him well. Live the life I couldn't have. Please. I beg you.

I don't answer, but at least I'm considering it.

• • •

Tuesday passes in the exact same manner; dark and dreary with a seventy-percent chance of despondency. Darlene is practically gushing when she calls twenty minutes after I get home, so excited to show me the ring Matt bought her that she asks if she can come straight over. The last thing I want is company right now, but I figure I could desperately use some girl time, so I tell her yes, figuring this will force me to eat something and be social.

I haul myself off the couch and trudge into my kitchen, listening to the TV droning away in the background. Somehow the sports channel got turned on, and I don't even watch sports. I think Grimm must have stepped on the remote, and I just didn't have the energy to change it back.

My kitchen is filthy; I haven't washed a single plate or dish or utensil all week, and pretty soon I think the landlord might have to declare my home an unsanitary disaster area and kick me out, so I run the hot water and squirt dish soap like hot fudge sauce over the mound of Corelle and let the sink fill with hot suds to soak them.

I turn off the water and move to the washer, where dirty clothes ease like *The Blob* from my overflowing baskets and slowly crawl across the floor, to Grimm's eternal amusement. This last week alone I've found him wrapped in my dirty t-shirts, towels, and once, even wiggling through my bra strap.

I make sure the cat is not in there before I kick them into light and dark piles and try to stuff one load into the washer.

When the doorbell rings, I pull it open.

Travis holds out another bouquet of flowers. "Rosie—"

He looks so beautiful I think my heart crashes to a halt. His eyes are forlorn, his lips turned down with his pain. All the bruises on his face have faded, and I think he's gotten a haircut. He looks better than I ever thought possible.

I see Darlene standing in the background, giving me a tentative finger wave from the end of my sidewalk while she sways like a little schoolgirl, knees together, and then clasps her hands before her.

I can't believe she's complicit in this.

I go to shut the door, but Trav holds it in place. "Rosie, you can't shut me out anymore. Not like this. I'm right here."

I'm so hurt I don't even know where to feel the pain. I feel like a car accident victim, so banged up and bruised that it's a week later before I realize I'm missing a fingernail. I can only stare at him, and he drops to one knee. "Please, Rosie, please, let me in."

Darlene grants an apologetic shrug to me, like she had no choice but to lure me to the door, and heads to her car to leave.

I shake my head at Travis, ready to close the door, but Titan runs out and jumps into his makeshift lap. Travis scoops him up and stands, holding both my dog and my eyes.

I order, "Come here, Titan."

I watch and hold Darlene's eyes as she drives away.

Travis holds my dog up and gives him a little kiss. "We men folk stick together. He wants to make sure you'll let me in."

I look at Titan, and dang if the dog doesn't seem to be thinking the same thought. Or maybe that's just my imagination.

I hold open the door and step inside, and Travis eases in and sets down my dog and closes the door. I look down at my feet as he bends to kiss my cheek, and even though he stops for a second, he does kiss me anyway.

He sidesteps the linen mountain and opens up an overhead cupboard in my kitchen and takes down a vase. I watch him open a drawer and pull out a sharp knife and whisk off the ends of the red roses and arrange them and the baby's breath in the vase, then set it on my counter and toss the scraps in my overflowing trash bin.

He grabs my nylon scrubbie and starts washing my dishes.

"What are you doing?"

He talks to the suds. "Dishes."

"Why?"

He looks over at me, his eyes filled with the pain I know mine must show as well. "I'm trying to make amends."

I try to scoff, but it sounds more like a sniffle to my own ears. I look away to dash the tears from my cheeks. "Do you have any idea how much you hurt me?"

He tosses the scrubbie into the sink and faces me. "Yes, RoseAngel, I think we're rather evenly matched in the pain department."

My mouth drops open as I stare at him. "I can't compete with your dead wife, okay? I get it. You still love her. She still loves you. You both win, I lose."

He snatches the towel from inside my sink cupboard and dries off his hands as he marches up to me. He tosses it on the counter as he reaches me and grabs my elbows. "This isn't a competition, Rosie. My wife died years ago, but you're here and alive and well." His fingers turn gentle, and his hands rub my arms. "I don't want to lose you, Rosie, I told you that before. But what you didn't let me share is what I'd been saying since the day I met you." His shoulders rise and drop, and I see his eyes drift outside. "For the last three years, I talked to Jaz, confided in her, pretended she wasn't dead. It got me through those first few horrible months.

Now I don't know if she was around or not, but after what you told me at the trial, maybe she was. Anyway, I told her all about you, Rosie." He meets my eyes then. "I told her that I could never replace her in my heart, but that my heart was large enough to love again. And I told her I was going to be moving on, putting her to rest inside, like she was out there." He points in a seemingly-random direction.

I feel a kernel of hope sprout one leaf in my chest and stall, like it's waiting for a ray of sunlight to help it grow the rest of the way.

He continues with, "Although some part of me will always love Jazzy, I can't live in the past any longer, not when the future is looking me in the eyes."

Mine start to burn. "You told her you'd love her forever, Travis. A girl doesn't easily recover from that."

"I was saying goodbye to her, Rosie. I just didn't realize I said it out loud until a few seconds later."

My mouth falls open, and I replay that over and over. Could I really have been that obtuse?

His hands slide down to hold mine. "You're the one I want to be with, RoseAngel. Please don't throw away what we have."

I am nothing grander than an artless harpy, and my guilt and self-loathing step to the fore. I tug away and start forcefully stuffing more clothes into the washer. He'd be better off with a woman with a working brain, not a doddering idiot like me. "We had a week."

He tugs me back around to face him, his voice gentle. "I thought we were headed for a life."

I tuck my head and lean back over the washer, staring at the colored swirl of clothes waiting to be agitated as I touch my stomach. *Life.*

I hear Ray send me a message: *Tell him,* and let out a groan. Damn, Ray knows Travis is here. I can't fight off two ardent men right now. I close my eyes and really try to snap my mental guards in place to block at least one of them.

A soft hand graces my shoulder. "Rosie, what's wrong?"

I feel mutinous as I whirl to face him, as if I hadn't made this abundantly clear over the last three weeks, but his head cock tells me he knows it's deeper than a slip of the tongue. I halt at his expression and turn back to my laundry.

He whirls me around once more. "Rosie, what is it? I know this is far deeper, whatever it is."

I turn away, shoulders down, feeling no more battle left in me, and dump some soap into the tub and turn on the water and let it run. Then I slide out from under his hands and walk into the living room, where I plop back on the couch. My pile of snot rags fills the ottoman and side table, and my blanket is covered with dog fur, and not one, but six empty glasses surround me, but I just don't have the energy to care right now.

Travis slides the ottoman away and kneels at my feet, gathering my hands in his. I can tell he's nervous, his hands feel a bit slick, but his eyes are so warm and filled with concern that I can't stop looking at him.

Three or four commercials play out, and I'm still mutely searching Travis' eyes. It's not until a loud car commercial comes on that Trav seems to hear the TV, for he snatches the remote and clicks it off and returns all his attention to me.

Titan invites himself into Travis' lap, curling up on his side despite the sharp angle. Softness edges Travis' features as he smiles down at my contented dog, and his head tilts in an invitingly charming way as he looks back up at me.

We're silent for far too long. His eyes melt into mine, soothing my soul, begging me to reveal what I'm so terrified to share. Perhaps this is why Trav leans forward and kisses me gently, and when I don't pull away, he does it again. "Rose?"

I hear Titan scramble to his feet after being tipped off and then try to get back into that moving lap. I totally understand the desire to be on that lap. I inhale a shaky breath and lean back into the cushions, studying him. Two words are all I have to say, two words that will totally change the course of my life and his. How he responds will either ruin my hopes and dreams forever or send me headlong on the happiest path I'd ever dared hope to dream.

I know which outcome I'm hoping for.

I'm terrified of how he's going to respond.

I hold my breath for a second before I open my mouth. I feel the air on my tongue, I feel my jaw moving up and down, but it's not until my lips feel about to crack like Sahara mud that I finally tell him, "I'm pregnant."

I watch his expression, like he's too afraid to show one extreme over the other. "It's mine?"

I part him the most mutinous, scathing glare I can muster, one intended to strip the skin off the living, the one Medusa employed as her baleful eyes turned people into stone.

He licks his lips, and I sense he knows how terrified I am of his reaction. I watch him shift back on his heels, his own mouth bobbing open silently. "When ... did you find out?"

I scoff. Well, maybe it was a sniff. Sniffle? "No secrets?"

He shakes his head, his eyes burning into mine. I know he means it when he says, "No secrets."

I lick my lips and pick imaginary dirt from under my nails until I think I'm able to be completely honest. My foot starts dancing away like it hasn't done since being on the stand. I glance up, a scared little girl move, because that's how totally insecure and terrified I feel right now. "The first time we made love. Charlie. He's ours."

I love the little grin he gives me. "Charlie? The little boy you kept seeing?"

I'm feeling a little hopeful, but I barely nod. I want him to be happy so much I'm afraid to breathe and ruin the moment.

His voice drops. "Is he a redhead?"

I have to hold in my smile. I'm afraid if I let it out, I might shatter apart into individual atoms, and then those atoms would collide at thousands of miles per hour and create antimatter, and a massive black hole would result and suck the planet into it, all because I dared hope that my pregnancy would make Travis happy. "Auburn. Caramel eyes."

I watch Travis melt with that. Then, "Freckles?" I nod, and he grins. Then my hands get a squeeze. "But, that means you were having premonitions all along."

I give a leaden nod. "I didn't know, though."

Now his smile drops, and both voice and eyes hold a twinge of fear. "Were you … making plans without me?"

I sense what he didn't want to ask: Am I pro-choice? Into selling babies on the black market? Lining up potential adopters? I shake my head. "No. Devoid of plans."

He seems visibly relieved, and then he kisses my knuckles, then stands and pulls me up to hug me. I keep my arms down, because I'm still frankly not sure how I feel about all this, but Travis is so excited I have a hard time being grumpy. He pulls me off my feet, along his chest, and when he drops me he kisses me so long and tenderly that I find my lips and arms betraying my head and broken heart as they eagerly participate.

Now Travis cups my face, and I feel my tears fall in earnest. I'm so terrified it's all going to fall away, that he's going to leave again, that we'll never be together because now I've told both my secrets and found him to be unworthy of them.

Travis scoops me up and lays me on the couch. I find my betraying legs spreading, and Travis' weight covers me like he never left. But he's not interested in making love—at least, not sexually. He strokes my temples and kisses my earlobe. He smoothes my hair from my face and kisses the corners of my mouth. He bumps his nose to mine and coaxes my lips to kiss his.

I love this man, even nineteen hundred miles away and a month of rejection later. I can't help it.

"Rosie, I'm so sorry for what you heard. I hope you understand what happened now and that you will forgive me."

I hold his eyes, feeling his pain like I refused to do that day last month. *He had been saying goodbye.* I let my head drop in a tiny nod, and then I keep nodding. I get it now.

His lips twitch in a little smile, and then his eyes grow warm. "I really will love you forever, if you'll let me."

I move a bit, and Trav eases up on his elbows to remove some of his weight from me. I say, "Forever's a long time."

"Yeah," he says, making it sound like three syllables. His eyes are bright and warm and completely inviting.

I like the images he's sending me, and I realize that perhaps the reason I thought my abilities were turned off is because I had no reason anymore to use them. Now, with Travis here, they're back on full force.

I see a Victorian house, yellow, with a large turret in front, blue shutters, white trim. A picket fence surrounds the front lawn. My little dog romps around the yard, along with a Golden Retriever. An improvised version of Charlie rolls on the ground, with a little redheaded girl in a blue frock toddling after them.

"I looked at a house today," he tells me.

I look up at him. "That was fast."

He shrugs. "I've been home for four days."

I crook a grin at him. "Does being a bank manager mean you don't have to prove steady employment prior to buying a home?"

He smiles and cups my nape. "The FBI cleared out my bank account for me. I have enough cash to only need a small mortgage, maybe two to five years or so."

I venture, "Why are you telling me this?"

He gives me a jaunty grin. "Why wouldn't I be telling you this?"

I feel my insides flutter like a butterfly wiggling free of its cocoon, like my heart just started beating today after a month of stasis. "What are you saying, Trav?"

He smiles, and my last wall melts like a chocolate bar dropped into the campfire. He braces my cheeks and says, "I told you, you were the girl I never wanted to let go."

"But you did."

He shakes his head no. "You and I both know you're bad at lying, Rosie."

I look down at his chest, noting a patch of black hair peeking out from the vee of his shirt. I want to bury my fingers in it, but they're busy holding onto his back. "You're right. I was the one who let go."

I sense his smile in the drop of his shoulders, the lowering of his taut muscles as he pins me to the couch. "You do know I wasn't going to let you get very far."

I hold his eyes.

"I'm a P.I. at heart, Rosie. Even if you moved away, I would have found you."

"Stalker."

"Lovelorn," he corrects, and I smile.

"Misha and Darlene have both been keeping me up to date on your activities, by the way. They were worried about you."

That surprises me, and I blink at him.

He shrugs. "I had to make sure you were okay."

Our eyes hold for another long moment, then Travis eases off me and pulls me gently to my feet. This time, I'm ready for his kiss, and when he pulls me back and swings me low in a dip, I'm hoping his kind never truly goes extinct.

Chapter 52

I'm blindfolded when the car pulls to a stop, and the excitement in Travis' voice feels contagious. He gets out and comes to my door and takes my hand. I'm cautious as I step out, and he warns me not to trip on the curb, so I slide out my foot and step over it.

I hear a lawnmower on the left, a hedge trimmer on the right, and a dog barking happily at what sounds like a kid or two on a skateboard.

"Ready?"

I feel grass beneath my feet, and he guides me up what I next assume is the sidewalk. "Yes."

He pulls off my blindfold, and I stare at a pink and purple Victorian house, two stories, with a "steeple" and third floor windows. A glass enclosure on the left could be a sunroom or porch.

I get a psychic punch in the gut and look to Trav. "Fixer-upper?" It needs a lot of work, from the peeling paint, to the cracked windows up front, to the missing shingles on the spooky roof. And that's just the outside.

He grins, and I see a stout man in his fifties in a brown jacket and black slacks coming from behind the house, and Travis waves to him. Must be the Realtor. Travis says, "I really like it. Wait 'til you see the beautiful woodwork. Oh! And it's got a massive staircase." He leans close and whispers, "I think Charlie would love to slide down it."

Before the Realtor draws near I whisper, "What about the ghost?"

His eyes snap to mine. "Really?"

I nod once, big and slow. "Oh, yeah."

He scratches his head. "I don't know how to fix ghosts."

The Realtor walks up and jangles his keys, and we shake hands with Mr. Mike Wallach. I'm feeling a little apprehensive as we approach the door, mostly because I'm not sure what to expect, but the closer we get to the front door, the homier this place feels.

Mike unlocks it, and I immediately fall in love with the deep curved oak staircase, the patterned hardwood floors, the oak and marble fireplace. This is good, because the peeling paint, the tattered wallpaper over the crumbling plaster, and the dangling curtain rod over the mystery stain offer a strong counterpoint to the more emotional part of my being.

Echoes of children racing through this house seem to resonate within the walls, and as I try to recall their happy cries, I think I see motion peripherally.

A child. A ghost child.

I smile. A ghost child would certainly like a few new young friends … at least, until I could figure out how to send him into the Light.

Trav and I explore room to room, and every step makes me more and more sure I want to live here. It has a dining room, a cozy living room, the ceilings in the sunroom are twelve feet high, and the kitchen, I note with envy, has a tin ceiling.

It also has Jasmine, beaming and circling and so happy she literally glows.

Trav is also glowing when he tells me, "The price is right. It needs updating—a new furnace, lots of electrical, but I can do that. Hell, now that the trial's over, I could probably get in touch with my old pals. A few of them owe me." He winks and smiles, his desire to live here and have me like it evident in the shine of his eyes.

He wants to be a family. With me. Just like that. After only a week of dating, and three weeks of avoiding him, and five days reconciling, Travis wants to spend his life with me.

I like how his brows waggle. "It's got four bedrooms. Room to grow," and he rubs my belly, making me weak with joy.

He must sense I'm wavering, for he grabs my hand and tugs me upstairs. "Wait 'til you see the master bedroom." We run upstairs, passing what I assume are the three smaller bedrooms, and Trav yanks me into the room and holds me still to face out the windows.

I point, at a loss for words. "Are those … doors?"

"Our own private porch." He opens the doors, and we step out onto a small balcony overlooking what I can tell was once a lovely sizeable yard. It needs work, now, of course, but—

We lean over the railing, and it's sturdy, not rickety like I feared. A sly glance from Trav, and then he glances down to my stomach. His voice is low when he asks, "If you're pregnant, that means you won't have your cycle for nine months, right?"

I give him a Pillsbury poke in his muscular belly. "What do you mean, if?"

He holds my eyes.

I give a small nod as my answer.

He sends me a sly, heated glance. "So I really *can* make love to you daily." A wolfish smile accompanies his words.

Ooh, my body clenches and dampens with the mere anticipation of that promise. "You can."

Trav faces me, rubbing my arms. "I put in an offer yesterday, but if you don't like it … " I can tell by his expression that he desperately hopes I like it.

I have to say, I like the idea of being a *family* in this house far more than simply living in any house could ever offer. To me, this represents *home*. My gaze takes in all. I nod, fervently. "I like it, Trav. It's beautiful."

Jasmine is nodding, and I think her eyes are filled with tears, if that's possible. *Do it, RoseAngel Marie. You will be blessed with happiness here.*

His hug is so joyous, so filled with relief, that I know he would have been truly devastated had I said anything else.

Wow! I never knew I had so much power over another human being. I don't feel stronger for it; I feel humbled, loved.

Graced from Beyond.

Jasmine is touching both of our shoulders, and I smile at her while I nestle into those manly arms. She says, *If you ever need me, simply call. Otherwise, live well, laugh often, love much. And enjoy Charlie.* She winks and says, *I sent him to you.*

I can only blink at her. When I open my mouth, she disappears, true to her word.

Travis draws back to smile into my eyes and says, "I knew you were a sensible girl the first time I saw you."

I feel a tease coming on, so I playfully swat him and say, "Girl? Girl? I consider myself a woman, or sometimes a divine empress, or possibly even smokin' hot tango dancer, but not once since high school have I considered myself a girl."

Oh, I love the smile he gives me with that comment, and he stretches out my right arm, laces our fingers, and draws me close. I feel his fingers spread wide across my back as he presses my hips to his, and a second later we're twirling around what will soon be our bedroom.

His movements are smooth and measured—mine, not so much. I'm breathless when I say, "You really can dance."

"Yup."

And he twirls me away from him, whirls me back into the shelter of his arms, and a second later he dips me.

It's really hard to refuse the man in this position, and I'm too breathless to do much more than look into his eyes and swoon.

I decide Dippers and Swooners are a natural combination.

He draws me up and takes me into the smallest room and says, "I was thinking about becoming a P.I. again, making this room my office. I really miss it." He gives me a devilish grin. "Scoping you out, learning about you like I did that first week, it made me realize how much I missed it. But I was thinking of taking only happier cases."

I frown at him. "Like what?"

He grins. "Lost and missing pets."

I know my eyes are bright when I smile at him. "Really?"

"Really." He looks down at my belly for a second, then says, "Maybe you'd like to help?" He lets the implication hang in the air a moment, granting me time to reply.

I shrug. "I like the shelter, and what I do. It's just—"

He nods in a knowing way. "You've had a grand taste of adventure. It's hard going back, isn't it?"

I think he's nailed it. I hold his eyes.

He pinches my chin and steps so close we'd need a stick of dynamite to blast us apart. "That's why I was thinking you'd be perfect as my partner in crime." He kisses my nose. "My partner in every way, actually. But I thought you'd like this, and it's something we can do as the occasional case pops up, maybe one or two cases a month. I even came up with a name for our new endeavor."

I raise one brow in query.

"Third Eye P.I. Like it?"

I smile. "I get top billing?"

He whispers, "You can be on top."

I laugh and playfully shove him away. I walk back out to the hallway, to the stairwell and look over the railing. (More railings. I'm really liking railings.) I see the house now for the potential, for the fresh palette it offers. Ivy could be twirled down the stairwell come the holidays, and the tree could go over there ...

I envision a glass coffee table in the living room, with one dark red accent wall.

This could be a fresh start.

I can check with work, see how many animals are declared missing, stolen ...

I know it's too soon to be physically possible, but I think Charlie just kicked. Psychically, at least. He likes this idea.

I face Trav in a stiff pose intending to show I'm battle-ready. "The bedroom has to be purple. No exception."

His eyes warm me straight through. He offers me his hand. "Deal."

I don't shake yet. "And I'm not going to be 'Miss Dobson' when I'm a mother, if you get my drift."

His hand moves a bit closer. His lips twitch. "Deal."

I lean forward, my finger pointing at his chest. "And the next time I tell you to get the hell out of Dodge, you better *git.*"

He laughs, stepping so close now I can feel his heat radiating from that wonderful chest. "Deal."

I stare at his hand, still open, still waiting for me to clasp it. I hold his eyes and shake my head. "I don't shake on deals; I seal my promises with a kiss."

Now his hands enfold my waist, and his lips hover a scant millimeter from mine. "You, Miss Dobson, definitely have a deal."

And he kisses me like the rest of our lives depend on it.

About Dorothy Callahan

I live in New York with my wonderful husband, a pride of demanding cats, and two loyal dogs, all rescued from shelters (not the husband). I married my husband because he brought a sword to our first date. This is a good thing, because the housecats turn into lions about one hour prior to feeding time, and sometimes I need to be defended.

When I am not writing, I enjoy shopping for antiques, trying not to kill everything I planted in the garden, and renovating our pre-Civil War house.

I also love ghost stories and spent more than a year ghost-hunting, and that enjoyment certainly leaks into my stories. Next on my bucket list is karate, fencing, and maybe a cruise.

I love hearing from people, so feel free to hunt me up! Some of my greatest pleasures are hearing how my stories make people feel, and a review helps me know what I'm doing right. Questions or comments? Visit me at *www.dorothycallahan.com*, email me at *dorothycallahanauthor@gmail.com*, or friend me on Facebook at Dorothy Callahan Author.

More from This Author
(From *Loving Out of Time* by Dorothy Callahan)

If Cody could make it there in fifteen minutes, he could save her life.

The sun bore down hot on the Oklahoma earth, and his horse's hooves jarred his teeth with the impact. It hadn't rained in three weeks, and by glancing behind himself, Cody could see a cloud of dust a mile long marking his run across the ranch lands.

A snort of pleasure preceded Sultan's mane toss, and Cody knew how much his horse loved a fast run. Today, though, was not for pleasure. He patted the shirt pocket under his linen vest, ensuring the vial was still there, wrapped in his red bandana. The apothecary had hastened to make the powder while Cody waited, and although he promised it would work, Cody was still not sure the conglomeration inside the tiny vial would reverse the disease.

She was all that was left of his brother's family.

He tugged the reins and leaned left as they breached the old oak tree, and Sultan responded by veering that way, his hooves sending a spray of dust and stone as they maneuvered the ninety-degree angle at a gallop. Next would be a right at the split, and Cody thought to take the deer trail and cut across the frontier. The path could be navigated by horse but not cart. He guided Sultan right at the fork and then leaned forward up the sharp incline, Sultan's muscles straining under the hard leather saddle as he willingly clambered up the slope.

Two strides later had them flying across the scrub land towards his old home.

He pulled out his fob. Five minutes left. He kicked Sultan's sides, urging his steed to greater strides. Sultan responded with the vigor of a horse half his age, and Cody gave another brief prayer of thanks to his brother for purchasing this fine Morgan just prior to his untimely death.

Young Annabel Lee missed her father terribly.

She often visited her parents' plots on the farthest side of their family's ranch. The pastor had advised Cody to loosen the soil beside Catherine's and Benjamin's graves.

His parents' ranch house came into view, and he noted their cart was still gone. They probably stayed in town, sending a telegraph to the city, looking for a more prominent physician, although Cody's fast horse would have beaten them back here anyway. Cody leaned lower over the black mane, noting the sweaty froth gathering on his horse's reddish-brown neck. Sultan would need a good rubdown from this exertion. But Annabel Lee came first.

The rough-hewn brown ranch house was silent. The chickens made no noise. The goats looked toward the house, contemplative in their cud-chewing. Even the wind had stilled. Chill bumps raced his arms despite the heat. He choked down the lump in his throat and kicked Sultan once more, not yet willing to concede defeat.

And then, a giant flat ball of fire appeared before his eyes, large and looming, with an ominous black center rimmed with flame. It was too late to stop, too late to turn. Sultan balked, and the last thing Cody remembered was flying straight towards his death.

Check out these books from Dorothy Callahan as well:
Taming the Stallion

In the mood for more Crimson Romance?
Check out *Embrace the Desire* by Spring Stevens at
CrimsonRomance.com.

Printed in the United States
By Bookmasters